Pushing on a String

Pushing on a String

Bruce Margulies

MARVINAL PRESS

Publisher's Cataloging-in-Publication Data
Margulies, Bruce. 1964-.
Pushing on a String: A Novel / Bruce Margulies
p.____ cm.____
ISBN 978-1-947834-67-5 (Pbk.) | 978-1-947834-66-8 (Ebook)
1. Fiction–men. 2. Fiction–coming of age. I. Title.

Published by Marvinal Press, Chapel Hill, NC.
Author photo by Mark Schultz
Cover Design by Lauren Faulkenberry
using photo by Radu Bercan via Shutterstock

When I started writing this, just out of college, my working dedication was: "To my parents, who I hope never read this."

Now I wish they were around to read it.

ONE

I wasn't *ringing in 1987* like everyone else. It felt like a hundred people had jammed into my friend's house in Maryland, just outside Washington, DC, though there probably weren't more than fifty. Big parties made me uncomfortable, so I was hanging in a pack with friends, drinking beer until I could stop worrying what people thought of me.

On my way back from the keg, a girl approached, wearing a black party dress with a black bow at the waist. She was smiling at me, probably amused because I bounced when I walked.

"Hi Bruce," she said, stopping near the bottom of the stairway. "I was hoping I'd see you."

"Oh, hey, how are you?" I said, surprised she greeted me because I didn't recognize her. "How'd you know I'd be here?"

"Mike said he had invited you."

She had a cute face, medium-long brown hair, and her sturdy calves indicated she was an athlete. Her warm smile made me feel like we were acquainted.

I was dressed up for New Year's Eve. For me, anyway:

jeans, a wool V-neck Gap tennis sweater over a t-shirt, and black penny loafers with dimes, not pennies, in the slots. Many years before, my cousin told me he put dimes in his penny loafers, so he had money to call for help when his younger brother got hit by a car.

Being six foot five, my heels made me feel particularly tall next to her. She might have been five foot seven, but most people seemed short to me, and I couldn't judge someone's height unless I was on a basketball court.

I never knew what to say to girls, so I was rambling on about the rec league basketball team Mike and I played on. She seemed to like basketball so I asked if she followed the NBA.

"I'm more of a college fan," she said. "I know Steve Alford."

He was a leading scorer on the 1984 Olympic team, but that seemed like a random thing for her to say, so I tried to clarify, "You mean you've *heard* of Steve Alford?"

"No," she said, laughing. "I know him from campus. We're seniors at Indiana University. The Hoosiers are nine and one this year and the Big Ten season starts Sunday. I can't wait."

I was completely embarrassed and since I didn't know anyone who went to IU, that didn't help identify her. Feeling self-conscious, I leaned back on the side of the stairs but misjudged the height of the stair behind me. Stumbling backward, I spilled beer on my sweater.

"Think maybe you've had enough to drink?" she teased, as I hurriedly brushed off the beer.

What a spaz, I thought, expecting her to excuse herself, but she smiled at my gaffe and said, "How is Louis doing? I saw him watching TV but haven't said hi to him yet."

Our group had taken over the TV set to watch a college football bowl game. We had to keep assuring everyone that once the game was over, we'd turn the channel to Dick Clark's New Year's Rockin' Eve.

"Louis is doing great. Maybe a little too great. He's at Montgomery College now, not Maryland. His parents told him if he didn't get decent grades, they were only paying for community college."

"That sounds like Louis."

"Remind me," I said. "How do you know Louis?"

"Right after he started working at the Boy's Club, I helped coach one of the nine- and ten-year-old basketball teams."

"How were you able to deal with the lack of focus and immaturity?"

"Those kids were so cute," she said. "Occasionally they'd run a play perfectly in a game and even if we missed the shot, I was so proud of them."

"I'm sure you were, but I was talking about Louis."

She grinned, but her mouth stayed closed, so I couldn't tell if she appreciated my joke or was being polite. She asked about some of my other friends from the neighborhood and as I updated her, I was going crazy thinking, *Who is this girl?*

When *this girl* asked how my father's low-fat diet was going, I became suspicious. She knew too much about me.

I was feeling guilty about acting like I knew who she was. Finally, I had to confess, telling her, "I'm really embarrassed, but how do I know you?"

Her smile grew bigger.

"What's so amusing?" I said, figuring she was helping someone play a joke on me.

"I could tell that you didn't recognize me, so I tried not to say anything to give myself away. I hope you're not angry, but I couldn't resist toying with you a little."

As I tried not to show I was hurt, she squared her

shoulders, looked me in the eye, and stuck out her hand. "I'm Amy Lawson."

"David's little sister?" I said, as I shook her hand. She had a good grip.

"Yepper," she said.

"I haven't seen you since junior high. How come I never saw you at Blair?"

"Because I went to Northwood. My parents thought that would be a better fit."

"That explains it," I said, and realizing that she had been talking to me because she was interested in me, I resumed getting lost in her warm blue eyes.

Her family had moved three blocks from my house when her brother and I were in third grade. David and I were good friends until junior high when he got into drugs. Back then, I barely noticed my friend's tomboy sister. She had my full attention now.

"What's David up to?" I asked.

Her face fell. "Not much. He dropped out of college."

"That's a shame," I said. "He was one of the smartest people I knew."

"My father says David's too smart for his own good."

"I get that," I said, speaking literally and figuratively. My dad said the same thing about me.

I was a senior at the University of Maryland Baltimore County, home for Christmas break. A week at my parents' house was the perfect time to fine-tune my resume and research companies to work for. At least that was my dad's thinking. My plan was to hang out with friends before returning for the January session.

I told Amy I was also graduating in the spring. Since she was a class behind me, she laughed and chided me for being on the five-year plan.

4

"It looks that way," I said. "But I took two semesters off through a co-op program and worked full-time at the FDIC."

"What did you do for the FDIC?"

"I wrote a computer program that measures the volatility of banks," I said, cringing at how geeky that sounded. "There weren't any bank runs on my watch."

"Gaining experience in your field is so important for getting the right job out of college," she said.

Uggh. She sounds like Dad.

"That's what they tell me," I said. "Unfortunately, my job experience taught me two things: school is way easier than working full time and that I hate programming computers."

"Oh no. What are you going to do now?"

"It's too late to change my major, so I'm planning on going to business school."

I was only considering business school but decided to say *planning* because Amy didn't seem like she'd spend time with a guy who had no idea what he wanted to do with his life.

"What would you do with an MBA?"

"I'm not sure, but I'll be working for a year before grad school, so I'll have time to figure that out. How about you?" I said, desperately trying to shift the conversation before she asked me where I saw myself in five years. "What are you doing after graduation?"

"I've been applying for dietician positions with DC area hospitals, but there aren't many spots available for someone right out of college."

She impressed me as she detailed her search efforts, particularly since I hadn't started looking for a job. Fortunately, she moved on from job prospecting and asked what my favorite New Year's Eve tradition was.

"The ball dropping in Times Square," I said. "I like seeing

old, black and white footage of the crowd celebrating. How about you?"

"Mine's the kiss at the stroke of midnight."

Woah! The thought of kissing Amy was thrilling, though overwhelming because I couldn't initiate physical intimacy. I had kissed girls at parties, but only after many beers. It was almost 11:50 and I was too sober.

"That one's important for you?" I said, downplaying it. "Sounds like a lot of pressure."

"A nice kiss at midnight sets the tone for the whole year," she said, smiling, before glancing at the tiny face on her dressy watch. "Thanks for reminding me. I'd better get going if I'm going to find someone."

I stared at her, dumbfounded. I had never had a better conversation with a girl and just as I was starting to get my hopes up, Amy was leaving me.

"Why don't we talk some more?" I blurted, then regretted how desperate that sounded.

"I guess I can stick around a little longer," she said, checking her watch again. "Besides, I probably don't have time to find an upgrade."

I must have looked close to tears because Amy slugged me on the arm.

"What was that for?" I said.

"I was totally kidding about looking for someone else," she said, grinning.

It was my turn to smile. I wasn't used to a girl being so playful.

"You had me going," I said, rubbing my arm in an exaggerated motion, although she had hit me pretty hard, right on the bone.

"I sort of owed you that," she said. "Seeing as you had forgotten all about me."

"I promise I'll never forget you again."

That came out so breathless I felt embarrassed again. I was constantly overthinking my actions, too worried about screwing something up. My mind was a crowded place, with little room for letting me enjoy things.

Thirty seconds before midnight, Amy seemed to be getting ready for her special kiss, looking up at me, moving a little closer. I knew I wouldn't be able to kiss her.

Ten! ... nine! ... eight! ... seven! ... six! ....

While the people crowding around the TV counted down, I was questioning myself. *What if I try to kiss her and she pulls away? What if I lean in and then lose my nerve? What if I'm able to kiss her and she's disappointed?*

As I reached behind me to set my empty beer cup on the edge of the stairs, Amy was looking at me and counting down with the crowd. I watched her lips as they shaped the numbers: *three .. two .. one ...* Horns started tooting throughout the downstairs of the house.

My heart was pounding as I leaned toward her.

TWO

My head veered past Amy's, my hands avoiding her shoulders and going around her back for a safe hug. Ordinarily, I'd be thrilled hugging a girl but after Amy had brought up the kiss, the blaring horns seemed to be razzing me.

Amy looked confused, but didn't say anything about missing out on her New Year's kiss. I felt terrible for disappointing her but couldn't reveal my anxiety. I had no idea what prevented me from making a first move with a girl and had never shared that with anyone.

"Do you want to sit down somewhere?" I said.

She agreed and I followed as she paused outside a large room with shoulder-to-shoulder people, some shouting over the stereo. Luckily, Amy kept walking and stopped in an empty study. I sat next to her on the couch and she tucked a strand of hair behind her ear and looked at me.

"Now that the New Year is officially here," she said. "You can tell me your resolutions."

Resolutions? As in plural?

If I had made any resolution, it would have been to keep

my life the same, which I didn't think even counted as a resolution.

At school, my main responsibility was maintaining a B average for a discount on my parents' car insurance, so I arranged my schedule to avoid morning classes and demanding professors. I had played on the tennis team for two years but preferred intramural sports with my fraternity brothers. I also wrote for the school paper and deejayed for the campus radio station.

My life centered on sports, which Dad couldn't understand because leisure time wasn't part of his mindset. He'd get up, read the paper while eating toast with jelly, and go to work. Then he'd return home, eat dinner, finish the newspaper, do the crossword, read a book, and go to bed. I didn't want my life turning out like that.

I couldn't tell Amy that I didn't want my life to change, so borrowing from my surprise at her question, I said, "My resolution is to anticipate situations better instead of just reacting."

"That's a good one," she said. "I can never seem to get completely organized. My planner is always a mess."

I suspected that her planner was leather bound, 8 x 10 or larger, with multi-color entries based on a longstanding coding system that incorporated tabs and highlighting.

I never used a calendar and avoided making appointments. If I did have some place to go, I remembered it in my head. If something was really important, I wrote it down. Somewhere.

Since we started talking, I had been avoiding going to the bathroom, worried that she wouldn't be waiting when I got back. But I had no choice and had to excuse myself. I snuck upstairs, where there was no line for the bathroom. While hurrying to get back, I decided against stopping for another

9

beer. I wanted to stay sober and sharp, plus I couldn't risk another minute away.

When I returned to the study, Amy was sitting there and my seat was empty. She smiled when she saw me and I felt giddy as I walked over to reclaim my spot.

"Hey," she said as I sat down. "While you were gone, I remembered that—"

"Bruce!" someone yelled.

I turned. Louis and Silk, my neighborhood friends, were standing in the doorway. Louis was blonde and blue-eyed, with a forehead so large, he called it an *eight-head*. Silk was 100 percent Cuban with dark features. He excelled at sports, school, and life.

"Hi Amy," Louis called, and as he walked toward us, he held his arms wide. She stood to give him a hug, which made me jealous. Not because I thought he was stealing Amy from me, but because he hugged her like it was nothing, while it had taken me twenty minutes of not saying the wrong thing, and a once-a-year stroke of midnight to get the nerve to hug her.

"What's up Lou? Hey Silk," I said, happy to see them but apprehensive about "sharing" Amy because I did better in a one-on-one conversation.

"*Silk?*" she said. "When did you go from Jean Paul to Silk?"

"You can always call me 'Jean Paul,'" he said. "*Silk* comes from my smooth as silk jump shot."

"Don't let him fool you, Amy," Louis said. "His nickname is sarcastic. He got it senior year in high school when he tripped on the sideline going into a basketball game."

Louis took a few pigeon-toed steps then pretended to trip, his arms flailing. He loved provoking Silk.

"Good one, Lou," Silk said, trying not to appear annoyed. Silk was too polite to start talking trash, but always gave it back to Louis. "You always had time to make things up while warming the bench."

I hadn't been at the game in question, but I suspected they were both right. I rarely got in the middle of their arguments because they were too much fun to watch.

"It's twenty degrees outside, Louis," Amy said. "Why on earth are you wearing shorts?"

"Because I never get cold," he boasted. "It's natural selection."

"I'll bite," Amy said, rolling her eyes. "How is that natural selection, Louis?"

"You'll bite?" I interrupted. "Who are you, Archie Andrews?"

Everyone stared at me.

I tried to explain my comment. "*I'll bite* is an expression they use in Archie comics."

Silk and Louis were used to me making references and jokes that no one understood. While I didn't have to be the smartest guy in the room, too often, I tried to be the wittiest.

"What did you say your secret was?" Amy asked Louis.

"See for yourself," he said, sticking out a leg. "I have the perfect amount of leg hair."

For the second time in thirty seconds, Amy was at a loss for words. This time, she burst out laughing. She had a wonderful laugh and I was jealous of Louis again. I wanted to make her laugh like that.

"Hey Lou. What about that night in Georgetown senior year?" Silk said, then explained to Amy, "The wind-chill was below ten and Lou was wearing shorts. Whenever anyone brought up how cold it was, Lou kept insisting that he never got cold."

"Is that true, Louis?" Amy asked him.

Louis smiled and nodded. "I won five dollars that night

when Jack bet me that I couldn't stay outside for five minutes without my shirt on."

"Nice going, Lou," Silk said. "Then you got sick and missed the next week of school."

"Missing a week of school was better than the five dollars," Louis said.

I was relieved when Louis said they were going to the keg. As they walked off, Silk called to me, "Can I get you a beer, Pretty?"

"No thanks," I said, happy to have Amy to myself again.

"Why did John Paul call you *Pretty*?" she asked.

"We call him that, especially when we catch him checking his hair, so if he ever sees me doing something to improve my appearance or talking with a girl, he turns it around on me. That's the second time tonight he's called me *Pretty*."

"Were you talking to another girl earlier?"

"Nah. He called me *Pretty* when he saw my preppy sweater."

"I do like your sweater," she said. "But it sounds like your friends miss you. Maybe you should spend some time with them."

"I can see those guys anytime," I said, trying to sound cool. But I was concerned that this outgoing senior at Indiana University would leave me and meet her "upgrade" at the party.

I stayed with Amy until her friend Ellen came into the study and said she wanted to go home. I waited on the main level as they got their coats from an upstairs bedroom.

Amy came down with her coat draped over one elbow. "Do you want to walk me out to the car?" she said as I opened the door for them.

"Sure," I said, relieved to have more time to figure out how

I was going to kiss her when we said goodbye. "Aren't you going to put on your coat?"

"You heard Louis. I don't need it."

Barely a few steps outside, Amy yelled, "Louis is out of his mind. It's freezing out here!" I held her coat as she put it on.

I was almost as crazy as Louis because I hadn't brought a coat to the party. But being with Amy, the cold didn't feel so bad.

Walking to Ellen's car, I was trying to convince myself that I could kiss Amy. We had just spoken for almost two hours, but I was too intimidated to ask her something as innocuous as: *Would it be okay if I kissed you goodnight?* If I had been drunk, I'd have kissed her in a heartbeat. But sober, I couldn't touch a girl unless I was sure that she wanted me to. A hint wasn't enough. Since Amy was so outgoing, I assumed that she would make the first move.

Two blocks later, we got to the car. Ellen went around to the driver's side while I opened the passenger door for Amy, who got in. It was more awkward with Ellen right there and as I stumbled over what to say to Amy, I looked into her eyes and said, "We should stay in touch."

"Sure," she said, looking puzzled.

I stared back, waiting for her to kiss me. Meanwhile, Ellen lost her patience, starting the car and turning the heater on full blast.

"Good night, Bruce," Ellen called over the groan of the heater. Then quieter, she told Amy, "Shut the door, I'm freezing my ass off."

"You'd better get inside and warm up, Bruce," Amy said.

Hearing her say my name gave me chills, though to be fair, I was freezing my ass off as well. She closed her door and I looked in at her, helpless. Amy was leaving me, and instead of doing something, I kept hoping that she'd roll down her window, motion me closer, and then lean out to give me a big New Year's kiss.

Instead, the car drove away.

Angry at myself, I hurried back to Mike's, unable to feel my arms by the time I got there. As I warmed up inside, my friends were joking about my new girlfriend.

"What were you and Amy talking about for all that time, Pretty Boy?"

"Nothing much," I said to Silk. "Amy's so easy to talk with, it was like hanging out with you guys."

"For two hours?" said Johnny Mac, our basketball team's elder statesman. "I have no doubt you can talk for two hours straight, but I can't imagine anyone listening for more than ten minutes."

"Bruce is in love," Louis teased, slapping me on the shoulder. "It's been nice knowing you."

"I hope Amy lets you hang out with us once in a while," Silk joined in.

"Don't worry," Louis said. "After a few dates, Amy will be begging us to take him off her hands."

"You guys are crazy," I said.

But all I could think about was how excited I felt when Amy smiled at me, how much I enjoyed talking with her, and of course, how I couldn't close the deal by kissing her. For years, I wondered why I never had a girlfriend. That goodbye was the reason.

At 2:00, Silk told us he was leaving.

"Your mom wants you home early?" Louis said.

"Good one, Lou," was all Silk could muster as he glared back.

Silk never stayed out until all hours and was my voice of reason, although too often I didn't follow his example. I was so mad at myself for missing my chance with Amy that I didn't feel like staying, so I asked him for a ride home.

As Silk drove, he asked what was going on between Amy and me.

"I don't know," I said. "We just have a lot in common."

"Come on, Pretty. I could tell by the way she was looking at you that she likes you and I know you like her. When are you going to see her again? Did you get her number?"

"I guess I should have," I said, trying to sound nonchalant, although failing to get Amy's number was bothering me almost as much as the kiss.

When we got to my house, I asked what he was doing for the bowl games that afternoon.

"Everyone's going over to Fletch's," he said.

"What time did he say we should get there?"

"We haven't told him about it yet," Silk said. "So don't show up before noon."

My parents had left the outside light on for me. As I approached the front door, I fished my keys from my pocket and waved back to Silk so he wouldn't wait.

After he pulled away, I became more critical of myself. *Why is a good night kiss such a hurdle? It could have been perfect with Amy, but I blew it.*

I opened the storm door and a piece of paper fluttered down.

Figuring that New Year's Day was the perfect time for a Jehovah's Witness flyer, I picked the paper off the concrete stoop. It was a handwritten note that read: *You'd better call me at school.*

I grinned, feeling giddy again. There were ten numbers, the first three I assumed were the area code for Bloomington, Indiana.

THREE

It was late February and with the sun setting around 6:00, it felt like winter would never end. After our Tuesday night fraternity meeting, four of us went to Shook's Lounge, located a mile from campus in a strip mall. Smoky and shrouded in dark paneling, its entertainment comprised a jukebox and a hazy old black and white TV over the bar that made people's bodies on screen look short and wide.

Most dive bars had their charm, but finding Shook's' *je ne sais quoi* was elusive. I suspected it never had a "lounge" section and that the person who ordered the sign out front just had a lot of chutzpah.

Six quick beers in, I got up from our table and as I approached the bathroom, a guy my age called, "Hey frat boy! What are you guys doing in here? This is our turf."

Claiming Shook's seemed like planting a flag in a landfill, so I thought he was joking. Besides, I didn't think that a bar could qualify as someone's "turf" unless it had a pinball machine. I mean, why bother?

The guy had acknowledged my purple sweatshirt with gold fraternity letters. I, in turn, appreciated his white

Embassy Dairy work shirt with its "Doug" patch over the heart because I owned several second-hand bowling shirts and work shirts with people's names chain-stitched on them.

"Nice shirt," I said. "Did you get it at a thrift store?"

"It's my work shirt. I don't buy my clothes at Goodwill."

"You're a milkman?" I said, thinking of one of my favorite Billy Bragg songs *The Milkman of Human Kindness*. "I've never met a milkman before."

"Don't call me a milkman, dipshit. I drive a truck for Embassy Dairy."

Free-associating and buzzed, I said, "When you're on break, do you guys play Truth or Dairy?"

"That's why everyone hates asshole fraternity guys," he said, moving closer. He was much shorter than me, though solidly built, probably from hefting thirty-five-pound milk crates all day.

"Hey, I was just joking," I said as he got in my face.

"Do you know anybody who actually works for a living?" he said. "Not everyone got a free ride."

I tried to defuse him, not sure why he was so upset, but he kept railing about privileged fraternity guys.

"Let's take this outside so I can show you how funny I think you are," he said. Our eyes locked and he said, "That's right, pal. I'm going to kick your ass."

I lunged past him into the bathroom and locked the door behind me. Breathing heavily, I surveyed the tiny room, with its sink, urinal and doorless stall. Upkeep at Shook's was like primitive medicine. Anything broken or damaged was removed and the area was splashed with alcohol to sterilize it. Then, fingers crossed, they hoped nothing worse would grow back.

While using the urinal, I glanced at the day's sports page taped to the wall, hoping the guy would cool down so I could rejoin my table. But he started rattling the doorknob so hard I thought it would break off.

"You coming out or what?" he yelled, pounding on the door.

Trying to ignore him, I finished at the urinal. My heart was still racing as I hunched over the sink, futilely pumping the empty soap dispenser. I looked into the cloudy mirror. Instead of checking my hair, I focused on the fear in my eyes.

The guy's cigarette breath took me back to junior high when Robbie Watts, in motorcycle boots, a brass Marlboro belt buckle, and the jean jacket he wore even when it was 90 degrees, would corner me in the halls. In seventh grade, his mouth reeked of cinnamon from Big Red chewing gum. Two years later, his bad breath smelled of cigarettes and minty Skoal smokeless tobacco.

"When I get my hands on you after school, your ass is grass," Watts would threaten, shoving me against the lockers, as his fellow greasers laughed. For three years, I had eluded getting punched by Watts, thinking I had won that battle. But running from fights had taught me to avoid confrontations.

My current incarnation of Robbie Watts continued banging on the door as I rinsed my hands. "Hey Bud, your only way out is through me. And I'm not going anywhere."

"Give me a minute," I yelled through the door, while staring at the fraternity letters on the chest of my sweatshirt. "Don't you have some milk emergency to get to?"

"What the fuck is a milk emergency?"

"I don't know," I said, chuckling at the thought. "Like maybe your dairy is forming a posse to track down a gang of cattle rustlers."

"You really are a smart ass, aren't you," he said.

Actually, I was hoping that my friends would notice him

yelling into the bathroom and realize I was about to get my smart ass kicked.

Resigned, I took a deep breath and pulled open the door. My heart was pounding in my throat when I saw him stand from his lean against the wall in the alcove outside the bathroom. He crushed out his cigarette in a round gold-tone ashtray atop the pay phone.

"Time to go, motherfucker," he said, advancing to block my path.

"Hey, I'm sorry if my joke offended you," I said, holding my hands open in front of me.

He smiled. "You're too big a pussy to fight me, aren't you, frat boy?"

Before I could answer, he lunged, grabbing the front of my sweatshirt and driving me against the wall. He turned me, and as I covered my face, he started hitting the side of my head.

All my life, I had been afraid of being punched in the face. But in the moment, I wasn't thinking about it. Each blow was making my skull feel squishy and I heard crackling when his knuckles smashed my ear. My eyes were watering, though I didn't feel the pain. As he pounded away, my instinct wasn't to hit back, but to break free.

Flailing, I ripped myself from his grasp. But after regaining my footing, I saw Tom, one of our pledges, wrestling the guy into headlock. Apparently, Tom had freed me.

If you had phoned Central Casting and asked for a surfer or a band front man, they'd have sent over Tom. He was solidly built and undeniably good looking, with black hair that nearly reached his broad shoulders.

"Let me go, asshole," the guy hissed, struggling to break Tom's grip. But Tom, who had trained in martial arts, was in control.

"You through fighting tonight?" Tom asked, as if he were disciplining a child.

The guy thrashed furiously, but Tom held firm, while mouthing a sarcastic yawn to me.

"Who the fuck do you think you are, getting in the middle of this?" Doug seethed. "Why don't you mind your own business?"

"Stop asking me stupid questions," Tom said. "Who the fuck are you, Columbo?"

The guy said something under his breath, but after struggling again unsuccessfully, he grumbled, "Yeah, I'm done."

Tom let him go and the guy stood up. Breathing heavily, he straightened his shirt while glaring at Tom, muttering, "It's fucking unbelievable the way you frat guys gang up on people."

"You mess with one of us, you mess with all of us," Tom said, as Doug walked away with two guys who had declined to step forward to take on Tom.

The crowd dispersed, probably disappointed that the fight had ended so soon. As my head began to clear, a sharp pain in my ear confirmed that I had lost badly.

"Thanks for bailing me out," I told Tom, as we walked to our table with two other brothers. After saving my ass, I no longer viewed him as a pledge. He was my brother.

He winked and said, "You can thank me by paying the tab."

Tom generally stayed in the background to avoid being hassled by the brothers, but you knew he was there. His gaze melted girls but what drew people to him was his palpable confidence. During rush week, he was the recruit that we wanted most.

We all sat down at our table as 38 Special's *Hold on Loosely* played on the jukebox. From across the booth, Fish was staring into my eyes.

Red haired and stocky, Fish looked comfortable dressed up, even when he was sweating through his shirt. He had come to the meeting from his accounting job wearing brown slacks and a white button-down shirt, his tie probably neatly rolled and sitting in his car.

"What are you looking at?" I asked him.

"That guy got in a few good shots, so you'd better stop drinking tonight. You might have a concussion."

I touched my ear. Seeing blood on my fingers shook me, but I tried to act unaffected. "My brain is fine. It's my ear that hurts."

"What were you doing back there?" Tom said, grinning. "You've obviously never been in a fight."

"Aren't I the fraternity's sergeant at arms?" I deadpanned, as I poured myself a beer from the "beehive," an ancient swirled green glass pitcher that for the same money, held two more beers than all the other plastic pitchers at Shook's.

"We don't have a sergeant at arms," CJ said. He was nineteen, but with his baby face, braces, peach fuzz mustache, and light brown widow's peak, he looked more sixteen than twenty-one, so he had a Coke in front of him. "You're our song master."

"And athletic chairman," I said, dabbing at my ear to check the bleeding.

"That won't do you much good in a street fight, Pilgrim," Tom said. He was also nineteen, but our waitress was too busy checking out Tom's smile to care about his fake ID.

How did the fight start anyway?" CJ said.

"Technically, I'm not sure that was a fight," Fish said.

Ignoring their laughs, I said, "I went to take a leak and that guy stopped me. His name is Doug and he drives for Embassy Dairy."

"Just the executive summary, please," Fish said.

"You know that townie's name and where he works?" CJ said. "Was there a ringside announcer before your fight?"

"I read the patches on his work shirt," I said, staring CJ down. "Anyway, I made a joke that Doug didn't appreciate. He told me that fraternity guys didn't have to work a day in our lives and that our biggest worry is what tie to wear with our blazer."

"That guy's dead wrong," CJ said. "I only have one tie."

Tom and I grinned, while Fish set his jaw and said, "Then what did you tell him?"

"That if he had joined a fraternity, he'd see we were regular guys. He said I was full of shit because regular guys like him couldn't afford to go to college."

"Boo fucking hoo," Fish said. "I work thirty hours a week and take twelve credits. That guy could do the same."

"He was so pissed, I was just trying to appease him."

"Take a stand, dude," Tom said. "If that gets you into fights, then at least you'll learn how to fight."

"I can't help it," I said, taking a gulp of beer. "That's why people call me Henry Clay."

"No one calls you Henry Clay," Fish said.

"Who is Henry Clay?" CJ said.

"Some US statesman," I said. "He was known as the Great Compromiser."

"Maybe if Henry Clay had taken a stand once in a while, we'd know who he was," Fish said. "They might have put him on the currency."

"Why are you accountants always talking about work?" I told Fish, who scowled at me.

"Speaking of work," CJ said, winking at Tom. "What are

you guys doing this summer?"

"I'll be at my bank," Fish said. "They offered me a post-graduation package I couldn't turn down."

A package? I thought. *All I want is a job.*

Bubbling over, CJ said, "Tom's hooking me up with a job parking cars at the Carousel. It's one of the best jobs in Ocean City."

Sitting back, Tom stretched an arm along the top of the wooden seatback. His glance at CJ, said, *No need to push. It's a great job.*

But CJ continued excitedly, "Tom was the valet supervisor last year. He shared a place with a bunch of guys and banked four thousand dollars."

Tom lifted his chin slightly to affirm.

"That's solid money," Fish conceded. "But what are you going to do in Ocean City for three months?"

"The three B's," CJ said. "Babes, bars, and of course, the beach."

Tom rolled his eyes while Fish and I chuckled at CJ's bravado because he wasn't a partier, and he didn't chase girls.

"Must be nice," I said, taking a swig of beer. "Party all summer, then back to school in September for more partying."

"Jealous?" CJ teased. "Don't worry. Graduating isn't the end of the world. Besides, you've got to grow up sometime."

"How would you know?" I said, swatting at him in a backhand motion. "You're only a sophomore."

"You didn't tell us about your job," Fish said to me, sounding like a guidance counselor prodding one of his laggards. "How are your interviews going?"

I paused, then admitted I hadn't scheduled any.

"What are you waiting for?" Fish said, his eyes bugging out.

"Motivation," I said. "Right now, I'm just trying to pass

COBOL II."

"Are you seriously not looking for a job?" Fish said.

CJ cut in, "Hey Bruce, if you come to the beach, you'd not only have a job but you could get rid of your pasty complexion."

"What are you laughing at, Pledge?" I said to Tom.

"You're so pale," he said, giggling. "Even my ass is tanner than you."

We emptied the Beehive one more time, and our waitress came by with the bill. Tom nodded toward me, and she tore a green sheet off her pad and slapped it on the table in front of me.

I pulled out my credit card and handed it to her without looking at the number circled at the bottom.

As we got up to leave, CJ asked me, "So are you in on Ocean City?"

"My dad would kill me if I spent summer at the beach."

"You should be living for yourself, not your father," Tom said.

CJ added, "You don't have anything else lined up, so this is perfect."

"I could use a break once I'm done with school," I said, glancing at Tom. He was too cool to say anything, but his eyes were telling me, *Come on, dude. You won't be sorry.*

"Of course you need a break," CJ said. "Tom owns that town and he'll be with us every step of the way. What do you say?"

Caught up in the moment, I said, "I'm in."

"Are you serious?" Fish shook his head in disbelief. "You need to get a real job."

"I will. But not in May."

FOUR

L auderdale! was the Spring Break destination touted by flyers blanketing every bulletin board on campus. But on spring break Monday, CJ was driving us to our interviews in chilly Ocean City. After not pursuing any other job prospects, Dad would have to deal with me living at the beach for the summer.

I hated job interviews. I was too honest and avoided hyping things, myself included. My biggest weakness wasn't that *I take on too much work because I have trouble delegating responsibility*. It was that I didn't feel like playing the game.

Before that day, I had only been to Ocean City twice. On both trips, I was probably drunk before we had gone thirty miles to the Bay Bridge and didn't sober up until the ride home. I had fun, but didn't get any feel for being at the beach.

On one drive, a fraternity brother, decided to steal a chicken from one of the chicken houses along Route 50 in Salisbury. It was dark outside when we stopped and he got out. Fortunately, he couldn't get into the building and his ill-advised plan fell apart. Later, he poached a plastic lawn chicken from a yard.

My drive with CJ was much more subdued. He seemed content to stare out the windshield for the 150-mile trip, while I was nervous about the interview and feeling guilty about not looking for a real job.

"How can you be so calm?" I said, trying to engage him.

"How hard can the questions be? We're parking cars."

"What do I tell them when they ask if I can drive a stick car?"

"They aren't going to ask that."

"What if they do?"

"Then tell them you can drive a stick."

"But I can't. You saw me yesterday."

The day before, CJ had given me a driving lesson. I had his old red Dodge Colt stalling and lurching while navigating our campus' empty parking lots. His car's nickname *The Doge* wasn't from a cowboy saying, "Git along, little Dogie." It was because the second metal "D" in Dodge had fallen off the hood, leaving two holes where the missing "D" had been fastened.

"Some people pick up driving a stick right away," CJ said, fingering his gear shift as he stared out the windshield. "Then there's you."

"You said I was doing fine," I said, agitated.

"What could I say? Did you think that curb just jumped into your way?"

He drove in silence for twenty miles. Then I said, "So what if they do ask me?"

"Stop worrying," he said, squinting his eyes at the road. "They won't ask."

As I rode, I thought about the past few weeks. How when I floated spending summer at the beach, most of my friends were excited for me and said they'd visit. While I still wasn't committed to the beach, there was nothing to stop me.

The Doge shuddered in the wind as we crossed the last bridge before Ocean City. I looked out the windows for a sign that I was making the right decision, but it was dreary. Seagulls were perched atop each highway light, puffed up, trying to stay warm. I didn't see any boats on the bay, but about a dozen twenty-story hotels dominated the skyline to our left, offering some promise of civilization.

CJ turned onto Coastal Highway, Ocean City's six-lane beach drag, at the town's midpoint and headed north. Nearly every traffic light was flashing yellow and swaying in a cold, heavy wind. Cars and pedestrians were scarce as we rode past three miles of closed restaurants, hotels, condos, bars, shops, and realty offices.

"Is this the right Ocean City?" I asked CJ, who ignored me.

We pulled up at a twenty-two-story building with CAROUSEL boldly spelled out in a column of large red letters reaching halfway up the facade. I was impressed, but then, I had never stayed in a hotel. On our infrequent family trips, we always stayed at relatives' homes.

The person at the front desk directed us to a small waiting area. Minutes later, an office door opened and a woman, around thirty with short, brassy blonde hair, stepped out. Seemingly in one syllable, she called, "Which one of you is Bruce?"

I raised my hand, then stood and tossed my Ocean City-themed magazine on a table.

"I'm DeAnne," she said, smiling and waving me over. "Come on in."

Her desk and walls were covered with family photos, most set at the beach. She asked where I was from and I told her I had grown up in Silver Spring, just outside D.C.

"I'm originally from Jacksonville, Florida," she said, in a southern accent. "But I've been an OC Local for years."

"You actually live here year-round?"

"I *actually* do," DeAnne said, her head down, scanning my application on her desk. "I just love Ocean City."

"What do you do here in the winter?" I said.

She raised her eyes just enough to peer up at me. That one, I wanted to take back.

"The Carousel is available year-round for banquets, conventions, weddings, *and* for people who enjoy the beach," she said. "It opened in 1962, before North Ocean City was developed. Bobby Baker, owner and LBJ's protégé, built here because he knew people would come." She sounded like the back of a picture postcard.

"That's impressive," I said, my words betrayed by my nervous monotone.

She leaned forward, likely expecting me to say more. When I didn't, she eased back and looked down at my application.

I'm bombing this, I thought. *I had prepared for real interview questions but can't hold a simple conversation.*

She leaned forward again. "What would working at the Carousel mean to you?"

"Umm... Working at the Carousel. I... uh... think that parking cars is an important..."

Her smile turned into a giggle and I gave her a *What gives?* look.

"I'm only pulling your leg because you looked so serious," she said. "Don't worry. You're not interviewing with Ernst and Whinney."

"You got me," I said, producing my first genuine smile of the interview.

Then she asked a few casual questions, probably easing into rejecting me. As she put her hands on her desk, I braced myself.

"Congratulations!" she exclaimed. "You got the job! Orientation is May second."

"Really?"

"Really. You brought proof of your clean driving record and you have a referral from Tom. That's all I need."

My interview felt like it lasted at least twenty minutes, but CJ's couldn't have been more than five. As we walked to his car, he said, "What did you tell her?"

"She didn't ask."

"I told you they wouldn't."

"I thought Tom was kidding when he said all the Carousel needed was warm bodies with clean driving records," I said. "You still think it's a good job?"

"It's a *great* job," CJ said. "It's not what you know but who you know. And we know Tom. Like I've been telling you, this is going to be the best summer of your life."

After hearing that for weeks, I was starting to believe him.

I got the job, but I never felt satisfaction from anything I achieved because something couldn't be that great if I could do it. On the drive home, I spared CJ my concern over telling my dad that my career job search wouldn't be starting until after Labor Day.

Having grown up in the Depression, Dad was all-encompassed with financial security. He never showed pain or missed work, and except for anger, rarely expressed emotion. As he got older, Dad occasionally conceded that his knees ached because of arthritis, probably from him carrying the weight of the world all those years.

An economist, Dad used to offer to take me by bus to the library and show me how to research stocks using the

ValueLine index. Our relationship might have turned out better had I gone more than once, though it was probably doomed when my first word was *Mama* and not *Dada*. He could hold a grudge.

I waited until 9:00 that night to call, figuring Dad might be less combative at the end of the day. I'd take my lumps from him now, then coast through the last six weeks of school and go to the beach where he couldn't reach me.

Mom answered. Tall and rail thin, she was a junior high school teacher. Months shy of her fiftieth birthday, her dark brown hair didn't have a strand of gray, though she may have plucked interlopers. Mom's pleasant face was scarred from more than a decade of skin cancer biopsies and removals of growths, so our family had fanatically avoided the sun most of my life.

"Should I call you back?" she said, which would cause C&P Telephone to bill my parents, not me, for the long-distance call.

"No thanks," I said, flexing my independence. "Well, I got the job."

"At the beach?" she said, though she knew. That was her way.

I ignored her question. That was my way. "What kind of mood is Dad in?"

"Par for the course," she said, sighing, then called upstairs, "Marvin, it's Bruce!"

Our house played to a par three. DEFCON 3.

He yelled back, "You're not on your father's front stoop in Brooklyn anymore. I will not have you shouting up here at me."

Undeterred, Mom called up again, "Pick up the phone. Bruce is on!"

"Alice, if you have something to tell me, then come up and speak civilly!"

I bristled, hearing Dad baiting her. Growing up, he always made me defend my actions so I constantly felt guilty about something. Eventually, I became fed up with his all-stick-and-no-carrot approach.

I nervously cleared my throat while waiting for him to pick up the bedroom extension.

"Hay-lo."

Dad's deep voice usually unsettled me and I pictured his stern face, clunky glasses, and short, dark, graying hair as he barked into the phone's mouthpiece.

Not bothering with a subtle build-up, I said, "Hey Dad. I got the job in Ocean City."

Dead silence.

"Will you be taking that job?"

Jesus Christ, can't he take an inference?

"Yes, I will be taking the job. As a valet. At the beach. Starting in mid-May."

"Where will you be working in the fall?"

"I don't know yet," I said. The only answer I had prepared that day involved my experience with manual car transmissions. "I'll guess I'll look for a job when I get back home."

"You're waiting until September to *look* for a job? Do you think they hand out good jobs like candy?"

"People hire year 'round," I said, as doubt crept into my mind.

"Doing what? You said you didn't want to be a computer programmer."

"That's right. I didn't find programming very satisfying, so I'll have to revisit my field."

"Just when are you planning to revisit your field?!"

"After graduation. Right now, I'm taking sixteen credits and I'm struggling in COBOL II."

"You have ample time for career counseling and job interviews. Without a good job, how do you expect to make a mortgage payment? Or the upkeep on a car?!"

"You need to calm down, Marvin," Mom interrupted from the kitchen extension. "Remember what Dr. Weintraub said about your blood pressure."

"It's pounding right now, Alice. How in blazes could I forget?"

"Dad, I'm graduating on time and I'm entitled to a break. I've worked every summer since I was fourteen and have never gone away for Spring Break. I'm not even asking you guys to pay for anything."

Those were my best arguments, but he wasn't impressed.

"When I was your age, I worked at Macy's for twelve cents an hour to pay my way through night school," he said. "I never had the luxury of a beach vacation!"

"It's not a vacation. I'll be working forty hours a week."

"Doing what? Parking cars? Alice, your son, who we just put through college, is going to be a car parker. You must be so proud. After you hang up, be sure to call everyone in your Mahjong group so you can toot your horn."

For Dad, working as a valet wasn't a real job because I wasn't bettering myself and there was no path to management or a pension.

"This not-looking-for-a-job nonsense has gone on long enough," Dad resumed yelling at me. "I forbid you from moving back into my house until you have secured career employment!"

"Oh Marvin—" Mom interjected.

"We've discussed this, Alice. There have been no

interviews. There's no plan. I'm not going to sit back and watch my son turn into a good-for-nothing bum."

Then back to me. "This is the thanks I get after twenty-two years?! Why is it so goddam hard for you to look for a job?!"

"I told you I was taking some time off!" I yelled back. "Why can't you accept that?"

"Because you think you know more about life than I do. Well you're not as smart as you think. Alice, I swear to God, this is more than I can take. I'm washing my hands of it!"

He slammed down the phone receiver. It was quiet for several seconds. Mom and I were used to Dad's outbursts, but this was one of his worst.

Finally, I said, "Why can't Dad leave me alone?"

"For him, a job, a *good* job, means everything. He knows what's best for you."

"How could he possibly know what's best for me? He doesn't know anything about me."

"He went through the same things when he was younger. And the world was much harsher then."

"Everything was harder back then," I said, tired of that trope.

"You need to listen to your father. He's been having a difficult time since Grandma Helen died."

Dad's mom had died four months earlier. Two years before that, Dad and his brother moved her from Brooklyn to a nursing home in our area. When I'd visit Grandma Helen, she'd unload on Dad and Uncle Morton about her aches and ailments, or her grievances with the nursing home. Dad showed great patience with her. I wished he had more patience with me.

"Grandma Helen had been in poor health for years," I said. "I thought her death was merciful."

"It was, but she left a void, especially with your father. You know he needs something to worry about and now that she's passed, it looks like that something is you."

"Wonderful," I muttered. "I don't know what field I want to go into and all his pressure isn't helping."

"That's your father's point. Saying that you don't know isn't an excuse."

"I can't believe you're taking Dad's side," I said, and as soon as I got off the phone, I wanted to call her back and tell her I loved her. But I had never said that to my parents, nor had they ever told me.

Alone in the front room of my row house on the outskirts of Baltimore, I picked up the phone and called Paul, my best friend from high school. I was too upset to wait until 11:00, when the long-distance rates went down to ten cents a minute.

We had little in common. He was free-spirited and intellectual, someone who rarely broke a sweat and couldn't read a box score. He drank in moderation, preferring to be tipsy, while I needed to be drunk. He got me into progressive music, so I was listening to Talking Heads and The Smiths before they were played on the radio. Meanwhile, Paul, who came out to me after we had known each other five years, *felt* The Smiths.

Senior year in high school, I was on the baseball team and joined Paul on stage crew. Trying to hang with both the jocks and the theater people was like trying to be a member of the Sharks and the Jets, a reference lost on the jocks. Both groups rejected me, so I spent most weekend nights alone, watching TV.

After gravitating toward Paul's worldview, I began pushing back on Dad, who resented Paul's influence on me. In frustration, Dad often referred to him as "That Paul."

Dad would growl, "If That Paul told you to jump off a bridge, you'd do it."

"Only once," I'd reply.

He lived in his parents' basement with no car and little money. Credit-wise, he was still a sophomore, chronically dropping classes and taking semesters off to work to pay for school. He wasn't as far along in college as I was. But he never seemed rushed, so maybe he just wasn't as lost as I was.

"What are you doing?" I asked when he picked up the phone.

"Relaxing and having drink."

"What are you drinking?"

"Coke and grenadine."

I immediately felt better, imagining the contemplative look on his round face as he held his highball glass.

"How are things in Bal-T-more?"

"That's Baltimore, Jack," I said, though he wasn't a Springsteen fan. "Actually, the news is out of Ocean City. I got the job at the Carousel this afternoon and just told my parents."

"How did Marvin take it?" He liked referring to Dad by his first name.

"He kicked me out of the house until I get a career job," I said, choking on the last few words.

"When *are* you going to start interviewing?"

"I don't know, but I can't back down now. I've bragged to too many people about living at the beach."

"Why is living at the beach so important for you?"

"I'm tired of my dad telling me what to do. Besides, what's wrong with the beach?"

"Nothing's wrong with the beach," he said. "The problem is you don't like it."

"Who said I don't like the beach? I don't like the pool."

"Down to a pool fraught with danger … is a pool full of

strangers," he sang the B-52's' *Private Idaho* in a loose Fred Schneider imitation. "What don't you like about the pool?"

"It's crowded and everything there centers on the water or the sun."

"I hate to break it to you, but the beach is one giant pool."

"I'll have cable TV," I said. "You won't see that at the pool."

"That's because people at the pool *like* being at the pool, so they don't watch TV. Why don't you tell me your favorite things about the beach."

"Drinking in the afternoon ... bikinis," I said, but couldn't think of anything else.

"You don't even like seafood. What are you going to do at a crab feast?"

"Drink beer," I said, realizing I had lost the argument. "Bottom line, Dad kicked me out and I'm not crawling back to him. Am I in for a long summer or what?"

"Or what?" Paul said, completing our inside joke.

The beach was everything that Dad wasn't: fun, relaxing, and impractical. I was going there to show him that I didn't need him.

The following week, I was deejaying my fraternity's happy hour, which I enjoyed because I was physically separated from the crowd. Behind my equipment, I had purpose. Hell, I had the mic so I was in charge. At least until someone asked me to play a song I was tired of hearing. If I gave in, then I turned into every other deejay.

One of the most insulting things someone could tell me was that I had done or said something predictable. I wanted to stand out, even if that meant standing by myself.

Tom walked up to my table, grinning. "Dude, everything's

set," he said, as we high-fived. "We're rooming together and I've got a line on a killer house."

"That's awesome," I said, trying to copy his vernacular, thrilled that he had chosen to room with me from among all his beach friends. "Who is CJ rooming with?"

"That's not my problem."

"What do you mean?" I said, my levity immediately gone.

Tom snorted. "CJ isn't twenty-one and his ID can barely get him into an R movie. I want housemates who can drink at bars."

"You promised him he'd be in the house with us," I said. "You can't do that to him."

"I already did," Tom said, staring at me. "Look, I told him I could only arrange roommates in pairs, so don't tell him the real reason he's out. I don't need that drama, understand?"

"What if CJ finds his own roommate? I can make some calls."

"Dude, it's over. Now if *you're* not in, I'll get another roommate and you and CJ can look for a place together." He picked up an album, absently glanced at it, and took another hard look at me. "Well? Are you in or not?"

"I'm in," I said, but couldn't believe he was screwing over CJ like that.

He nodded and tossed the album back on my pile. "Okay then," he said, smiling, like the conversation about CJ had never happened. "Wait until you see the place I'm working on. It's just off the beach, close to the Carousel. It's perfect."

But if it was perfect, then CJ would be living there. I felt terrible for not standing up for him, but I couldn't get on Tom's bad side. Spending summer at the beach was my last waltz and I knew the closer I was to Tom, the more fun I'd have.

FIVE

A couple of days later, I was watching *Letterman* by myself in my house's front room. It was the last Monday in March, just after 11:30 p.m. When the phone rang, I knew it was Amy.

We spoke by phone every week or so, and always talked and talked, though never about how we felt about each other or about dating. I liked Amy, but whenever a girl was interested in me, I'd look for flaws in her because why else would she be interested in me?

But Amy was polished, outgoing, and happy—three things I wasn't—so instead, I questioned whether I was worthy of her.

My usual pattern after a couple of dates was not getting as far as second base unless I was drunk. Both the girl and I would get frustrated that things weren't progressing and it was easier for me to break up than to explain my issues. I wasn't shying away from Amy because the distance between us removed the pressure of physical intimacy.

My first crush was in ninth grade. Shari Dunning was a freckled, strawberry-blonde jock who looked great in her tight, navy-blue tracksuit. After agreeing to go to the spring dance with me, she backed out at the last minute. The *Grease* soundtrack had recently been released, so my broken heart was further tormented by my AM radio, which wouldn't stop playing Olivia Newton-John and John Travolta's vocal flirtations on *You're the One that I Want*.

Getting jilted made me even more hesitant around girls and my losing streak continued through high school, where I didn't go to a prom and had been kissed exactly once. That had been on the cheek, which didn't really count. And she had kissed me.

Having a girlfriend sounded nice but wasn't really an option for me. I didn't know how to flirt, ask someone out, or date. In college, I had sex with several girls, but our relationships ended soon after the sex. One girl kept me around, mostly for booty calls, which at least confirmed that I wasn't bad in bed.

With few girls as friends or acquaintances, I was never relaxed around them. Amy was different. She was patient with the random thoughts that popped into my head. She knew sports and my music, so talking with her was easy. Still, as great as she was, I couldn't get too close to her, because she'd expect more than I was able to give. My biggest fear was disappointing her.

I had been expecting Amy's call because an hour earlier, her Hoosiers had won the NCAA basketball championship.

"Did you see that game?" she said, more excited than usual.

"I did. Congratulations to you and your school. Your campus must be going nuts."

"Bloomington has been crazy for weeks," she said. "They'll probably burn down Disco Briscoe tonight."

"What's a Disco Briscoe?"

"It's a high-rise, high-testosterone dorm near Assembly Hall. All the jocks live there."

"Got it," I said. "I'm glad you called. Now I feel like I'm part of the celebration."

"Go Big Red!" she shouted.

As we discussed key plays from Indiana's one-point victory, she impressed me with her basketball knowledge.

I updated her on my plans for the beach and she asked if I knew where I'd be staying.

"I'm rooming with Tom. He's working on getting a place, but CJ won't be living with us."

"Why not?"

"Because he doesn't have a solid ID," I said.

"What does that mean?"

"Tom wants housemates who can get into bars and drink."

"You can't shut CJ out like that," she said, surprising me with her anger.

"I agree with you, but Tom's mind is made up, so I'm caught in the middle."

That didn't satisfy her, so trying to change the subject, I brought up my fraternity formal. I told her how it was a month away, and since I didn't have a date, I was thinking about putting an ad in the school newspaper.

"Are you seriously taking a blind date to your formal?"

"Why not? I don't have anyone to go with."

"How about me?"

I hadn't considered asking Amy. She was a thousand miles away and I hadn't asked anybody to a dance since Shari.

Caught by surprise and feeling I had no choice but to accept, I said, "That would be great."

"It sounds like fun. I've never been to a fancy fraternity event," she said. "I already have a dress, so I just need a cheap flight to D.C."

Once again, Amy had impressed me. While I rarely traveled more than forty-five minutes from the house I grew up in, she was booking flights and crisscrossing the country.

"There is one catch," I said. "Our formal is on a Friday and I have to leave the next morning for orientation at the Carousel. Make that two catches. There's also my hair."

"What about your hair?"

"Last week, our rec league basketball team won our final game but missed the playoffs by one point in a tie-breaker. We were drinking afterward, frustrated at going 9-1 and still finishing in second place.

"I'm sure you guys were upset. But what does that have to do with your hair?"

"Well, Louis decided to shave his head."

"Why on earth would he do that?"

"He said he was going to shave his head before the game to psyche out the other team. He didn't go through with it but after the game and after a bunch of beers, he decided to go through with it."

"And you thought that was a good idea?"

"I didn't think it was a good idea, but Louis looked so silly, I couldn't leave him hanging."

"Oh, Bruce," she said, sounding as disappointed as Mom had when I had told her.

"Don't worry. It's got another month to grow back."

"Leaving early the next morning is one thing," she said. "But your hair has me reconsidering."

After hanging up, I was thinking about how Amy coming all that way for a date would raise expectations for our relationship. While I could be attentive and considerate on the phone for ten or fifteen minutes, I doubted I could sustain a dating relationship, even with someone as great as her.

Late afternoon on May first, I opened my front door and a smiling Amy dropped her purse and garment bag and extended her arms out to her side, clearly signaling me. I stepped forward and hugged her. She didn't unpack because to avoid driving drunk I had booked us a room at a motel a quarter mile from the formal.

We arrived at the motel and I couldn't tell if Amy was serious when she said, "You needed a reservation for this place?"

Inside the tiny office, the middle-aged woman checking us in asked to see our IDs.

"What for?" I asked, as she popped her gum.

"To make sure you're both consenting adults, Hon," she said, straight-faced.

Turning to Amy, I said, "Are you a consenting adult?"

"I guess I am," she said, laughing as she produced her ID from her purse.

Amy's consent was more of a joke, but as the clerk handed our licenses back, I was struck when she said, "As long as you're both twenty-one, I don't care what you kids do in there."

Having sex was more aspirational for me than imminent. The biggest significance of sex was prompting emotional consequences that I wasn't prepared to deal with. If I happened to be in bed with someone, even drunk, I focused on pleasing my partner and was too inhibited to tell her where or how I wanted to be touched. I didn't want to be selfish or treat her like a prop.

Of course, sex was certainly a big deal, mostly because my brothers talked about it constantly, making it a currency that they traded in. The first question many brothers asked me about Amy wasn't: *What do you like about her?* It was: *Are you getting laid?*

I opened the door to our ground-floor room and was greeted by the stench of cigarettes. Amy put down her bags and picked up the brown plastic wedge lying near the front door. I was thinking: *What a trooper. Once she props open the door, the place will air out.*

But she positioned the wedge under the *closed* door and kicked the wedge with the toe of her sneaker several times to secure it in place. Then for good measure, she slid in place the chain lock on the back of the door.

I sat down on the queen-sized bed, nervously smoothing the top of the bedspread with my hand. I had chosen it instead of two singles when I reserved the room. Amy didn't seem concerned by the one bed, while I was feeling overwhelmed thinking about us sharing the bed later.

I changed into my charcoal gray interview suit while Amy put on a red dress with a white jumper flap on the back and white hose. I wasn't wowed by what she was wearing, so alluding to the red and white, I told her, "Your dress and hosiery are very Hoosiery."

We walked along the heavily cracked pavement in the motel parking lot. After stepping around some broken glass and debris, Amy said, "I hope there's enough lighting when we walk back. I don't want to turn an ankle in these heels."

"Don't worry," I said, feeling guilty about our seedy motel. "I'll carry you all the way back."

As directed by the motel clerk, we crossed the street and followed a dirt path. Once clear of the industrial area and on the grounds of our venue, I felt better seeing mature trees, gardens, a gazebo, and pathways dotted with slate stepping stones, all accented by beautifully maintained grass. Glancing back toward our motel, blocks away, I was trying to remember if I had locked my car.

The ballroom was faux-Venetian, tall enough to play basketball in with vast chandeliers, their brilliance enhanced by ceiling mirrors. The walls featured soaring windows with swooping curtains and elaborate woodwork trim. It was grand, but I was more impressed by the alcohol selection at the open bar.

In our room, I had no perspective for Amy's dress. But under the bright lights, her dress looked modest, almost Christmassy, compared to the glittery, clingy, and revealing off-the-shoulder dresses worn by most other dates.

I introduced CJ to Amy and she told him, "You must be a great salesman."

"Why do you say that?"

"Because Bruce doesn't strike me as the beach type."

"He'll do fine there. He just needs to relax more."

"Do you guys mind?" I said. "I'm standing right here."

"See what I mean? Too high-strung," CJ said, grinning. "Did Bruce tell you about the fight he got into the night I told him about the valeting job?"

"You got in a fight?" Amy asked me, clearly amused.

"I wasn't in a fight. First, I'm minding my own business, then I'm joking around, next I'm getting punched, then Tom's pulling some guy off me. I still don't know what the fight was about."

"It was about your privilege," CJ said.

"Privilege? I'm working as a valet this summer. How is that privilege?"

"I think that's the definition of privilege," Amy said, smiling.

"Not twenty minutes into the event and she's already turned on me," I told CJ.

"Don't look at me," he said. "Tom said you've got to learn to fight your own fights."

A little later, I introduced Amy to Tom and his girlfriend Erin, a pretty, dirty-blonde, wearing a low-cut, mini cocktail dress that matched her blue eyes.

"Bruce has told me a lot about you," Tom told Amy, flashing his dazzling smile.

That seemed sociable of him, since all he knew about Amy was her name and that we hadn't slept together.

"I've heard about you as well," Amy replied, her cool tone surprising me because she got along with everybody and people usually fawned over Tom.

Tom looked at Amy suspiciously, so I jumped in, "I've been telling Amy about how much fun we're going to have at the beach this summer."

That broke the tension and the rest of the conversation was cordial, but something was going on between them.

As spring Athletic Chairman, I had to present our Athlete of the Year award. I was uncomfortable speaking in public but I felt better after several trips to the bar. Standing behind the podium, I rambled on about our successful semester, particularly our intramural basketball and softball championships.

With my speaking commitment behind me, I was able to relax. I had been introducing Amy as my date. One time, I accidentally referred to her as *my girlfriend* and Amy smiled knowingly. She didn't miss much.

My slip may have been the alcohol or maybe wishful thinking on my part. Seeing Amy's assuring smile and watching her face light up when she got excited made me realize how much I had been missing when we spoke by phone.

Some brothers were testing Amy, either telling her that she

was the first girl they had seen me with all year, or that she was the fifth girl I had been with that month. Faced with boasts, sarcasm, and bravado from a roomful of inebriated guys, she showed she could hang.

Jim Murray, our newly-minted Athlete of the Year, sidled up to us, saying, "It's good they cut your mic, or you'd still be up there. All you had to say was, 'The athlete of the year is Jim Murray.' Actually, you could have just said, 'Jim Murray.' I need no introduction."

"What do you care?" I told him. "You got your precious award."

"Jealous?" he said.

"I'm not jealous. I'm outraged. I should have won."

"What are you complaining about?" He laughed. "You had the only vote, so it was unanimous. Just like I had planned."

"How did you plan that?" Amy asked.

"Bruce knows I served as Athletic Chairman in the fall instead of spring so I could win Athlete of the Year. I'd have looked like a jerk if I gave it to myself instead of this guy," he said, patting me on the back.

"Since when were you concerned about looking like a jerk?" I said. "At least you acknowledge that I deserved the award."

"I hate to say it," he said to Amy. "But your giraffe of a date is wrong. I had a better year than him."

"A better year?" I said. "In football, I was open on every play. If anyone was near me, all you had to do was throw the ball nine feet high in my direction. A monkey could have done that. Then in basketball, you inexplicably forgot how to pass the ball into the post."

"I'm a shoot-first, pass second point guard," he said, laughing, as he walked away.

"Were you serious about the award?" Amy asked me.

"I had a better year than Jim. But he's right, I couldn't have voted for myself."

"But wasn't he your team's point guard? And didn't he play quarterback?" she said, playfully repeating his arguments.

I stared at her, still annoyed with Jim, but her teasing smile took my mind off Jim. We were standing close, gazing at each other. It was a perfect time for our first kiss.

When I didn't act, Amy reached and tightened my tie. "You're usually so modest," she said. "I didn't know you had such an ego."

"I'm proud of two things. My athletic ability and the fact that I can outdrink anybody in this room."

"Drinking a lot doesn't mean anything, so we'll have to expand your skill set," she said. "I'll bet you're also good at kissing." And she kissed me on my cheek.

CJ, who was walking past, yelled, "Hey. Get a room, you guys!"

"We do have a room," I called back, which reminded me that I'd be in that room with Amy later that night, so I went to the bar. I joined Tom and Erin in line.

"Why haven't you told me about Amy?" Erin said. "She's perfect for you."

"Amy's great," I said, nonchalantly posturing for Tom. "I don't know how you can tell she's perfect for me after five minutes, but I'll trust your judgment."

"If she's the one for you, then have at it, dude," Tom said, sounding detached. "But in two weeks, you'll be meeting dozens of girls at the beach."

He obviously hadn't been impressed by Amy. Not only had she been indifferent toward him, but the things that attracted me to Amy—her sense of humor, her intellect, how down-to-earth she was, and most of all, how special she made me feel—

were not on Tom's short list of female attributes. Amy was pretty, but she didn't look or act like the hotties that got his attention.

Tom talked the bartender into giving us our own pitchers of beer. Erin didn't look happy as we exchanged toasts and bumped our pitchers before drinking directly from our half-gallon mugs.

When I rejoined Amy at our table, she glanced sideways at the pitcher in my hand.

"It's more efficient," I said. "I hope you're okay with all the drinking here."

"You're just starting to consider that?" she said.

"Well, I uh—"

"Don't worry, we drink at IU as well. At least you're not driving."

Hoping to clear the air, I asked what she thought of my new roommate.

"Tom? You had described him pretty well, although I don't find him as attractive as you seem to think he is," she said, giggling. "He's pretty slick, though. Maybe a little too slick for you."

"You didn't have any problem with Jim," I said, concerned by the strained feelings between two prominent people in my life. "What's wrong with Tom?"

"He shut CJ out of your house," she said. "Jim may be egotistical, but you're not rooming with him at the beach. Plus, Jim's different because I've always been a fan of shoot-first, pass-second point guards, though Steve Alford is a shooting guard."

"Just how well do you know Alford?" I asked.

"Not well enough. He's marrying Tanya in July. They didn't invite me to the wedding but I'm thinking about crashing."

"I'm sorry you don't like Tom," I said. "He's a good guy. He just likes being the center of attention."

"I'm sure he'll get over not being the center of *my* attention," she said. "I'm glad CJ will be with you at the beach. He'll keep you grounded."

A little later, Amy and I were dancing when the deejay put on *Take My Breath Away*, a slow song by Berlin.

"Do you want to stay out here?" I asked her, as the dance floor cleared out.

She agreed, and I realized I didn't know how to slow dance.

Unsure where to put my hands, I settled awkwardly on the sides of her waist, barely touching her. When she put her arms firmly around my shoulders, I instinctively pulled her close. After leading her back and forth with a couple of choppy steps, I whispered, "I should warn you that I'm a terrible slow dancer."

"I never would have known," she said, straight-faced, and we both laughed.

At first, I was just holding on to her, but I quickly started enjoying embracing Amy, smelling her lilac shampoo, and feeling her body leaning into me.

She looked at me and reached up to rub my hair, which had surprisingly little growth after six weeks. I looked into her eyes and without thinking, moved my arms up to her shoulders. Then I leaned over and kissed her. It was more of a peck, but it was on her lips.

Amy didn't flinch. She put her hand behind my head and gave me a nice, long kiss. My legs got a little wobbly and as we separated, she said, "You can add kissing to the list of things you're good at."

Cutting loose with my brothers was fun, but I did that at every party. Being with Amy was special. I had a *date* and as we got drunker, we were holding hands, cuddling and smooching a little, even while not on the dance floor. I hated public displays of affection, but I wasn't so concerned by my own.

When the event ended, I wanted to go to Howard Johnson's for food with the crowd, but Amy said she was tired. I wasn't used to being part of a couple and hadn't considered how long her day had been: getting on a plane and then going to a formal event where she only knew me.

I swept her off her feet and holding her aloft, I reminded her of my promise to carry her back to our room. Underestimating how drunk I was, I dropped her before we got out of the ballroom. We were laughing as I helped her to her feet. When we got to our room, I insisted on carrying her across the threshold.

I went into the bathroom to pee and when I came out, Amy was standing at the foot of the bed, her hands behind her neck.

"My zipper is stuck," she said. "Can you help?"

I hurried over and stood behind her, unfastening the zipper with little effort. I couldn't call her out for being manipulative because I was feeling terrible for dropping her.

With her back to me, she removed an arm from her dress and then the other. Then she did a little shimmy and her dress fell in a tantalizing pile up to her shins. It looked better on the floor than on her.

Amy slowly stepped out, one leg at a time. She reached down, peeled off her hose, and tossed them on the floor. Her bare legs looked great, and as she turned and faced me, I couldn't help but glance down at her white bra and panties. Up close, her body was sexier than anything I had ever seen in a magazine.

With my anxieties drowning in alcohol, I embraced her. We started kissing and intertwined, we fell onto the bed.

SIX

I woke the next morning and looked next to me. *Holy cow. That's Amy.*

She was asleep, turned away from me, her dark hair scattered against the white pillowcase. My eyes followed her red IU t-shirt down the outline of her body under the covers, back up to the top of her head. I wanted to reach over and detangle her hair with my fingers but didn't want to disturb her.

Lying there, I was nervous about what to say and how to act. I had never spent the night with a girl and the movies and TV shows I saw didn't depict couples waking up together the morning after and hanging out.

I couldn't remember the sex, so I felt guilty. I couldn't tell Amy that I had been too drunk to remember something so special for us.

If I had been sober the night before, I would have been too shy to touch her, so we probably would have laid next to each other, talking until the sun came up. Then as we fell asleep, I'd have been trying to get the courage to put my arm around her.

I was afraid that things had changed and that now, she

would want me to dress better, or talk with her on the phone all the time, or stop drinking. I wasn't ready for someone to change my routine. I was too comfortable hanging out with the guys or being alone so I didn't think I could be happy spending so much time with a girl.

We hadn't closed the curtains so the room was filled with sunlight. Our formal clothes were strewn across the floor and on my way to the bathroom, I bent down and carefully picked a used condom off the rug and flushed it. My head was pounding, but I didn't have any quarters for the soda machine so I drank water directly from the faucet.

Walking back, I paused and stood over the bed. Instead of hopping under the covers like I belonged there, I crawled in, staying close to my side.

When Amy woke up, she looked terribly hungover but she smiled and scooted over to hug me. As we laid there, instead of whispering in her ear an affirmation so resonant she'd remember it on her flight back to Bloomington, I asked how she had slept.

"I wish we could stay in bed a few more hours," she said, yawning. Then, as we chatted about the night before, avoiding the fact that we had just *slept together*, she seemed like the same old Amy,. Maybe sleeping together hadn't ruined our relationship.

Then she shook me with four words: "What are you thinking?"

I had been fretting over our alcohol-fueled hookup, how we had gone way too quickly from our first kiss to sleeping together, and I was still doubting that I'd be able to initiate physical intimacy with her while sober.

Trying to sound comforting, I said, "Last night was special. I'm really happy you came to the formal so we could be together."

As we lay there, we weren't talking like lovers or like a couple after a flirty date. Instead of feeling euphoric about committing to a girl that I really cared about, I was trying to sort things out after having my emotions shaken like a snow globe.

I had to meet CJ at 10:00 to leave for orientation, so Amy and I didn't even have time to shower. We modestly alternated getting dressed in the bathroom with the door closed and then, both looking disheveled, we left.

Amy stayed in the car as I went into the office to turn in the key. The woman from the day before was there.

"How'd you make out, Tiger?" she said, grinning as she worked her gum.

"Not bad," I said, too embarrassed to look her in the eye. I signed the bill, put my key on the counter and walked out.

As we drove to my place to get her car, I shared something that I had been afraid to admit to anyone. That I was having doubts about living at the beach.

"Just go there with an open mind and you'll be fine," Amy said, giving me her supportive smile. "Besides, after talking with CJ and Tom last night, those guys would never forgive you if you backed out."

"You're right," I said, smiling back. "I gave them my word. That's all I've got."

We got to my place and I put Amy's garment bag in her car. "Thanks again for coming all this way," I said, wishing I could tell her how much I liked her, though I assumed I had probably avowed my love for her while drunk during sex. "I'm sorry we can't spend more time together today."

"I knew this visit would be a whirlwind," she said.

"Call me when you get a break from finals," I said, and as we stood close to each other, her eyes fixed on me, I was too intimidated to move.

She leaned forward and kissed me on the lips, making it easy for me to put my arms around her. Holding her felt so nice, I didn't want to let go.

"I can't wait to see you at Tamara's wedding next month," I said.

"Cool beans," she said, to affirm.

As she drove off, I was already starting to miss her. Erin was right. Amy was perfect for me. Amy understood me better than any girl I had ever met.

But I was also relieved to be by myself. Around Amy, I felt pressured to act more responsible and mature. I was afraid that if we started dating, she'd see how lazy and unfocused I really was, and she'd break up with me.

CJ suggested I drive The Doge to Ocean City to practice driving a stick. With each hop, rev, and stall, I thought I was burning out his clutch or destroying his engine, but he didn't say anything.

"How did the end of the night with Amy go?" CJ said, grinning.

"You know I don't kiss and tell," I said.

"You guys were swapping spit on the dance floor so it's not exactly a secret."

"Last night was great. Amy let me hang with you guys without reminding me that we were on a date. But this morning, I felt trapped, like she had pinned me."

CJ looked confused. "You mean like wrestling?"

"No. *Pinned*. Like when people used to exchange their fraternity and sorority pins as a sign of commitment."

"Why don't we just use expressions that our generation understands?" CJ said.

"I thought you might find my reference relevant, seeing as you're in a fraternity," I said.

He glared back but being so easygoing, he ignored my remark and said, "So is Amy your girlfriend now?"

It would have been easy to say that she was, but I knew better. Since I didn't want to tell him about my difficulties with intimacy, I avoided his question. "Amy's great, but I'm not ready for someone telling me I have to dress better or eating off my plate like Rodney's girlfriend was doing last night."

"Rodney and Jill have been dating since sophomore year in high school," CJ said. "Not all girls are rushing to get married. Besides, Amy's pretty cool. Does she think she's your girlfriend?"

"You'll have to ask her the next time you see her."

"If I see her again, then I'll have my answer." CJ said.

Driving on the highway, I felt better not having to shift so much. We sat in silence for several miles, but then I sensed him staring at me. "What are you looking at?" I said.

"You look awful," he said, chuckling. "You sure you're okay to drive?"

"I'm fine," I said. I was hurting, but my drinking pride dictated that I always got up and functioned, no matter how hungover I was.

"You ever think that you drink too much?" he said.

"Sometimes. But if I have a drinking problem, then so does a third of our fraternity."

"I'm not worried about a third of the fraternity. I'm worried about you."

I looked at him. "Seriously? You're bringing this up on our way to the beach?"

He nodded. "No one in the fraternity drinks as much as you do."

"That's true," I said, smiling.

"That wasn't a compliment."

Most of the drive was on Route 50, a lazy cross-country highway that passed through a few decent-sized towns. Forty minutes out, there wasn't much to look at besides farmland. I was fighting the tedium of the trees lining the road. CJ was squinting into the distance and I couldn't tell if he was asleep, so I asked if he needed glasses.

"My eyes are fine," he said.

"I just got glasses," I said. "I think it comes from looking at a computer screen so much. I had to pick out frames and they're —"

"Cop!" he yelled, pointing.

A trooper's car was in a clearing on our left.

"Shit!" I said. The speedometer read seventy-five miles per hour. My eyes went to the rear-view mirror, watching the trooper's cruiser. It sat. Then it pulled onto the highway. The blue lights went on, it accelerated quickly, and got right on my tail.

"Damn it," I said, clumsily shifting into neutral while braking before pulling onto the shoulder. I watched in my side mirror as the trooper finally got out and marched up in his heavy black boots. Tall and wiry, he wore a beige, high-brimmed hat over close-cropped hair. When he stopped next to The Doge and made a precise half turn, I knew I wasn't getting off with just a warning.

I rolled down my window and smiled. He didn't remove his aviator sunglasses as he bent to say, "You boys going to the beach?"

"We are, Officer," I said.

"I clocked you going 72 in a 55," he said. "What's the rush? The beach isn't going anywhere."

I just nodded as I handed him my license and CJ's car registration. The officer pivoted and returned to his car.

As we waited, I told CJ, "I should have told the cop I was going so fast because of beach erosion."

"What are you talking about?"

"I read in the *Washington Post* that Ocean City is spending fifteen million dollars on a beach replenishment program. When the officer told me that the beach wasn't going anywhere, I should have said I was in a hurry to get there before the beach erodes."

CJ stared forward, so I explained, "The beach literally *is* going somewhere. I'm just overstating the urgency."

"I got your joke," he said. "Keep it to yourself. That guy looks pretty uptight and I hear that police don't like getting chummy while they're busting someone."

The trooper returned, ticket book in hand. I signed and he handed me the carbon copy, along with my license and CJ's registration. Then he marched back to his car.

"How much is the ticket?" he asked.

"I don't know," I said, putting my license back in my wallet and shoving the ticket and CJ's documentation at him.

"One hundred dollars?" he said. "Ouch!"

I winced. "According to Tom, I'll make that back with a couple of days' tips."

As I stared into my rear-view mirror, he said, "What are you waiting for?"

"That trooper to leave. I don't want him to see me shifting as I pull away. There's probably some law against driving when you can't drive a stick shift."

But the trooper wouldn't budge. Sighing in frustration, I started The Doge and shifted into first. It stalled.

"Give it more gas," CJ said. "Or let the clutch out slower. Whatever's comfortable."

"Nothing's comfortable when I'm driving a stick," I muttered, then stalled it again. On my third try, the Doge bucked forward but I coaxed it into first and eased it back onto the highway. We were on our way.

Sunny and sixty degrees, Ocean City had a different vibe than six weeks before. As we headed north on Coastal Highway, traffic was steady and people were walking around as stores, restaurants, and bars were open for weekend business.

At the Carousel, they directed us to a conference room where about twenty clean-cut college-aged guys were assembled, with Tom right in the middle of the action. The bellmen knew each other from the summer before, while valets were the newcomers.

Sitting there, not saying anything, I felt the same sense of not belonging as when I started college. Back then, I had tried meeting people by playing pick-up basketball in the field house. Most had Baltimore area high school sports and parties in common, while I was from the DC suburbs. Between games, talk centered on girls and sex, but I didn't have anything to say, being a virgin. Those guys were already hooking up with girls at college, while I was still buying my textbooks.

Since March, Tom had been warning us about Gary, the bellcaptain. When he strutted in, his face was stoic but the bellmen started chanting, "Gar-y, Gar-y, Gar-y" and he broke character by smiling. He was nearly thirty with stringy brown hair and a scraggly mustache, looking like Sonny Bono without hair volumizing spray.

"Welcome to the Carousel," Gary addressed us, then paused for effect. "That's the first thing you will say to every guest you see. Listen up and I will share the tips of the trade for providing the Carousel total guest experience."

Gary introduced his favored bellmen—his lieutenants, as he called them. Tom, one of the elite, beamed obediently at our leader. Short and in need of a few solid meals, what Gary lacked physically, he made up for with pluck and bluster, mixing overzealousness with a pedantic tone. He spoke in great detail. Mostly about details.

"The Carousel's guests and condo owners are our biggest assets, and why must we give them so much attention?" Gary asked, before answering his question, "Because if we don't treat them like VIPs, they won't come back."

Duh. He was peddling common sense like a trade secret. As Gary droned on, some lieutenants started mocking him behind his back. I joined by making faces back at Tom.

"Every week this summer, a quarter-million people will visit Ocean City and my job is to make sure that the Carousel's bellstaff is providing the best service at the beach," Gary said. "Your response to every guest request will begin with the word certainly. If you can't back that up with *certainty*, you *certainly* will be fired."

He grinned at his wordplay and one of his lieutenants shouted, "You tell 'em, Gary!"

"As long as I've been here, the Carousel has been the top resort in OC and this season will be no exception." He turned briefly to gesture at the line of bellmen flanking him, "The bellmen are our backbone, but you valets are on the front line. One of you valets sitting here will be the very first person every guest sees…"

After Gary said, "OC," he turned back to face us valets and one of the lieutenants mouthed "Ocean City." Those of us who noticed tried to keep from snickering.

Sensing a distraction, Gary stopped pacing and asked, "Do you have something to add?" No one responded.

Why is he staring at me? I thought, as I sat up straighter.

"Are you sure?" he said, taking a few steps toward me, his lowered eyebrows showing he was daring me to challenge him.

"I'm sure," I said quietly, sneaking a look at the lieutenants. They were frowning at me because I had gotten caught and spoiled their fun. One was slowly shaking his head. Even Tom looked pissed.

"What's your name?" Gary asked.

"It's Bruce."

"Your name is *Spruce*? Like a tree?" he said, prompting laughs from a crowd eager to make points with him.

"Bruce."

"Bruce," he repeated. "That's good, because I'm sure as hell not putting *Spruce* on a name tag."

More laughter. Then Gary said, "Well, Bruce, what's the first thing you say to a guest?"

"Welcome to the Carousel," I said.

"That's correct, but I can barely hear you. We have to greet guests with enthusiasm. Try that again."

"Welcome to the Carousel!" I shouted.

"Whoa, whoa, whoa!" Gary chided, pumping his hands downward several times. "You must never raise your voice to a guest," he said, almost in a whisper. "Just act like you're happy to see them. You can do that, can't you?"

"Yes sir," I said, as chuckles filled the room.

"Okay Bruce," he said, grinning. "What's the *next* thing you say to a guest?"

"I…umm. I'm not sure," I stammered. By then, everyone was laughing at me, except maybe CJ.

"Then do me the courtesy of paying attention and you'll find out."

Everyone laughed again.

After speaking for more than an hour, Gary concluded his talk by reading passages from a photocopied five-by-eight-inch pamphlet, grandly titled *The Carousel Total Guest Experience*.

"Read this before you start work," Gary kept repeating, as he handed each of us a copy on our way out. It was a good bet he had both authored and memorized its contents.

"Just what I need," I told CJ, as I tossed the pamphlet into the backseat. "Next week, I have three finals and a paper due, and Conrad Hilton here wants me to do a book report on parking cars."

"Gary may seem like a hard-ass," CJ said. "But he just wants us to follow his directions."

"Sounds like someone's already sucking up to the boss," I said, but smiled so he would know I was kidding.

We hadn't left the parking lot before I realized I had just traded my dad for Gary.

SEVEN

Late the following Friday afternoon, Tom and I packed his borrowed pickup and my eight-year-old Impala. Before taking off, I rolled my windows down as far as possible without anything falling out and cranked a mixed cassette.

After we crossed the Chesapeake Bay Bridge, Tom was flying. As I struggled to keep him in sight, my speedometer was flirting with 90 when we weren't weaving through local traffic. I wasn't worried about ticketing cops because Tom had also borrowed a radar detector.

In the long stretches between towns, the roadside was a blur of billboards and sporadic gas stations with their hand-painted "live bait" signs. Looming among endless furrowed cornfields were vast silver metal-pipe irrigation systems, broad and arched like giant beetle skeletons.

Applying at the Carousel had been my response to a dare and became my excuse to not look for a job. Since calling Dad in March, I had been racked with guilt. I knew he was right, but I didn't feel like listening to him.

With each town we passed through, I relaxed a little more. As we approached the spot where I had gotten my ticket with

CJ, my heart was beating faster but when I didn't see a trooper, I felt like I was in the clear. My summer vacation had begun.

On the outskirts of Salisbury were compounds of chicken houses with rusty tin roofs, some as long as a city block. Once through the town, traffic cleared up, just like Tom had said it would. It was early evening, but the sky seemed to be getting brighter. I was breathing deeper at the air rustling in from outside and couldn't wait to get there and celebrate with a few beers.

We pulled up in front of our house on Shipwreck Road, the last street before the bay. Ocean City was a barrier island and we were about a mile from the ocean. Our side of the street had duplexes with front yards dominated by concrete driveways. Across the street were three-story condos overlooking the water.

Normally laid-back, Tom couldn't suppress his goofy smile as he got out of his pickup and we exchanged high-fives. He was *stoked* to be at the beach.

"I thought I lost you a couple of times back there," he said, his tone somewhat derisive, like I was a liability. It felt strange because Tom was masterful at communicating his preferences and dislikes without seeming either overbearing or whiny.

"I was a little gun-shy because of my speeding ticket," I explained. "But after waiting months for this, I couldn't wait to get here."

"That's what I keep telling you, dude," he said, building me back up. "You're going to have an awesome time this summer. *There's no way you can't.*"

I cringed at his double negative but didn't mention it because Tom bristled whenever I corrected someone's grammar or their facts as they told a story.

His guarantee of an awesome summer wasn't hyperbole. I was being indoctrinated. I didn't mind because I wanted to prove my friends wrong who had doubted that I could hang at the beach.

Our house slept eight—we were four guys and four girls. Tom knew two girls from school and the other two sets of housemates were friends of friends. Since Tom had arranged everything, he and I got the main bedroom with our own bathroom, phone extension, and balcony. But as we wandered through the upstairs, I left one bedroom thinking, *This should be CJ's room.*

Downstairs, I walked into a living room furnished in 1970s castoffs, with a heavy nautical theme: white wicker chairs, fisherman-themed wall clock, swag lamp, lighthouse bookends, glass lamps filled with seashells. The couch had a blue and white floral print with fabric as coarse as the kneepads on an old pair of Sears Toughskins jeans.

"Where do the owners get this stuff?" I called to Tom the kitchen. "It's like Shirley Partridge hired Jacques Cousteau as her interior decorator." He was too busy checking out what had been left in the fridge to acknowledge my schtick.

There was no TV, so Paul was right. I had brought my ancient twenty-five-inch model, that I had paid a dollar an inch for at a Value Village thrift store. Ocean City had no reception without cable, so I'd have to wait for installation.

A waist-high railing separated the living room from the dining room, which had an eat-in counter and a large wooden table that looked perfect for quarters, though I didn't have a coin to test its bounce. The kitchen looked serviceable, but all I needed was a refrigerator and a microwave.

The house wasn't run-down, but $3,000 a month, split eight ways, was still $275 more than the $100 I paid at my row house.

"How can they charge $3,000 a month, plus utilities, for this dump?" I asked.

Not realizing I was kidding, Tom went into sales mode. "Dude, this place is a deal. You're lucky I found it. It's big, it's on the water, and it's only half a mile from work. Let's sign the lease, get a couple of cases of Schaefer, and fill up my mini-fridge."

That made me feel better. Not because he had convinced me that the place was so great, but because he was trying to win me over.

He sat down at the head of the dining room table and without a cursory look, flipped to the end of the densely typed lease and signed the document. I was standing over him, glancing at an accompanying sheet with yellow highlighting emphasizing certain Ocean City noise ordinances.

"Hooting is an offense?" I said.

"Just sign and keep quiet," Tom said, handing me the pen. By *keep quiet*, he may have meant so as not to violate the ordinance in general, but he might have been telling me not to question him.

After cramming for finals, I was in no mood to read anything with yellow highlighting, so I leaned down and signed without asking for clarification.

When I had met Tom in late January, he was a pledge, so any brother could tell him to do anything, like *get me a beer* or *go tell that girl you still wet the bed*. As coach of our fraternity's teams, our relationship had developed while he was dependent on me for playing time. But at the beach, he wasn't going to let me call him out for not wearing his pledge pin. Here, he was both captain and cruise director, while I was starting to feel like a pledge.

The next day, I went to "Carousel Beach," the stretch behind our hotel, with Tom, CJ and our housemates Lisa and Sue. Lisa, who had grown up on a farm, was contemplative and reserved. Sue was outgoing, ditzy, and attractive.

After laying out our blanket and towels, I removed my shirt and CJ was joking that my pale chest was blinding him. I was thin and muscular but I rarely took off my shirt. CJ was as skinny as me and wasn't athletic, but he was tan, which trumped my pale muscles at the beach.

Little kids were digging in the sand with plastic shovels and wading in shallow water, while older kids were boogie boarding. Most beachgoers were reading and tanning, and there was a steady parade of beach walkers near the water. A mix of rock and easy-listening music converged from nearby boom boxes, and when the breeze was right I could smell the burgers from the Carousel's outdoor grill.

Tom asked if I was going swimming, but I declined, content to lay on my towel, drink beer, and read *The Sporting News*. I hadn't swum in ten years and had developed a significant fear of water.

Tom, CJ, and Sue headed into the ocean, with Sue pirouetting in her bikini. She was a dancer, seemingly in perpetual motion as she followed some internal beat. They stopped beyond the breaking waves and the boogie boarders, looking like specks against the vastness of the Atlantic.

Lisa stayed behind with me, reading her book, not removing the t-shirt she wore over her swimsuit. I enjoyed talking with her. She had an unburdened approach to life, a refreshing contrast to my constant indecision, regret, and unease.

The squealing kids, screeching gulls, persistent *whoosh* from the foamy tide, and music from nearby boomboxes blended into the background. But every ten minutes, I'd hear what sounded like a lawnmower and immediately look up, my eyes following a tiny plane flying over the ocean, pulling a banner touting a rib place or a bar on the nearby boardwalk.

Hours later, I got tired of re-reading my magazine and combing through the weekly baseball statistics. But instead of walking the mile home, I stayed because everyone would have been offended if I told them I was leaving because I was bored.

"Dude, it's time for you to get wet," Tom prodded me.

I couldn't tell him about my fear of the water, so I waded out with him and CJ for my first time in the ocean while sober.

I wasn't sure what I was supposed to be doing. They were bobbing, chatting casually, diving into the waves, while I was standing stiffly in four feet of water, trying to avoid getting dragged under. As the waves surged past every five seconds or so, with water swelling above my chest, I kept taking deep breaths but didn't feel I was getting enough air.

"You're getting crushed, Dude," Tom told me. "Turn sideways when a wave hits."

Whenever a wave rolled past, I turned like a weathervane. Tom's advice helped with the pounding, but I still wasn't relaxed.

"Check out those two," CJ said, and we watched two girls walking in the wet sand on shore.

Tom and CJ were expressing their preference for the well-endowed blonde. I was enjoying the view but didn't say anything. While distracted, a wave knocked me off my feet. With my head underwater, I panicked, swallowing water while flailing my arms, trying to swim. Tom's voice was eerily distorted from above. It sounded like he was saying, "*Stand up, Dude.*"

When I realized what he was telling me, I scrambled to my feet, gasping for air. After thinking I had been caught in a rip current, it was a comically simple resolution.

"I'm going back," I said, trudging toward the sand. Tom

and CJ were cracking up at me, oblivious to how terrified I had been.

As I walked up to Lisa, who hadn't moved from her spot in hours and apparently hadn't seen me go under, she politely asked, "How is the water?"

"A little choppy," I said.

Tom and I lifted weights that evening. We benched about the same amount and our camaraderie was great, so I enjoyed feeling like his equal at something at the beach.

After lifting, we went to Popeye's for dinner. Driving back, I got pulled over at a speed trap on Jamestown Road, unofficially 118th Street, a quarter-mile from home. Jamestown connected our street to Coastal Highway and with four unpainted lanes, it was as straight and wide open as an airplane runway.

I slammed the column shifter up into the park position and gave Tom a *What the fuck?* look. He shrugged.

The officer, who didn't look old enough to drink, told me I was going thirty-six in the twenty-five-mile-per-hour zone.

Before I could protest that there was no way I was going that fast, Tom called, "Joe! Don't tell me the OCPD is letting you back again."

The cop slouched to look in at the passenger seat. "Hey Tom," he said, grinning. "I'm thinking of doing this when I graduate. What other job would let me carry a gun besides the Army?"

To meet summer demand each year, the Ocean City Police Department hired dozens of college students as seasonal officers.

Tom laughed much more than the joke warranted, before

saying, "Joe, this is my roommate, Bruce. We're fraternity brothers."

I didn't point out that Tom was still a pledge.

"Sorry I had to pull you over," Joe told me. "But I can just consider this a warning."

"I really appreciate that," I said, extending my arm out the window. "Nice to meet you."

His body snapped backward.

"What are you doing, dude?" he said under his breath, glancing over his shoulder. "My patrol supervisor's right there. He'll write me up if he sees me shaking hands with someone I just pulled over. Now I have to write you a ticket."

"Are you serious?" I said. "What's wrong with shaking someone's hand?"

"Oh, for Christ sake," Tom muttered.

"License and registration," Joe said, sternly. As I rummaged through my glove compartment for my registration, Tom was looking out his window, disassociating himself from me.

Joe snatched the documents from my hand and pulled his ticket book from his back pocket. With an exaggerated motion, he flipped open the cover, quickly filled out a ticket, and ripped it off the pad. "Welcome to Ocean City," he said, stone-faced, and shoved the ticket at me.

In a friendly tone, he said, "See you around, Tom," and walked back to his police car.

I looked at Tom. "Since when is it a capital crime to shake someone's hand?"

"Dude, you're not at a mixer. Now the next time I see Joe, I'll have to buy him some drinks to make this up to him."

"Make this up to *him*? I said, agitated. "He's the one who gave me the ticket."

Back at home, we were on the deck, drinking beers, getting primed before going out. In a better mood, Tom said, "Don't worry about the ticket. Just take it to court and they'll throw it out." I nodded and he said, "But dude, you've got to be cooler than that."

Thanks. If I could just make myself cooler, I'd have started years before.

Being cool came naturally to Tom, which made him even cooler. Sometimes, I couldn't stop myself from making comments or jokes even though I knew people wouldn't understand them or understand me. I hated to filter out my quirkiness because the watered-down version that remained wasn't really me.

That night, we went to the Angler, a crowded bar near the boardwalk with an outdoor section along the water. Meeting so many people was like going on a bunch of mini-interviews where all the questions were the same.

I had trouble getting my point across quickly because I spoke in paragraphs, not sentences. Tom often answered with one word: *Chill, Dude, sick, psyched, stoked, later*; his brevity was often punctuated by a grin, wink, or nod, though never a wave.

We stood around as everyone sized each other up: Does this guy belong? Should I acknowledge him? Like him? Shun him? Conversations centered on opinions and boasts. Whose favorite beach was the best, whose bartender friends got them the best deals, which bars were the most fun. Most people had persistent smiles and laughed at things that weren't funny or clever.

They were extroverts who walked all over guys like me who were shy, humble, and— *shudder* —made self-deprecating jokes. It might have been my body language or that I rarely smiled, but they could tell right away that I wasn't beach A-list and knew they could crush me with a sideways glance or dismissive stare. They chose the topics, spoke with authority, and their opinions were accepted as fact.

I marveled as Tom glided in and out of clusters of people, smiling, nodding, shaking hands, backslapping. His words had instant credibility and some were even sucking up to him. Everyone noticed Tom and when he told girls that he had a girlfriend, he was even more alluring.

I was in a group without Tom. One guy was from Pittsburgh, so I asked if he was a Pirates fan.

"I go to a couple of games a year," he said. "I got Bill Mazeroski's autograph once. He hit that home run to win the World Series. You heard of him?"

It was an insulting question. Every baseball fan knew about Mazeroski's home run to win the 1960 World Series. That and Bobby Thompson's *shot heard round the world* in 1951 were baseball's most storied at bats.

"He was known for that home run," I said. "But Maz won eight Gold Gloves and turned the most double plays in history. Do you think the Pirates can finally get out of the cellar this season?"

"I haven't had time for baseball lately, with finals and being at the beach," he said, sounding miffed that I knew much more about Bill Mazeroski than he did.

"Are you following the Niekros?" I said, happy to talk baseball. "Phil and Joe Niekro now have 528 pitching wins combined, one behind the Perrys on the all-time wins list for brothers."

"Are you serious, dude?" he said, scoffing. "I'm not twelve. I'm not obsessed with baseball like you."

The rest of the group smiled or laughed at me and I was relieved Tom wasn't there to see that.

As the conversation flowed back to something more *appropriate*, like the weather that day, I kept thinking about the Niekros tying and then passing the Perry Brothers in the next week. The prospect of both sets of brothers being tied for wins reminded me of when Franken and Davis went on *Letterman*, billing themselves as "the comedy team that weighs the same." Then they got on a scale and actually did weigh the same.

The more I thought about it, the angrier I got. *The guy was acting like a baseball fan, so why was my talking about baseball trivia so nerdy?* I noticed that no one was talking with me unless I asked them a direct question. I needed Tom with me because he'd make eye contact with me and bring me into conversations.

It was a long night, but I got through it. After last call, Tom and I left the bar and climbed into my Impala.

"You need to speak up more in conversations," he said, as if that had never occurred to me.

"Yeah, I know," I said. "I'm getting adjusted to things here."

"What's there to adjust to? Just go up to people and start talking to them like you know them."

"You're right," I said, but knew I couldn't pull that off. Tom and I had different personalities and different levels of self-esteem. He thought I wasn't trying hard enough to fit in, and I was already doubting that I'd be accepted.

Traffic on Coastal Highway was steady, with so many people leaving bars. Everyone was driving gently, trying to avoid getting pulled over for a sobriety test. After turning onto Jamestown, I saw the speed trap ahead. Tom started laughing about my ticket from earlier. As we approached, an officer waved his flashlight.

"He's pulling you over," Tom said.

"What the hell for?" I said.

The cop informed me that he had clocked me going thirty-three.

"There's no way I was speeding," I argued. "Besides, I got a ticket at this speed trap not five hours ago."

"Then hopefully, you'll learn your lesson this time," he said, as he wrote the ticket.

After the cop handed me the ticket and walked off, I crumpled the paper and threw it at Tom's feet. "I never went over thirty!" I yelled, pounding on my steering wheel.

"Two tickets? In one night? At the same speed trap?" Tom guffawed. Then he sang Sammy Hagar's hit, subtracting thirty miles per hour. "Take my license, all that jive. I can't drive twenty-five!"

I glared into my rearview as I pulled away. The cops had stopped the guy behind me. And he was riding a bicycle.

Friday night, we went to Harpoon Hanna's, a seafood restaurant two miles north of our place, near the Delaware line. On Mondays and Fridays, Hanna's offered two-for-one drinks from 10:00 until 11:30, so around ten, the dinner crowd was replaced by bar-hopping locals.

We were in line to get in and CJ stepped forward first, pulling his ID from his wallet. Tom nudged me as CJ haltingly handed the ID to the doorman, a chunky guy with curly hair who looked burned out from too many summers at the beach. Tom seemed to be enjoying the spectacle. My stomach was in knots.

The doorman reflexively extended his hand to accept the

ID. Looking at CJ, the guy's eyes narrowed, and he pulled his hand back before touching the ID, like it was radioactive.

"Good luck starting college this fall," he said with a smirk. CJ's head dropped. He turned and walked away.

"Brutal," Tom said under his breath.

"I've never seen a doorman refuse to look," I whispered back.

"He should have shoved his ID in the guy's face and made him look at it," Tom said. "He can't just back down without trying."

CJ was separated from the herd like a wounded antelope in one of those wildlife shows that never ended well for antelopes.

"*That's* why CJ isn't living with us," Tom whispered.

It was bad enough when Tom was laughing at CJ, but now he was trashing him. Since I didn't have a solid ID until I turned twenty-one, I knew how lousy it felt to be turned away.

"CJ, Wait up!" I called, stepping out of the line.

"Dude. What are you doing?" Tom hissed.

"I can't leave CJ hanging," I said, and Tom gave me a death stare.

I wasn't choosing between them. I just wanted everyone to be happy and knew that Tom would be fine in a bar without me.

CJ's posture improved when he saw me approach. "You don't have to leave with me," he said, as we walked past the end of the line to the parking lot. But he looked happy I had.

Back at my place, we drank beer in my room while I finished unpacking and hanging band posters. Tom's two walls were already covered with pages of swimsuit girls cut from surf magazines.

Around midnight, CJ went home. He had an early shift the

next day and didn't mind missing the almost nightly partying that started at our place after the bars closed.

Shortly after 1:00 a.m., our storm door opened and slammed, followed by loud voices. Minutes later, the door rattled shut again, and the voices got louder. The distinctive sound of a quarter hitting glass told me there was a quorum, so I went downstairs.

There were about twenty people, some on the back deck. I joined the quarters game at the dining room table and after several rounds, the guy sitting next to me gestured at Sue, standing in the living room, and told his buddy, "I'm going to fuck that blonde tonight."

I looked over at Sue, dancing in place as she chatted in a small group. She was wearing a t-shirt and short shorts, unaware of the guy's remarks, but she seemed oblivious to most things, often flitting around erratically like a butterfly.

"Think she's worth the effort?" the guy's buddy asked, from two seats over.

"I'll tell you tomorrow," the guy said, his smugness enraging me.

No one else heard their conversation, so I walked over to Sue. Not sure what to say, I tried warning her about the guy sitting next to me.

"Eddie? What are you talking about?" she said, her eyes bloodshot. "I just met him at Hanna's. He's a sweetie."

"He's not a nice guy," I said.

"How do you know?" she said. "You're drunk."

I wasn't that drunk, but she was too drunk to listen to me. I thought Eddie was a dick, but Sue didn't know me well enough to trust me and I was too embarrassed to tell her what he had said. Frustrated, I went back to the table and sat down.

Eddie kept calling to Sue. Eventually, she came over and sat down between him and his friend. They kept picking her to drink and as she and Eddie flirted, his buddy kept talking him up. I couldn't ignore the guy as he lied, bragged, bullshitted, and most of all, charmed my drunk housemate.

Trying to distract Eddie, I kept asking him questions, mostly about Towson State, where he went to school. He answered several, then pointed at me and loudly announced to the table, "Slim over here has a couple of drinks and now he thinks we're best friends."

I was already mad at Eddie and now he had embarrassed me. Instead of confronting him, I decided to drink him under the table. After almost every shot I made, I gestured at him with my elbow, knowing that in retaliation, whenever Eddie or his friend made a shot, they'd pick me to drink.

"Thanks, asshole," or "Lucky shot," Eddie would say. Then he'd drink, put down his beer, and sneer at me.

I overheard him tell his buddy, "This asshole is crushing me." Eddie had stopped taking nips from a bottle of Southern Comfort he had been drinking in addition to his beer from the game. Feeling guilty, I let up on him.

A little later, Eddie held out the bottle of Southern Comfort. "You're a drinker," he told me. "I'll bet you five bucks you can't kill the rest of this in one minute."

I saw a few good-sized shots remaining in the bottle.

"You're on," I said, happy to take his money. After drinking for a few seconds, I held the bottle in front of my face, expecting to be finished, but several shots remained.

Eddie and his friend were laughing so I realized Eddie must have tilted the top of the bottle away from me to hide how much was left.

I waited ten seconds, took a deep breath, and guzzled. The alcohol burned all the way down. I was gagging as I struggled to swallow the last of it and had to close my lips tightly to keep it from coming up. Luckily, Eddie was talking with Sue and didn't notice my difficulty.

"Done," I said, slamming the bottle on the table in front of him. "You owe me five dollars."

"No way you finished that. You must have poured some out."

"Where would I have poured it?" I said, leaning back and gesturing with my arm at the wall behind me. "You were sitting next to me the whole time."

"I didn't see you finish, so I'm not paying you!" Eddie shouted. "Since you poured it out, you owe *me* five bucks."

"Admit it," his friend jumped in. "You poured it out."

"I didn't pour—"

"Liar!" Eddie yelled, as everyone at the table seemed to be laughing at me. "You poured it out!"

I was having trouble thinking straight. Each time I tried to respond, Eddie and his friend shouted over me.

"Fork it over! Fork it over!" Eddie started chanting. By then, the whole room was watching. I had been right. Eddie *was* a dick.

"Fuck you guys!" I shouted. Feeling dizzy, I stood to go outside for air. The room was spinning as I walked through the living room and I fell. After crawling onto the couch, I stared at the TV until I realized it wasn't turned on. Then everything went black.

EIGHT

I opened my eyes and glanced at an IV bag dangling from a metal stand next to my hospital bed. I followed the plastic tube from the bag as it went below the bed and then back up and into my arm. Usually, I was squeamish about needles but was too out of it to freak out at the one sticking into me.

"Do you know where you are?" a nurse asked as she put a blood pressure cuff on my bicep. She looked about forty, with a white nursing cap atop her expressionless face.

"I'm in a hospital."

"You're at the Peninsula Regional Medical Center," she said, enunciating the name. It meant nothing to me.

"What am I doing here?"

"You were brought here by ambulance overnight for alcohol poisoning." Her tone was clinical, as she squeezed the bulb to inflate the cuff.

"Am I going to be okay?"

"I can't say."

"What?!"

"I meant that's for a doctor to say," she said, unapologetic for my misunderstanding.

She looked at her watch and shook her head. "That's not good."

"What's not good?!" I shouted again.

"You're too agitated for an accurate reading," she said, removing the cuff. "I'll have to try again later." She picked up a clipboard and glanced at it. "I need you to answer some questions."

I candidly answered her questions about my health and drinking habits. Until she asked if I had ever thought about killing myself.

In high school, I started thinking about suicide after feeling rejected by everyone. I was convinced that no one but Paul and Silk would miss me.

"Well, *have* you?" she said, bringing me out of my thoughts.

"Sorry. What was the question again?" I said, pretending I hadn't heard her, as opposed to having been reflecting on her question. I was coherent enough to realize that if I had answered *yes*, I wouldn't be leaving the Peninsula Regional Medical Center anytime soon.

She rephrased her question to lead me. "You don't want to kill yourself, do you?"

"No," I said, and with a flourish, she checked the last box on her sheet, put the clipboard on a counter, and left the room.

I fell asleep, dreaming I was at my dining room table, playing quarters with Eddie and his buddy. Then my dad walked up to the game and sat down without a word. He was wearing a black suit, a white button-down shirt, a thin black tie, and a black fedora. No one reacted to the old guy in work clothes, though if Dad had on sunglasses, he could have passed for a saxophonist in a ska band.

"What are you doing here?" I asked him. "You never spend any time with me."

Dad stared at me, ignoring my question.

Someone slid the quarter in front of Dad and said, "You're up."

"What do I do?" Dad asked, in his deep voice.

"Bounce the quarter off the table and try to get it into the glass," someone explained. "If you make it, you pick someone to drink. If you miss twice, then you drink and lose your turn."

I was embarrassed that Dad didn't know the rules. Everybody learned how to play quarters in high school or by their first weeks away in college. But no one else seemed to care and I was relieved that no one realized he was my dad.

He picked up the quarter and positioned the glass in front of him. Then he stood up, looked at the glass, and moved it back a couple of feet.

Just shoot already, I thought, as he held the quarter between his thumb and index finger, yo-yo-ing his arm up and down about a foot. Finally, he slammed the quarter onto the table. It bounced four feet in the air and landed in the glass with a loud clink.

No one else reacted to the miraculous shot. I grabbed my beer, knowing Dad would pick me.

He pointed at me from across the table.

"Gladly," I said, and took a big swig.

"I don't want you to drink anymore," he said.

"Then why are you pointing at me?"

"Because I want you to listen to me."

"You can't make me listen to you," I said. "That's not in the rules."

"We play by my rules," he said. "We've always played by my rules."

I tried to yell, "I'm not listening to you anymore," but no words came out.

I woke up, still in the hospital bed. CJ was peering down at me like he had just trapped a bug in a jar.

"How did you know I was here?"

"Tom told me at work. I just got off."

"What time is it?"

"About 3:30. What happened to you last night? Did you drink too much or is something else wrong?"

"It was just alcohol poisoning," I said, gesturing with my free hand at the clipboard with my paperwork.

"*Just* alcohol poisoning?" CJ said, picking up the clipboard and glancing through the papers. "This says that your blood-alcohol was point three."

"What's the big deal? I wasn't driving."

"Because you can *die* from that," he said, his voice cracking. "I've never heard of one that high."

I didn't say anything, so he pressed, "Don't you care what your drinking is doing to you?"

Again, I didn't respond and CJ shoved a quarter-page note at me. I didn't extend my hand, so it floated down on my chest. I picked it up. Under *Recommendations*, it said: *Stop drinking*.

I tossed the note on the shelf next to my bed.

"You can't keep ignoring your drinking," he said.

"I don't want to talk about it."

"You never want to talk about it," CJ said, but didn't push it, maybe because I was lying on my back in a hospital bed.

When the nurse returned, I asked if I could leave.

"I still have to get your blood pressure. If that's normal, you can be discharged."

She put the cuff on my arm and several seconds later said, "One-ten over seventy."

"What do those numbers mean?"

"Your pressure is normal," she said. "That's good because we're going to need this bed for real patients."

Man, was she pissed at me.

After watching her remove my IV, I felt lightheaded.

"You look pale," she said, concerned, as if she had just realized I was her patient.

"I don't do well with medical stuff," I said, swinging my legs over the side of the bed and putting my head down between my knees. "Can you get me juice or a Coke, please?"

I expected her to say that the Peninsula Regional Medical Center was not a luncheonette, but she nodded and left. She returned with a Dixie cup full of apple juice.

Ten minutes later, she came back and said the color was returning to my face. I told her I wanted to leave.

"Are you sure you're okay?" she asked.

I nodded and when I got to my feet, my head was killing me. CJ stepped forward and supported me under my arm as we walked out of the room.

When we approached the bursar's station, the woman smiled and asked if I needed to sit down.

"I'm okay, thanks," I said, leaning heavily on the counter. It was too late to turn back. The nurse had probably already given my bed to a *real* patient.

"Very well," she said. "Do you have medical insurance?"

I reached for my pocket, which was empty. "I have insurance," I said, reflexively patting my shorts pockets. "But I don't have my wallet with me."

She glanced through my paperwork. "I guess you didn't have a chance to grab your wallet before coming here," she said. At least she said it in a friendly way.

I looked at the plastic identification band on my wrist. It read *John Doe*. A chill went down my spine as I realized that when I had arrived, passed out, they couldn't identify me.

I gave her my name and beach address and must have looked pathetic because she said, "I can wait two days before processing your bill. Call me tomorrow with your insurance information."

As we walked out of the hospital, I pointed to the Band-Aid and cotton ball covering my IV cut and told CJ, "That was a rough night but I'm leaving here unscathed."

"Hopefully, you learned your lesson and you'll stop drinking like that."

"I plan to." But I only said that to appease him.

When Tom came home from work that afternoon, I was in bed. He stopped in front of the mini fridge in our room and plucked out a beer.

"Want one?" he said, pointing the top of the can at me like a flashlight, grinning like the devil looking to make a deal.

"No thanks," I said. I had a splitting headache but shifted around and sat up, not wanting him to see how affected I was.

"Dude, I wasn't letting you have a beer. I just wanted to see your reaction." he said, snapping open the can and taking a gulp. "What did the doctor say?"

"He said that I should stop drinking."

"*So are you going to stop drinking?*" he said, in a patronizing tone.

"For the rest of the day anyway," I said.

"How'd you get so bad? I thought you were just playing quarters."

"I was, but the guy next to me bet me I couldn't finish his bottle of SoCo. I did it, though."

"You showed him," he said, scoffing.

"Actually, I *didn't* show him. Since he didn't see me finish the bottle, he wouldn't pay me. Next time I'll make sure he's watching."

"*Next* time? Don't be stupid, dude. Drink when you want to, not because someone challenges you."

It was good advice for most people. But for me, being a drinker was a big part of how I felt noticed and accepted. Whenever I drank, I kept track of how many drinks I had consumed. That gave me some purpose, so I certainly wasn't backing down from a drinking challenge.

"Who called the ambulance?"

"I came in from the deck and you didn't look good," he said. "You were passed out on the couch, pale as shit."

"I always look pale to you," I said, trying to smile at my joke. "Besides, how good could I look, passed out?"

"Dude, you looked bad," he said, his tone ominous. "We were going to let you sleep, but some girl, I think she was a nursing student, insisted we call 911. The paramedics came and put you on that thin white stretcher and wheeled you out to the ambulance with your feet hanging over the edge."

After Tom went downstairs, I started shivering, thinking how I might have died if they had let me sleep. I walked across the room to call Paul, but forgot to include his 301 area code. When the call didn't go through, I started to redial, but hung up, figuring he'd press me about my drinking like CJ did. I knew I couldn't stop drinking while living in Ocean City.

Paul had been promising to come visit me at the beach, so that would be the time to talk with him about my drinking.

I got back in bed and pulled the covers over me, picturing myself passed out on the couch, as the party from the night before continued without anyone calling 911. Then I imagined Paul, CJ, and Silk at my funeral, telling Mom what a good friend I had been.

NINE

Tuesday was my first day at the Carousel. I put on my burgundy Carousel polo shirt and regulation beige shorts with their hem so high, it would make a Dallas Cowboys cheerleader blush. Looking into the bathroom mirror, my dark brown hair was sticking up, still too short to brush. I couldn't get used to seeing me in my glasses, with their thin black frames and large round lenses. Along with my long, thin legs, I looked like a burgundy flamingo with bad eyesight.

At 9:00 a.m., I walked through the front door into the lobby and bounded up to one of Gary's lieutenants standing behind the bellstand podium, his muscular arms folded, his tan a deep bronze.

"I'm ready for work," I said.

"You sure look happy to be here," he said, his tone mocking. "What's your name?"

"Bruce."

"That's right. My boy, Spruce," he chuckled, as he picked up a piece of paper and looked at it. "What are you doing here, anyway? You aren't scheduled today."

"But Gary told me I was starting on the nineteenth."

"Well you're not on the schedule," he said, putting down the paper.

"Then when am I scheduled?"

Put-upon, he sighed, and lifted the sheet like it weighed several pounds. "Friday," he said. Then he put down the paper and with great precision, rolled his short uniform sleeves up, further enhancing his huge biceps. The discussion was over.

I walked outside, muttering, "Thanks for telling me the nineteenth, Gary."

I wasn't looking forward to killing three days at the beach with no cable TV. I spent the morning buying groceries and beer, had house keys made, and opened a savings account. I also bought a Pen-Tab composition book. I had never kept a journal but was emulating Tom, who said he kept one every summer.

When I got home, I looked at *The Washington Post* I had bought. There were no baseball scores from the day before because the Ocean City edition was published so early the day before. I was probably the only one who missed the scores because the national pastime here wasn't baseball—it was getting a tan.

Late that afternoon, Tom and I lifted weights in our room. Just inside our door was Tom's mini fridge and one stride further was the "gym," where we lifted and played Nerf basketball. Along the wall to the left of the door was Tom's bed, and across from Tom's bed was a sliding glass door that led to our balcony. Across the golden-brown shag carpet from the fridge, was my bed, and near the foot of both beds was our bathroom door.

The room wasn't tiny but it felt small because the only other time I had shared a room was freshman year in a dorm.

Growing up, I spent plenty of time alone in my room, so I needed my space.

Tom asked if I was going out that night.

I had planned on taking it easy for a few days, but apparently, I could only milk my alcohol poisoning excuse for so long. Hell, I even had a doctor's note. But I agreed to go out to avoid disappointing Tom.

We began at the Carousel Club because Tuesday was employee night. Per our employee handbook, a hotel-wide manual that was different than Gary's *Carousel Total Guest Experience*, Tuesday night at the Carousel Club was the only time that off-duty employees were permitted in the hotel.

Onstage was a cover band called The Shades. Several band members were wearing sunglasses, so they could have called themselves The Cli-Shades. The crowd was mid-twenties and older, and nobody from the bellstaff was there. Worst of all, the drink specials—dollar-fifty imported beers and two-dollar rail drinks—weren't that special, so we left after one drink.

Our next stop was Scandals, a nightclub on 65th Street. "You're gonna love Scandals," Tom said. "Everyone goes there on Tuesdays."

It bothered me that locals had a prescribed bar for every night of the week. But the weekly crusade coincided with the best drink deals, so economics outweighed my inclination to reject conformity.

After paying the cover, I followed Tom inside. The music kept getting louder and when he opened the door to the club area, the music washed over us. The place was huge, with the ambience of an airplane hangar. I glanced at Tom, his eyes were wide, like he had just passed through the entry gate at Disneyland.

Waitresses at Scandals trolled the floor, carrying trays with metal grids housing thin plastic test tubes filled with dark blue Windex-colored shooters. At a buck each, they weren't a bad deal since the bar lines usually went two-deep. The blaring music, fog machine smoke, and flashing lights seemed better suited for a Kiss concert, but locals loved Scandals. A shrine to overstatement, it was Ocean City in a nutshell. The town was happiest when a deejay was shouting at them, telling them how much fun they were having.

We stood in small packs with people constantly coming and going. Tom seemed to know everybody, while I felt like I had tagged along to the prom with my much older brother. Since I didn't feel like drinking heavily that night, I volunteered to be the designated driver.

I wasn't saying much, but when one conversation turned to roommate quirks, I joked, "Tom never met a mirror he didn't like," which got some laughs and even a grudging smile from Tom.

But then his eyes narrowed. "Give me some space, dude," he hissed. "Are you going to be hanging on me all night?"

I took his hint and walked off. But separated from him, my social training wheels were gone.

Circling the dance floor, seeing people's put-upon expressions as I approached kept me from stopping. When I did join a group, I didn't have much to say and once I felt sufficiently awkward, I'd move along, trying to find dead spots around the dance floor. After absorbing enough stares —*Who stands by themselves at Scandals?*—I'd leave to look for another place.

Being alone and sober at a crowded nightclub fed my self-consciousness. There must have been an unwritten rule about where I should be standing, but my expert on unwritten rules at the beach had just told me to take a hike.

Feeling sadder by the minute, I went to the bar. Ordinarily, I'd be frustrated waiting in line as girls and pushy guys who schmoozed bartenders arrived after me and got served first. But I didn't mind waiting. I was happy to have a place to stand where no one was staring at me.

After more laps, I saw three guys I had met earlier. One seemed to be smiling at me, so I stopped, casually shifting my beer to my left hand, in case someone wanted to shake hands. I usually didn't greet anybody before being acknowledged, but trying to be outgoing, I said, "What's going on, fellas?"

They all stood up straighter. "Do I know you, *fella*?" one replied, his smile gone.

"Sort of," I said. "Tom introduced us earlier."

"What do you want with us, Lanky Boy?" asked another. He was short, his pecs straining against his tight polo shirt, and was full of himself. I remembered his name was "Steev-o" because it sounded like "Speedo," and he seemed like a dick.

"Nothing," I said. "I'm just hanging out, having a beer."

"Aren't you the guy who just went to the hospital for alcohol poisoning?" Steev-o said, as his friends laughed. "What do you have against being sober, Lanky Boy?"

"Nothing. I just like to drink."

"Drinking's one thing," Steev-o said, grinning. "Getting shit-faced and ending up in the hospital is another."

"Thanks for the advice," I said, but with no place to go, I remained on their periphery and as they resumed their conversation, I stood there, feeling stupid.

The deejay put on an Erasure song. There was a lull in their conversation, so I said, "This song is way too dancey for this crowd."

They all looked at me. Then one guy, wearing a cropped

mesh football jersey, smirked and told the others, "Did you hear something?"

Another shook his head slowly.

"*Dancey?*" Steev-o said to the others. "What's up with this guy?"

"No idea," the head shaker said, laughing.

Two of them resumed talking like I wasn't there, while the smirker stared at me, mouth agape, baiting me to say something.

Instead, I slinked away, glancing at my watch. It was 11:30 and Scandals didn't close until 1:00.

Whitney Houston's *I Wanna Dance with Somebody* was blaring and I stood alone, watching hundreds of people having fun. Nobody wanna-ed dance with me. Nobody wanna-ed talk with me.

Why is everyone here so happy? Why can't I be happy like everybody else? How can they talk for ten minutes about how great the waves were that day? Who the fuck cares?

I had just experienced the four stages of *bar loser*: feeling excluded, then self-conscious, then frustrated, then resentful.

If I joined a group, I was just watching conversations. When I'd make a comment, I noticed that no one was making eye contact with me. *Did they hear me? Are they ignoring me? Am I smiling enough?* Unable to hear over the music, I'd pretend I was hearing what people were saying. But I could only smile and nod for so long before moving on.

With no one to check in with and acknowledge me, I became more self-conscious and frustrated at my inability to engage with people. I had a long time to consider that for the next three months, Ocean City was my home—and it didn't want me. I missed my friends. I missed playing basketball, softball, poker, and watching baseball.

I had been trying to look calm but now I was trying to *stay* calm. I was through killing time, running, feeling rejected and ignored. Disoriented by the pounding music, I was taking deep breaths, struggling for air. I had to get out of there.

But I couldn't leave Tom stranded. If I did that after ditching him with CJ at Harpoon Hanna's, he'd know he couldn't count on me to be his running mate. I decided to go outside, clear my head, and return before closing time. I strode out of the club area and as I approached the exit door, a bouncer said, "Hey buddy, if you leave, you have to pay the cover again."

I stopped. Not because of the money but because I saw the huge line of people waiting to get in. I was afraid that if I couldn't get back in before closing time, I wouldn't be able to explain to Tom why I was waiting for him outside.

"Thanks," I told the guy before slinking back to the club area. I had been caught trying to sneak out of Scandals.

After another drink, I was standing alone, watching girls dancing on top of the huge speakers surrounding the dance area. Someone shouted, "Hey wallflower!"

I turned to see who was hassling me.

"Why are you by yourself?" Tom said. "Come on. There's some people I want you to meet." He was smiling, so I must have been back in his good graces.

"How do you know so many people here?" I yelled, over the music.

He shrugged. "This is my third summer in Ocean City. I go out and get seen. It's why we're here."

By *here*, I didn't know if he meant Scandals, the beach, or the planet. Flourishing in that environment came so naturally to him, he couldn't have explained it. Even if he had tried, his advice wouldn't have helped me. I didn't have a Scandals attitude and couldn't fake one.

If I had told him, "I'm struggling in here, dude, let's leave," he probably would have laughed at me. Then he would have kicked me out of the house, like he did to CJ.

As I waited for last call, I hung on Tom's words like everyone else. He reciprocated by pulling me into conversations, if only to verify a detail in one of his tall tales. "Isn't that right," he'd say, clapping me on the shoulder.

I was happy to back him. After I received his stamp of approval, his friends treated me differently. Tom's endorsement validated that I was worth hanging out with. Without it, I didn't exist.

———

When Scandals closed, I was done for the night. But Tom wanted to go to the Greene Turtle, which was across Coastal Highway from the Carousel. Most Ocean City bars closed at 1:00 but it was open until 2:00, offering a second chance at last call.

The last thing I wanted to do was go to another bar, but I couldn't deny my roommate. When we walked inside, the music was low and there were open tables. I looked at the walls, cluttered with lacrosse sticks and curios from University of Maryland and Baltimore-area sports items. I felt at home.

Leaning into the bar, I ordered two pitchers.

"How many cups do you need?" asked the bartender.

"None," I said, and if I had more confidence, I might have winked at him.

When I brought the beer to our table and sat down, Tom said, "It's dead here, but at least it's open." Then he grinned. "What did you think of Scandals?"

I grabbed some peanuts from a bowl and considered my response.

"That place was packed. And loud," I said, trying to be truthful without offending him.

"I told you Scandals was awesome," he said. "You know, there were times this spring when I wasn't sure you were committed to living in Ocean City. But now that you're here, I'm glad we're roommates."

He was wasted but hearing him affirm our friendship felt great, especially after feeling so alone at Scandals. We were bullshitting, just like at school, and I went back to thinking that with Tom by my side, I could adapt and fit in at the beach.

The lights went on at 1:45 and we had to chug to finish our pitchers. We ditched my car and staggered the half mile home, close as brothers.

Most nights, and particularly Thursday through Saturday, our house served as a hostel for visiting friends. With eight of us, that meant a lot of bodies.

Two mornings after Scandals, I was in bed, pillow over my head, trying to muffle the music, yelling, whooping, and blender from downstairs. That goddamn blender had to be in violation of some noise ordinance.

Sleep was futile, so I brushed my teeth and went downstairs. At the bottom of the stairway, I was greeted by a pungent combination of spilled beer and B.O.

The couch and love seat cushions were arranged on the floor as makeshift mattresses. Travel bags were scattered along the walls and a mound of beer cans lay in the far corner behind the TV. Dirty clothes were strewn about, with a t-shirt dangling from a floor lamp. My mom would have observed, "It looks like a bomb went off in here."

Van Halen was playing on a boom box. The volume was

somewhere between *conversation muffling* and *party hearty*. I walked over and turned down Eddie and the boys.

"That's a good tune, dude," said a guy who was stretched out on our cushion-less couch, speaking quietly to avoid disturbing an empty beer can balanced on his forehead.

"It's a little early," I said, foregoing the harsher *My house, my rules*.

I went to the kitchen to nuke a frozen pizza. The counters were buried under pizza boxes, sub wrappers, beer cans, plastic cups, and dirty plates. A splattering of light brown clumps intrigued me and I bent for a sniff, confirming it was peanut butter, not vomit. Despite our huge green outdoor trashcan parked in the kitchen near the sink, there was trash all over the floor.

I didn't care. It wasn't my week to clean and there was a path to the microwave.

As I sat at the counter eating my pizza, a guy came over. "Come on Bruce, drink with us." Shirtless, he was talking like we were lifelong buddies.

Who is this guy? I thought. *No really, who is he?* We had been drinking buddies the night before, but I couldn't remember his name or who he knew at my house, assuming he knew someone at my house.

"Thanks," I said. "Maybe later in the afternoon."

"You can't be *that* hungover," he said, holding a plastic Spuds Mackenzie cup in my face. "Come on. Hair of the dog."

He thought I was a *partier*. But I was a *drinker*. Drinkers were introspective, lonely, troubled, complicated. Partiers were carefree, outgoing, popular, and used full-throated expressions like *damn straight, kick*-ass, and fuckin-*A*. They were having all the fun and knew nothing about drowning their sorrows.

"Thanks, Beerman," I said, finally accepting the seafoam-colored slushy vodka drink. Too embarrassed to ask his name,

I kept calling him *Beerman*. He didn't mind. He was a partier, so nothing fazed him.

After finishing my pizza and drink, I declined another drink.

"Hey guys," Beerman said loudly. "Bruce is too hungover to drink with us."

Too hungover to drink? I couldn't let that stand and just like that, my drinking cycle continued.

Whether they were there for the weekend or longer, everyone else in the room was enjoying their vacation while I felt anxious, like I was waiting for a bus that was behind schedule. I knew my ride would be coming in September, but I had no idea where it was going.

Just after noon, the phone rang. Someone picked it up and yelled, "Bruce! Amy wants to speak with you. She sounds *nice*."

I went upstairs, away from my booze-soaked living room, to take the call.

"Your answering service seems to like my voice," Amy said, chuckling. "Are you guys having a party at this hour?"

"It's hard to say. People keep coming into town and cutting loose, so it's not really a party, just Thursday afternoon. Whatever you call it, I don't think I can keep up this pace much longer."

"You aren't getting any sympathy from me," she said, laughing. "I called to let you know I got an internship. It's six months with VCU's hospital in Richmond. It's starting right away so I'm going this weekend to find an apartment."

"That's great, but six months in Richmond? When will I ever see you?"

"It's a great opportunity and I'm lucky it's only two hours from home," she said. "Besides, you were the one who left me to go to the beach."

She was right, but I had committed to the beach before considering that we could be an *us*. Now I was wondering if she thought we were an *us*.

"You're right," I said. "I'm really happy for you."

I was also jealous. Amy knew where her bus was going. She even had exact change ready.

"How's your job going? Has anybody yelled at you for stalling their car?"

"Not yet, but only because I don't start working until tomorrow."

"So are you settled there yet?"

"It's very different from what I had expected," I said, not wanting to admit that I had made a big mistake by moving to Ocean City. "You're the one who should be living here. You're much more outgoing than me."

Why didn't I tell her that she should be here <u>with</u> me? That would have been perfect.

"Three months at the beach is too much for me," she said, which was what people kept telling me in spring when I told them about my summer plans. After a little more than a week in Ocean City, I was starting to understand what they meant.

"Will you be able to come back to DC for The Cure?" I asked.

Months before, I had bought us tickets for the August concert.

"Yepper," she said. "But your sister's wedding is next month. You didn't forget that, did you?"

"Me? Forget? I might skip it, but I'd never forget it."

"I'm glad to hear that," she said. "I've already bought my dress."

Of course she already had her dress. Amy faced responsibilities and challenges head-on. Her life was so together, and as I sat on my bed, I couldn't imagine what she saw in me.

After we hung up, I was thinking about how much I missed her and tried to downplay my feelings for Amy by attributing them to how alone I felt at the beach. I wasn't letting myself admit that we were an *us*.

TEN

Clack. *Clack, clack.* Instead of my clock radio alarm, I woke the next morning to pebbles crackling against my balcony's sliding glass door. Tom, who could sleep through anything, wasn't stirring, so I wobbled outside to see what was going on. It was CJ, so I leaned my forearms on the railing and stared down at him.

"I just got off the graveyard shift," he said.

"You woke me to tell me that?"

"You can thank me later," he said, ignoring my schtick. "You're working at 9:00 today, not noon."

"Seriously? They'd better get their shit together. That's twice they've screwed up my schedule and I haven't started working yet."

His message delivered, CJ turned up his palms and left.

I parked in the Carousel garage and walked through the front of the hotel. Gary was chatting with an older couple, looking more in his element than during orientation, but he certainly wasn't relaxed. His eyes were scanning the lobby like he had Terminator vision, seemingly monitoring dozens of monitorables. When a bellman emerged from an elevator, pushing an empty cart, Gary urgently waved him over.

Gary and I trailed the trio outside. "I moved you up to 9:00 because we have 150 check-ins today with the holiday weekend," Gary said. "Did CJ let you know?"

No, I show up to work three hours early whenever I have a hunch things might be a little busy.

"CJ told me," I said.

"Humph." Gary reacted, probably sensing that I wasn't on board with his agenda. Shifting from guest services to personnel, he said, "You punched in, right?"

"No, I just got here."

The squint in Gary's eyes showed that his question had been a courtesy. Trying to prod me, he said, "You know you don't get paid until you punch in."

At $2.01 an hour plus tips, I didn't share his urgency. But in an effort to please him, I said, "Where do I punch in?"

Gary glared at me, the veins in his skinny neck rippling.

"What were you doing during orientation, besides clowning?" he said, then pointed toward the garage. "Run, don't walk, run. At the end of the hotel, turn right. Go inside the door marked *Carousel employee entrance* and turn right." He held his palms a foot apart and pivoted his body to the right, like he was doing *The Robot*. "Ask the person behind the glass for your time card."

As he spoke, a car pulled past us, stopping in the drive-through lane. A valet greeted the driver.

"Sure thing, Gary," I said and strode off past the car, eager to at least show him that I could run fast.

"What are you doing?" Gary called, sounding exasperated.

I stopped abruptly and looked back. *Didn't he just tell me to punch in?*

"Get that door!" Gary yelled, pointing to the passenger door.

I shuffled back and opened the door, making sure to say, "Welcome to the Carousel." Then I resumed running but had forgotten Gary's directions.

After punching in, I walked through the employees-only area before entering the hotel's guest area, where the Carousel's opulence was on display. I gazed up at a dramatic five-story atrium with hallway railings overlooking the main-floor shops, restaurants, bars, kiosks, eateries, pool, gym, arcade, and ice rink. Looking around as I walked, I imagined I was inside a gigantic machine with burgundy-clad Carousel employees performing their duties with precision. That was how Gary demanded his bellstaff operate. Like clockwork.

Out front, I walked up to a valet who smiled and said, "Welcome to the Carousel, my bruh-thah. I'm Dave."

He had short, receding brown hair and a wry smile, like Bruce Willis, from *Moonlighting*.

"Gary was right," I said, as I shook Dave's hand. "Hearing that does make me feel like a VIP."

We were leaning against a four-foot-high retaining wall near the front door when Gary emerged from the lobby. My body tensed as I braced for his instructions. I got the same feeling when Dad would come home from work each evening.

"How's it going, Gary?" Dave said, casually engaging him, which was something I couldn't do.

"No leaning on the facing wall," Gary said, and we hopped forward and stood up straight. "Looks like you valets need to re-read *The Carousel Total Guest Experience*."

Gary removed a quarter from his pocket and flipped it over his head. After snagging the coin, he opened his palm to look at the result. "Dave, cover the door. And you, Mr. Timecard..." his voice trailed as he strode a few steps to the end of the retaining wall and pulled a squeegee and Windex bottle out of a wooden phone box. Gary walked back, handed me the implements, and said, "Go clean the vans' windows."

After cleaning the windows, I returned to the front of the hotel and said to Dave, "Don't tell Larry, but before I can re-read *The Carousel Total Guest Experience*, I'll have to read it first."

"Don't worry about Gary," Dave said. "He's always bunging." Apparently, *bunge*, which rhymed with *sponge*, was the bellstaff's term to describe Gary's mania.

Hours later, I had to park a tiny 1970s Datsun hatchback, my first clutch. Rushing to move it from the loading zone, I stalled it. *Not enough gas*, I thought, and stepped on the pedal. The motor revved loudly. *Damn. Forgot to put it in gear.*

I took a deep breath. *What does CJ always say? Feel the clutch. Find that balance—*

Tap. Tap.

Startled, I reached over and rolled down the passenger window.

"What are you doing, Dweeb?" asked Jon, a solidly built bellman, with military-short light brown hair and an impressive tan. "Don't you know how to drive a stick?"

Instead of posturing and saying something like, "Of course I can. This car's just a piece of crap," I said, "I'm getting better at it."

"Are you serious? You really can't drive a stick?!" Jon howled, then looked around for someone to share his amusement. Seeing no one, he stuck his head in the window and shouted, "Come on Dweeb. Put in the clutch! Shift into first! A moron could do it!"

Flustered, I pushed in the clutch and shifted into first. The car lurched forward, but it was moving. I gave it more gas and it stopped bucking. As I advanced down the drive-through lane, I decided against trying to shift into second.

After a rolling stop at the end of the hotel, I turned right, made a left and another quick left into the parking garage. The garage guard stopped me until he noticed my name tag. I had to get it back into first gear before turning right to go up the garage ramp.

Pulling into an open space, I set the parking brake and turned off the ignition. Breathing heavily, with my shins crammed against the bottom of the dashboard, I paused to reflect on my first week at the beach. I had been hospitalized, ticketed twice, humiliated at a bar, and picked on at work. I wanted to leave town without telling Tom. But I'd still have to face Dad.

I punched out at 5:00, I pulled my crumpled tips from my front shorts pocket. I counted eleven dollar bills, figuring at that rate, I'd have to work three weeks just to cover my rent.

The Carousel did give us a meal in the employee cafeteria each day we worked. All my life, Dad had been harping that there was no such thing as a free lunch, so on my days off, I planned to put on my uniform and go to our cafeteria for a free lunch. Just to prove him wrong.

A couple of nights later, I tore the cellophane off my GMAT study guide. It had never occurred to me to study *how* to take a test. The practice tests reminded me of the SATs, so all I had to do was review formulas from junior high, like area of a circle.

I wasn't sure if I was cut out for business school: wearing a tie to class, reading the *Wall Street Journal*, using corporate buzzwords, and being so damn serious. But I needed a plan and when I told people I was going to business school, it seemed to impress them, or at least appease them.

Sitting on my bed, I worked on practice tests for two hours before stopping for my first graveyard shift. In the spirit of the GMAT, I prepared a sample question:

The Carousel employs twelve valets, including a supervisor and an assistant supervisor. Supervisors do not work graveyard shifts, which run from midnight until 8:00 a.m. How often does a non-supervisor valet work a graveyard shift?

A) Every 12 days; B) Every 10 days; C) Eight hours; D) All night long

In recognition of Lionel Richie, the correct answers are B) or D).

I arrived at the Carousel at midnight and after punching in, I walked past nearly a dozen eggs splattered in the drive through lane. CJ told me that guests had been throwing the eggs off a balcony. The front of the hotel continued rollicking for hours, with drunks coming home from bars, toting cases of beer. Some invited me to parties in their rooms, but I declined. Gary forbade us from sitting down at work, even on the graveyard shift, so attending parties was probably a no-no.

By 3:00, things were dead and I felt like the last one up in town. Leaning against the retaining wall, I stared at our electronic message board alongside Costal Highway until I had memorized the order: "Ocean Front Dining … Carousel Club featuring The Shades… Indoor Ice Skating Rink … Piano Master Raif Jenkins appearing at King Al's Pub …"

Hours later, two older women came out of the hotel, cheerfully greeting me before their walk on the beach to watch the sunrise. I was a night person, so for me, sunrise was an ending, not a beginning. That morning, I was looking forward to the sunrise because it meant I was almost done with my graveyard shift.

The sun came up, glinting off the metal sign atop the Carousel's five-story garage that read: "Next to the ocean, we're the main attraction." Tom used that line, substituting *I'm* for *we're*. It was an audacious boast, but he seemed to believe it. At times, so did I.

After closing down bars the following night, Tom and I were doing Bacardi 151 shots in our living room. I offered him another, but he declined.

"I'll fetch your shawl if you want to take your nap now, grandma," I taunted.

He laughed, but avoided my challenge. "Do me a favor," he said.

Curious, I followed him up to our room. He picked his Carousel name tag off his shelf and handed it to me. "Here. Pierce my ear."

"I'm not sure I—"

"Don't worry, dude. I've had done it before. It doesn't hurt."

"It's not that," I said. "It's just that in some cultures, I think that would mean that we're married."

"You think you can do better?" he said, with a perfect deadpan.

Too drunk to object, I went into the bathroom and rinsed the point of the pin in lukewarm water to disinfect it.

He crowded in front of the mirror with me to show me where he wanted his second earring to go. I marked the spot on his ear with my green Bic pen. Then he sat on his bed, while I stooped over him, touching my finger to the point, trying to gauge how much pressure I would need, though I was too drunk for any precision.

With my right thumb holding his earlobe between my index and middle fingers, I aimed with my left hand and stabbed. The pin went completely through, miraculously avoiding my fingers on the other side. Tom's head moved slightly in response but didn't say anything.

"You're right," I said. "That didn't hurt at all."

He went into the bathroom to wipe off the blood and put in an earring.

"That looks good," he said, walking out and holding a bag of ice to his ear. "I can do yours now if you want."

Letting him pierce my ear would have been a nice bonding moment, but I declined. My hair was months from growing back, so I was still living with the consequences from my last drunk fashion statement.

ELEVEN

The next morning, the phone kept ringing downstairs. I looked at my clock radio and closed my eyes with the red LED digits 7:22 burning into the blackness of my mind. Remembering my seven o'clock shift, I jumped out of bed, hurried across the room, and picked the phone receiver off the mini-fridge, its ringer turned off for the summer.

"Gooood Mooorning," a syrupy voice greeted me. "This is Dave from your Carousel bellstaff with a friendly nudge because you are tardy for your seven o'clock employment appointment. Bell Captain Gary Adams requests your immediate presence at the bellstand. Dress is Carousel casual."

I rushed to put on my uniform, hustled out the door, and punched in thirty-five minutes late. Dave was leaning against the retaining wall as I walked up to the front of the hotel.

"You look terrible, my bruh-thah," he said, laughing.

"Thanks," I said. "It's not easy getting my hair to look like this."

He nodded. "I'll bet you have to sleep on it a certain way."

"Where's Gary?" I said, not wanting to wait to face his wrath.

"He's not here. He isn't scheduled until 9:00," Dave said, smiling mischievously. "If you're seeking forgiveness for being late, just say twenty Hail Garys. That should cover it."

"I'm not seeking forgiveness. I'm seeking salvation," I said. "Salvation from this hangover."

I was seeing double, so I drove my first cars to the garage with one eye closed. I told Dave I was "double-parking" them.

At 8:00, Dave's housemate Flec came in for his shift. Flec had short, curly blonde hair, suspicious eyes, and fair skin that flushed easily when he got annoyed.

"Uggh," Flec said, scrunching his nose as he neared me. "You smell like a brewery."

"I can't argue with that," I said. "Have you ever been to a brewery?"

"Umm... no," Flec said.

"Me neither," I said. "But out of respect, I slow down whenever I drive past the Schaefer brewery on 695."

"That stuff's nasty," Flec said, still scowling. "How can you drink it?"

"It's six dollars a case, which is so cheap, they're paying me three dollars for every twelve-pack I drink. "Besides, I don't drink beer for taste. I drink it for effect."

"You need help, my bruh-thah," Dave said, laughing. As he walked off to punch out, he called back to me, "By the way, Flec's right. You do reek."

As we stood around waiting for cars, Flec asked several questions about my alcohol poisoning, including, "Was your blood alcohol content at the hospital really point three?"

"It was when they measured it," I said.

"Of course it was when they measured it, you muttonhead. How could it be anything else?"

"I meant it must have been higher, but by the time I got to

the hospital and they measured, it must have gone down some."

"Then why didn't you say that in the first place?" Flec said.

"I don't know," I said.

But I did know. Sometimes it was hard for me to phrase things while avoiding setting off Flec. But I couldn't explain that to him without setting him off.

Lightheaded, I was sweating out the alcohol in the sun. Running back from the garage after parking a car, I almost plowed into three beach patrols who had just come off the beach.

"Whoa, dude," one of them said, stepping back to avoid me.

Another asked me something that I didn't hear. I responded, "What was that?"

"Never mind, dude," he said.

"Dude's wasted," the first one said, and they walked away, laughing at me.

Back out front, Flec, who seemed to notice everything, asked, "What did you tell those guys that was so funny?"

"What was that?" I said to Flec.

"What did you say that made those beach patrol laugh?" he repeated.

Again, I told Flec, "What was that?"

He stared at me, his face getting redder as he kept ripping and reattaching the Velcro band of his Swatch in frustration.

Speaking slowly, I told Flec, "I didn't hear what they had asked me, so I asked those guys *What was that?*"

Then I stared at him until his glower faded. Finally he said, "That's actually funny."

What did he mean by _actually_?

Gary had been keeping a low profile, but when Tom showed up two hours late at 10:00, he immediately came outside. The bellstaff gravitated closer to see if Gary was going to bunge at his golden boy.

"It's ten o'clock," he greeted Tom.

"I know," Tom said, grinning. "When I punch in, the machine prints the time right on my timecard."

"You were scheduled for 8:00," Gary said. "Where were you?"

"In bed. I was drinking late last night and got my ear pierced again. Here, check it out," Tom said, folding the bottom of his ear forward to show Gary.

Ignoring our laughter, he told Tom, "You need to let me know before you drink so I can adjust your schedule."

"I drink every night," Tom said. "Besides, what's the big deal? You have two other bellmen scheduled this morning."

"Right now, I have two bellmen scheduled. Total," Gary said. "Go punch out."

"Ooooh," we all exhaled, validating his line.

"Thanks for the day off, Gary," Tom said, turning and slowly walking off.

Fuming, Gary went inside. Despite his constant insistence that the valets spread out and cover our zones, the bellstaff was congregating at the bellman's island, a cement median at the top of the drive through lane.

"Did he send Tom home for being late or for being hungover?" I asked.

"Gary did Tom a favor," a bellman said. "There's no way he makes it through his shift today without yakking." His eyes narrowed at me as he said, "You don't look so great yourself."

A little later, a guest came outside and fished a pink ticket from his pocket. I was *up*, so I trotted over for the ticket. After running to the garage, I ducked into the guard booth and grabbed the car keys and matching ticket off the hook.

The matching ticket read, "Black Porsche." *Shit.* I found the car and the 944 was gleaming importantly, even in the shade of the garage. I opened the door. There was a clutch. *Shit.*

In no mood or condition to drive a fifty-thousand-dollar stick car, I tumbled into the low-slung seat while squeezing behind the steering wheel. Already sweating, I took a deep breath, shifted into neutral, and turned the key. The engine rumbled and I pushed in the stiff clutch and shifted into reverse. Easing off the brake, I stepped on the gas.

The Porsche pitched *forward* onto the cement barrier, accompanied by a high-pitched scraping sound. I had shifted into first gear.

The car's incline made it feel like it had been hooked up to a tow truck. *Gary's going to kill me,* I thought, as I cautiously climbed out, the chest of my Carousel shirt damp where my sweat had soaked through.

I saw that the Porsche had a front-end spoiler. Afraid to look too closely, I didn't see any damage, but the spoiler was resting on the barrier, so I couldn't see its underside. I quickly climbed back in, praying that the spoiler wouldn't crack under my weight, then reviewed the path for reverse on the shift knob. *All the way to the right and down.* I had read it wrong when I glanced at it the first time.

I pushed in the clutch, shifted, and gave it gas. The car didn't budge. I gave it more gas but it remained stuck. *I'm going to need a tow to get it off this barrier,* I thought, squinting as I tried to keep the sweat out of my eyes.

On my next try, the Porsche moved, followed by the same grating noise as the front end dragged backward across the concrete slab. There was a jolting, though cartoonish, *ba-dump,* as the front wheels landed on the pavement, bouncing slightly.

Unable to see the row of cars behind me in the mirrors, I backed out, my foot cautiously alternating between the gas pedal and the brake. Once clear of the parking spot, I cut the wheel and coaxed the car into first, before easing down the garage ramps.

At the bottom, I had to wait for the motion-sensor chain-link exit gate, which rattled loudly as it slid open. I turned right, onto a side street a half block north of the Carousel. The Porsche's engine revved noisily, urging me to shift into second gear, but I wasn't taking any chances.

I pulled into the lot and purposely parked just past where the driver was standing so he'd have to walk up from behind the car. Pulling up the parking brake, my right hand was covered in sweat, as the whizzing handbrake signaled that my ride was over. I climbed out, dazed, like I had just stepped off a roller coaster.

The owner stepped off the curb as I got out to wait by the open driver's door. I couldn't look the guy in the eye as he handed me a dollar, folded in quarters, and got in. Then, as the Porsche drove away, I exhaled in relief, feeling like a shady used car salesman. *Once it leaves the lot, it's no longer my responsibility.*

Later, I was standing in a clump with the bellstaff. As they were bullshitting, I was thinking how lucky I had been to have gotten away with dragging that Porsche over a curb.

"Bruce!" Gary screamed.

Startled, I looked toward the front door as he made a beeline toward me. Luckily, I was no longer seeing double by then. One Gary was enough.

"Over here," he snapped, leading me away from the others. I walked behind him, as enthusiastically as a cat on its way to the vet. When he stopped, I stayed a few feet from him, but he moved closer, like the street fighter he was. I strained to get separation, concerned he would smell the rum I had been sweating out all morning.

"Are you feeling okay?" he said, his mouth clenched in

front of my face as he waited for my answer. Like a barking drill sergeant, Gary often flustered me. This time, I couldn't tell if his question was sympathetic or if he was about to bunge.

After I had hesitated too long, he said, "You need to get going now."

The guys listening in from the bellman's island started snickering.

"Get going on what?" I said, confused. I knew I was in trouble, which was confirmed as the laughter got louder.

Gary's beady eyes got smaller and he pointed to the garage. "Next time you show up for work this hungover, I'll send you home for good. Understand?"

"I understand, Gary," I said, trying to sound contrite. But I didn't understand Gary.

Hours later, Tom and I were sitting at a table under an umbrella at BJ's, enjoying the bay view. For him, BJ's Wednesday afternoon deck party was among the holiest of the holies, the laid-backiest of the laid backs.

"Do you think Gary will fire me?" I asked, after worrying for hours that my dad would question whether I'd be able to hold a real job, seeing as I couldn't keep a fake one.

"If he does, just get another one," Tom said, scoffing. "You should be more concerned that you can't handle your alcohol. Last week, you were in the hospital. This morning you couldn't even sober up for work."

"My problem isn't tolerance, it's intake," I said. "Anytime you want to lose a drinking competition, just name the time and the alcohol, you lightweight. Check that. Any alcohol but Southern Comfort."

"I could have worked today," Tom said. "But Gary sent you

home because he was afraid you were going to have a stroke and sue the Carousel."

"Like you told me back in March, if anybody on the bellstaff is going to have a stroke, it's Gary," I said. "Besides, you weren't even there. How would you know how bad I was?"

"I saw you stumble into our room after work. When you fell into bed, you almost missed," Tom said, standing up. Then after two sideways hops, he fell on the deck, curled up, and started snoring.

After he got back in his chair, I said, "Speaking of March, what happened to those big bucks you were promising back then?"

"You have to work harder if you want to max your tips," Tom said. Annoyed that I was questioning him, he shifted the blame to me. "You ever tell a guest his car drives nice?"

I shook my head. "For the two minutes I have a car, I only care if there's a clutch, whether the AC works, and what station's on the radio."

"Just tell them their car looks great. You'll make more in tips."

"I can't just lie like that," I said.

"You need to get over that. How else are you going to close deals when you're working?"

"Sincerely," I said, and took a gulp of beer.

"Then good luck when you're working at a Hallmark store," he said, grinning. "You'll fit in great there. I'll bet you're a wiz at gift wrapping."

As I stared out at the bay, Tom may have noticed that I had taken his remark personally because he said, "Okay. Here's all you need to know."

This is it, I thought, leaning in. *On May 27, 1987 at 3:46 p.m.,*

Tom's going to tell me the secret of life. Or at least the secret of life at the beach.

Grinning, he said, "Always tell people what they want to hear."

Realizing that was the extent of his advice, I leaned back, underwhelmed. "But how can I say something if it isn't true?"

He snorted. "Truth has nothing to do with it, Opie. Come on, try this: 'Gary, your haircut looks great.'"

"Gary, your haircut looks great," I repeated.

"That sounded like you read it off an index card. Come on, look me in the eye. Chin up. Be confident. Sell it!"

"Gary, your–" I couldn't finish without laughing. "Did you see his hair today? It was so greasy and matted down, he looked like he was wearing a hair net."

"You'll never get ahead in life if you can't lie about something as insignificant as someone's hair."

"Since when was hair insignificant to you?"

"You got me," he said. "I meant someone *else's* hair."

Back at our place after BJ's, I saw a note on the eat-in counter that read: *Bruce, call your mom.*

My buzz effectively killed, I picked up the phone.

"Are you moving back home?" was the first thing she said after "Hello."

Apparently, no one thought I could survive at the beach. Mom's monthly Mahjong game probably had a betting line on how long I'd last in Ocean City.

"No Mom, I'm staying at the beach."

There was a pause. "Have you at least changed your mind about graduation next weekend?"

"Sorry, Mom, I'm still not going."

"Even after we paid for your college?"

Ouch.

"Are you at least coming home for Tamara's wedding? It would be nice to have the family together."

"I'll be there, Mom. Though a reunion would be easier if Dad hadn't kicked me out of the house."

"Your father's been so upset about your job search. He just got home from work ... hold on a second... *What's that Mawv?* He has something to say to you."

My lucky day. Dad usually left me alone and never said much until I really annoyed him. Then, as he lectured me, I never got "I like what you did, but…" I only got the *but.*

"*Hay-lo.*" Dad's deep voice filled my ear. I greeted him and he asked what progress I had made with my career.

"Right now, I'm studying for the GMAT."

"You're not looking for a job?" he said, sounding surprised, as if I was skipping weekly career fairs at the beach. "If you weren't so coddled, you'd have found a job months ago."

"Don't worry. I'll be working soon enough. What's wrong with doing something this summer that makes me happy?"

"There's more to life than being happy," he said, and as I considered that, he added, "You must think I'm an idiot because I work."

"I don't think that, although I don't understand why you and Mom never spend any money on yourselves."

"Spend money on what?"

"How about a vacation?"

"Like at the beach? I'd rather sit at my desk at work. The pay's a hell of a lot better. One day, you'll learn that everything in this world revolves around money and that you have nothing without financial security."

"But if I'm not happy, then what else matters?" I said, but

my logic was useless with Dad. He had plenty of money but no happiness.

"I told you in March that you were on your own," he growled. "I read that Thomas Edison left his son a single item in his will: a gold button. That acknowledged the son while writing him out of an immense inheritance. Not that I'm saying that as a threat."

Then he hung up.

Not only did that sound like a threat, but apparently, Dad had put some thought into it. One reason I had gone to the beach was to get away from him. But he was right there with me on Shipwreck Road, reminding me that I had no career plan. I knew I needed to find a career job, but I wasn't letting him dictate everything to me.

TWELVE

O f all the prescribed weekly Ocean City bar destinations, the most sacred was Trader Lee's. It was only open on Fridays, so if you weren't there on a given week, you'd better have an iron-clad excuse. No place was bigger, rowdier, or more beloved than Trader's.

Located a few miles west of the Boardwalk in the middle of nowhere, Trader's was a collection of barns loosely converted into a sprawling bar. The gravel parking lot couldn't handle the more than a thousand revelers, so the overflow parked in surrounding fields.

I had gone there the week before, which was enough for me. But all day at work, Tom had been getting CJ fired up for Trader's, saying things like, "They don't care how good your ID is. You could write 'I'm twenty-one' on a piece of paper and you'll get in."

That night, Tom drove separately with Jon, my bellman nemesis, while I rode with CJ. We parked in a field, a quarter mile from the entrance. As we got out of his car, we heard the music blasting in the distance and CJ couldn't wait to get there.

When we got to the front of the line, CJ asked what I was laughing at. I pointed to the long, narrow wooden sign atop the entrance proclaiming: *The Home of Rock Music.*

I told him, "I was expecting something more palatial."

The doorman barely glanced at CJ's sketchy ID and waved him in. Tom had been right.

A tradition at Trader's was tossing cups of beer on others, resulting in muddy patches on the dirt floor. As people got drunker, some were occasionally wrestling in the mud, while others played *king of the table*, with drunken combatants claiming and defending a spot atop a designated picnic table.

CJ and I were hanging with Tom and Jon and some of the guys from the bellstaff. CJ was enjoying the action, but for me, Trader's was just like Scandals, only bigger. At least I hadn't driven, so I could drink as much as I needed to get through the night.

Around midnight, CJ said something I didn't hear over the music. He started walking toward one of the keg stations, so I called to him, "Hey, get one for me as well."

Ten minutes later, I was still waiting for him to come back. I got a beer and returned to where he had left me. It seemed strange, so I walked around, trying to find him. It was after 1:00 when I checked back with Tom.

"Dude, you've been looking for almost an hour. He's not here."

"It's a big place," I said. "Besides, CJ wouldn't leave me without saying something."

"Maybe he hooked up," Tom said, smirking.

"There's a first time for everything," Jon said, flashing the fake smile he used on Carousel guests in hopes of turning a five-dollar tip into a ten.

"He'd have told me if he was leaving with a girl," I said, angry that they weren't concerned about CJ.

"Maybe he didn't say anything because she was hideous," Tom said, laughing as I walked off.

"Did you see my friend leave?" I asked a bouncer who looked like all the other Mark Gastineau muscleman wannabes: mustache, no neck, and poufy, shoulder-length hair with bangs. "He's about six foot one, thin, with short, light-brown hair."

"Was he wearing a white t-shirt, light shorts and white sneakers?" the guy asked.

"He was, yes," I said, getting excited.

"I've seen about a hundred of him tonight," the bouncer said, laughing in my face.

After last call, I ran into Tom and Jon as they were leaving. "I told you he wasn't here," Tom said. "You coming with us?"

"Thanks," I said, tired of his know-it-all attitude. "But I'll get a ride with CJ."

With so few people left, it soon became clear that Tom had been right that CJ wasn't there. The bouncers, having lost their patience, were screaming at everyone that remained. "Clear Out! Leave! Go home!"

I drifted outside, realizing I didn't have a ride. My fellow stragglers were looking rougher and dirt-baggier than my usual crowd. Standing near the entrance, I was asking the safer-looking ones if they were going over the bridge to Ocean City. The few that replied said they didn't have room.

Minutes later, the bouncers were wielding metal rakes, physically prodding people from the entrance toward the parking lot. Desperate, I started asking everyone passing by.

A short guy, wearing a jean jacket with cut-off sleeves, replied, "I got room, Stretch."

His face was twitching and he looked like he was on something, so I said, "Thanks, but I'm okay."

"You fucking with me, Stretch?" he said, moving closer.

"I wouldn't do that," I said, trying to avoid setting him off. "I thought I just saw someone I knew."

"That's good, Stretch. I don't like people fucking with me. You're coming with us."

He didn't say *or else*, but didn't need to. He looked menacing, like he'd bring a two-by-four to a fistfight. Besides, I didn't have any other options.

He was among two couples. The other guy had a chain running from a belt loop to a wallet in his back pocket. Both wore jeans and well-worn wheat-colored Timberlands. Either of the girls could have kicked my ass. One had straight black hair and bangs, her eyes buried under black eyeshadow, looking like a heavy Joan Jett. The other wore a black Harley Davidson sweatshirt and had a red bandana in her blonde hair.

"Hey Stretch," the driver said, as I walked through the empty parking lot behind one couple and in front of the other. "Did your mom give you that sweet buzz cut?"

"One of my friends did."

"What do you think Johnny?" the driver called to the guy in the front.

Johnny turned around and said, "Makes him look like a ree-tard."

They both laughed, their high-pitched cackles reminding me of the way Robbie Watts and his buddies used to laugh before they'd beat up somebody. As we walked, the only other sound I heard came from frogs croaking in the surrounding woods.

Do I run? If I don't get away, they'll probably knife me. If I do get away, then what?

As we neared their car in the dark field, the driver's girlfriend said, "You sure you're okay to drive, Bobby?"

Finally, someone has the sense to stand up to this guy.

"Why the fuck do you ask me that every time I get into a car?!" Bobby screamed at her. "I'm good enough. Any cop wants to pull me over is gonna have to catch me first."

Bobby got behind the wheel of an old four-door Dodge Dart, with Bandana Girl riding shotgun. I sat behind him, sharing the backseat with the other couple. Just before Bobby started the engine, there was a conspicuous click from my seatbelt.

"Afraid I won't get us there, Stretch?" Bobby said. "Well we're gonna find out, ain't we?" He cackled so loudly, the frogs stopped croaking. They knew something was up.

"Roll down your windows. It's hot in here," Bobby said, turning on the AM radio. Then he yelled to Bandana Girl, "Gimmie some dust!"

"You need to lay off that shit." she told him.

"Please can I have my dust?" he said, sweetly. "It helps me drive."

"I hate when you act like a little pussy," she said, but pulled a baggie from her purse and handed him a pill. "You happy now?"

Bobby downed it. "I'd like a little pussy right now," he said, grabbing at her crotch.

She laughed and pushed his hand away.

"Whooo-eeee!" Bobby shouted, as the car sped through the pitch-black field, bottoming out in ruts. Back tires screeching, we skidded onto a paved two-lane road. After turning onto Route 50, he accelerated as fast as the Dart could handle. It was shaking so much, I didn't need to look at the big rectangular speedometer to know we were going close to eighty.

Bobby's girl hollered at him to turn down the music and he yelled back at her. The backseat couple was making out, so I was the only one terrified by Bobby's driving. The car would veer to one shoulder and Bobby would jerk the steering wheel, slamming me against the door. We'd careen toward the other side of the road, he'd overcompensate, and I'd fall against the guy on my right. Bobby wasn't driving, he was constantly re-aiming the car toward the middle of the road.

My body's going to be under a sheet in a driver's ed crash movie, I thought, clasping my hands in my lap. With each swerve, I gripped my hands tighter.

Bandana Girl saw the sign for the Route 50 Bridge and yelled. "Slow down Bobby! You know I'm scared of bridges!"

"Stop nagging!" he yelled, raising his fist at her. She stared back at him, bracing for him to hit her, as if it was no big deal. Seeing him threaten her so casually was appalling. I had to get away from them.

The bridge had two lanes in each direction but no median. The car was drifting and bouncing over our side. Then he veered right, toward the three-foot guard rail.

"Go left!" I shouted.

"Shut up, Stretch!" Bobby yelled, and eased the wheel to the left, keeping the car partly on the shoulder, probably just to taunt me. I reached to find my door handle in case the car flipped off the bridge.

Bobby got us across the half-mile span. Then the constricted streets in downtown Ocean City forced him to slow down.

"You can drop me off anywhere!" I shouted over the music.

"No can do, Stretch. We got some partying to do and you're our guest of honor."

I quietly unfastened my seatbelt and tried to steady my nerves. When Bobby stopped for the light on 28th Street, I pulled my door handle and threw my shoulder against the door, tumbling onto the road.

"I didn't know that was your stop Stretch," Bobby said,

laughing as I ran away. The car peeled off with the back door still open. Bobby yelled, "See you next Friday at The Barns!"

"Think CJ's okay?" I asked Tom the next morning when I went downstairs.

"Don't be dramatic, dude," he said, as I followed him out on the deck. "I called him at work and he's meeting us at the beach after his shift."

Tom's girlfriend Erin was in town. She looked at home lounging on the deck, wearing a sleeveless blue sundress and oversized sunglasses, her hair tucked beneath a floppy white hat.

I mentioned that my friend Stephanie, who was visiting Ocean City for the weekend, was joining us. Erin asked why I had never told her about Stephanie.

"There isn't much to say," I said. "We worked together last summer and went out a couple of times, but she's always been lukewarm toward me."

"Come on, dude," Tom said. "She's here, looking you up. Take charge like I tell you and she'll be staying over with you tonight."

Rolling her eyes at him, Erin said, "Why don't you let Bruce go at his own pace?"

"He just said he couldn't figure her out. Our son is crying out for help."

Around 11:00, Stephanie arrived with her friend Julie. Tom subtly raised his chin at me, clearly impressed by Stephanie. She was the best-looking girl I had ever dated, with reddish brown hair cut in a wavy elongated bob, a big toothy smile, and Bambi-like eyelashes. She was five feet ten and I was a pushover for tall girls. Julie was pretty, with blonde hair and an easy smile.

Once Stephanie saw me, she sounded horrified as she said, "What happened to your hair?"

"I made a bad decision while drunk," I said, forgoing the details. "Does it look that bad?"

"It's *different*," she said, laughing. "You might wait until it grows back before calling me again."

That shook me, but Tom smoothed things over, saying, "Come on, Cueball, grab a hat and let's get going."

At Carousel Beach, we spread a blanket and everyone arranged their towels. Then Stephanie flung off her cover-up, revealing an electric blue one-piece swimsuit. "Do you like it?" she asked me. She had a killer body so it was a ridiculous question. Stephanie wasn't content with being beautiful. She needed constant attention and compliments; two things I wasn't big on.

"It looks great," I said, looking, but trying not to stare. "What do you think of mine?" I said, extending a leg to accentuate the rumpled 1960s-era brown and tan plaid trucks I had bought at a Salvation Army thrift shop.

"I think you should learn how to iron." she said, laughing.

Hours later, CJ emerged from the back of the Carousel and joined us. I watched him methodically shake his twenty-five-dollar beach towel, with its large, circular Vuarnet logo, and lower it to the ground. The towel floated down and he smoothed the sand underneath, before sitting down.

"What happened to you last night?" I finally said, trying to sound detached.

"You mean after I told you I was going out to my car?"

"Is that what you said? I thought you said you were getting a beer. Why didn't you come back?"

"I was waiting in the line outside and when it didn't move for a half hour, I left."

"What were you doing in your car?" Tom asked.

"Looking for my comb. It had fallen out of my pocket and I found it on my seat."

Everyone else laughed at CJ's vanity. But I was pissed, having gone through that ordeal just because he had to comb his hair.

"Weren't you concerned I'd be stranded?" I said.

"I figured you'd catch a ride with Jon," CJ said.

"I told you he was okay," Tom told me, confirming I had overacted. I couldn't stay mad at CJ for a misunderstanding, though it would have been better if the reason had been a girl and not his stupid comb.

"Who took you home?" Tom asked me.

"I caught a ride with some crackhead who almost drove us off the Route 50 Bridge," I said, trying to sound like I was exaggerating so nobody would press me for more details.

With Stephanie there, the beach was more appealing than usual. The sun was bringing out the red highlights in her hair and the tanning oil glistening on her arms and legs was driving me crazy. But after a few hours and little reciprocation to my flirting from Stephanie, I grabbed my towel and put on my flip-flops.

"Where are you going?" Tom said. "There isn't a cloud in the sky."

"To the Turtle to watch the Celtics-Pistons game. It's Game 7 of the Eastern Conference Finals." Trying to be courteous, I asked if anyone wanted to join me, but they looked at me like I was crazy. Maybe I was, but I was doing exactly what I wanted.

Stephanie gave me a pouty look. "Are you still going dancing with Julie and me tonight?"

"I'll pick you guys up at 9:00," I said, and walked off. As I rinsed the sand off my legs with a hand-held shower outside the Carousel, I realized why I couldn't be a good boyfriend: No girl was more important to me than a Game 7.

After being in the sun for hours, it took my eyes several seconds to adjust to the darkness inside the Turtle. I sat down at the bar and ordered a pitcher from a bartender I didn't recognize.

"I can't serve you a pitcher," he said. "The alcohol board was in here last week emphasizing an ordinance that prohibits serving a pitcher to one person."

I flagged down the other bartender, who knew me, and pleaded my case. He tapped a pitcher and put it between me and the guy to my right. "You guys can share this," he said, winking.

The guy next to me was slumped forward, like he had spent a lot of time sitting at a bar. He was retirement-age, with a round face, ruddy cheeks, and a ribbon of white hair that looked like it came out of a can of Reddi Whip.

He smiled and stuck out his hand. "I'm Gerry with a 'G.'"

"Gee?" I said, shaking his hand.

"No need to be awestruck," he said. As I laughed politely, he said, "It's a corny joke, but I can tell a lot by how someone reacts to it."

The Greene Turtle mug in front of him looked the same as mine: ceramic, cream-colored, green printing, and a fancy gold rim on the lip. But when he drank from it I saw a number, handwritten in permanent marker on the bottom, signifying it was *his* mug. The Turtle had stopped issuing member mugs but I wanted one. I wanted to belong somewhere.

Throughout the game, Gerry kept a series of stubby cigars going. Sometimes, when the front door opened, his smoke would blow in my face. The smell reminded me of Dad, who had smoked cigars for years before quitting because of his heart. I didn't have a bad association with Dad's cigars. In fact, they made him seem more like a regular guy.

Gerry and I had a great time, watching the game and talking sports. He was probably surprised that someone my age knew so much about the history of the Celtics, his favorite team. I could talk about Cousy, Russell, the Jones brothers, Havlicek, and Cowens. What I didn't tell him was that I'd be rooting for the Lakers against the Celtics once the Finals started.

For me, Gerry was a treasure trove of knowledge of 1950s and 1960s sports.

"What can you tell me about Bill Mazeroski?" I asked him. "All I know about him comes from the back of his baseball cards and that one replay of his home run they always show."

"He had the best hands of any middle infielder I've ever seen," Gerry said. "When he turned a double play, he was so smooth, it was like he never touched the ball."

After the game, we made plans to meet for happy hour the following week. Gerry promised he'd talk with Karen, a daytime bartender, about getting me a mug. I left the bar wondering why I couldn't hang out like that with my dad.

———

That night, I picked up Stephanie and Julie at their hotel.

"How do I look?" Stephanie greeted me as she opened the door.

"You look great," I said. Her hair was crimped, and she wore a pressed white sleeveless blouse, and beige culottes that set off her long, tanned legs. To meet the dress code minimum, I had on a collared blue polo shirt with black drawstring shorts.

The weekend traffic on Coastal Highway was heavy. Then someone cut me off, veering across two lanes to make a right turn. I had almost gotten back up to speed when Stephanie screamed, "Look, a podiddle!"

I slammed on the brakes and looked around but didn't see any danger.

"What's a podiddle?" I asked, trying to stay composed after she had scared the hell out of me.

"There," she said, pointing across the median. "A car with one headlight on and one headlight off. When you see one, you're supposed to kiss the person you're with."

"So what are you waiting for?" I said.

"No. You kiss me," she said, sounding playful.

I leaned over and kissed her cheek. But I didn't feel any closer to Stephanie. It may have been the resistance across my chest from my seatbelt, but it was probably her indifference in general.

The Play Pen, the dance club they had chosen, was hotter than a summer basketball league gym. Instead of following Tom's *take charge* advice, I was a Ken doll being posed and positioned for Barbie's pleasure. If Stephanie wanted to dance, we danced. As soon as she cooed, "I'm thirsty," I was in line at the bar, getting her a drink.

I was trying my best to please her. We danced most of the time, even though I hated dancing while sober. As *Walk Like an Egyptian* blared, I further swallowed my pride by joining everyone and displaying my "Egyptian" hand gestures.

I drove them home and walked them to their door. Julie went into their hotel room, finally leaving Stephanie and me alone.

"I had fun tonight," she said, batting her eyes and putting her arm on my shoulder. She craned her mouth close to my ear to whisper, "I'd invite you in, but Julie's here."

"We could take a walk on the beach," I suggested.

"That sounds wonderful. But it's been a long day and I'm exhausted."

I turned to leave, disappointed, though not surprised.

"Aren't you going to kiss me goodnight?" she purred, her glazed Barbie smile saying, *Not tonight, but I might let you take me out again.*

I leaned over and kissed her on the lips, but it felt more transactional than anything. She pushed open the door and I admired her long legs. Then the heavy door swing shut in my face and I walked away, humming nervously. After spending the day questioning whether Stephanie was interested in me or if she only wanted me around for attention and free drinks, I had my answer.

The next day, I met Stephanie and Julie for lunch at The Landing, a seafood place. I had never ordered fish at a restaurant except Filet-O-Fish at McDonald's. But trying to fit in, I ignored the "For the Landlubber" section and ordered a basket of steamed spiced shrimp.

"What a perfect beach day. It's a shame we have to drive back," Stephanie said, "You're so lucky, Bruce. You get to spend the whole summer here."

She didn't know me very well.

The waitress set a red plastic basket in front of me. My shrimp, buried in brick colored Old Bay, smelled like low tide mixed with wet dog.

I picked one off the wax paper liner and stared at it. My parents kept a Kosher house and I had never eaten a shrimp.

Too embarrassed to ask if I should eat the tail, I ate what was soft and the girls didn't seem to notice. Slimy and salty, each bite was a challenge. After forcing down several, I stopped expecting the next shrimp to taste better and gave up about a third of the way through my basket.

We talked about our fall plans. Julie had her senior year at UVA and Stephanie was starting law school at Penn. I mentioned I'd be taking the GMAT in two weeks.

"What will you study in business school?" Stephanie asked, mildly intrigued.

I cocked my head, then said, "Business." I hadn't thought much about it.

Julie was nodding at me, anticipating more details, but I didn't have any.

Stephanie's laugh broke the silence. "You can always get a job in ... *business*."

"I hear you need a strong quantitative background for the GMAT," Julie said politely.

"I'll be fine," I said, although I didn't know what *quantitative* meant. From context, I figured it dealt with math.

"Getting an MBA isn't a bad move," Stephanie said, looking down at her cocktail as she stirred it with a short red straw. "Especially if you have no idea what you're doing."

Julie winced and I finally felt I done with Stephanie, although her criticism of my business school plan was justified. It reminded me of my poorly thought-out decision to major in computers. I feared I was as clueless as everyone thought and with the GMAT approaching, I'd be finding out soon.

THIRTEEN

That Tuesday at happy hour, Gerry vouched for me but Karen, an easygoing bartender around thirty, assured us that the Turtle was no longer issuing mugs.

"It's ironic," I mused to Gerry. "A drinking club I can't drink my way into."

"I noticed you were pretty handy with a mug," he said, as we gulped our beers. "How many days a week do you drink?"

"Two or three days."

"That doesn't sound excessive," he said, looking me in the eye. "Are you being truthful?"

"Sort of," I said. "I also drink five or six nights a week."

"Haw haw haw!" Gerry's hearty laugh rumbled through the bar. "How much do you drink each day—I mean, well, you know what I mean."

"I consider twelve to fifteen drinks to be a decent amount."

He whistled. "Are you depressed?"

"I'm not necessarily happy but my mood's okay," I said.

"Just okay?" he said, his eyes challenging me.

"What's wrong with *okay*?" I said, somewhat annoyed as I rocked on my barstool. I was in familiar territory, defending my drinking, though I was flattered that someone was paying so much attention to me. "I can't lie like everyone else here and say that I'm feeling super."

"Fair enough," he said, unruffled. "When was the last time you felt super?"

"The last time I was drunk," I said, unable to avoid smiling at his impish expression. "I'm sorry I lost my temper, Gerry."

"Not at all," he said. "But you haven't told me whether you're depressed."

I shrugged. "I get depressed sometimes, sure."

"Have you ever thought about why you drink so much? Is it for attention or as a crutch?" he said, extinguishing his cigar in an ashtray.

"I don't know. Except for sports and drinking, I don't have much of an identity. At bars and parties here, everyone sizes each other up. Who has more status, who gets more girls, who is more popular. I was losing all those battles, but at least I can win when the question is who drinks the most."

"So you like out-drinking your friends when you're out drinking with your friends?"

"That's not bad Gerry," I said, raising my mug to toast him. "Like the farmer who was out standing in his field."

"The $64,000 question is what that crutch is for," he said. "Have you ever tried to quit?"

"I don't need to quit," I told him. "Drinking isn't a problem for me. It's environmental. My friends drink, so I drink."

"Then why not just drink less when you drink?" he said, fishing another cigar from his jacket pocket.

I looked down, concentrating on the grain pattern in the wooden bar and thinking about how I drank to avoid most social settings. I wasn't sure why I drank *that* much, so I shrugged and told Gerry, "I think *that's* the $64,000 question."

"And yet you don't have a fifty-cent answer for me?"

"Living at the beach has been so foreign for me. I don't feel accepted, so I drink a lot to cope."

"You're struggling socially?" he said. "Are you dating anybody?"

He looked so serious, I paused to pick a peanut from a bowl atop the bar. Then I said, "Well, you aren't exactly my type, Gerry."

"HAW, HAW, HAW," he laughed so hard, he spit his unlit stogie on the bar. Composing himself, he reinserted it in his mouth and said, "Well, are you?"

"Not really. Well ... no," I said.

"You're going to have to choose between drinking heavily and that girl you want to date," he said.

I couldn't tell him how I needed to be drunk to initiate physical affection with a girl. Instead, I said, "I don't think my drinking is hurting me with girls. Besides, it's like therapy for me."

"Leave the therapy to the professionals. How long have you been drinking excessively?"

"I didn't have my first beer until I was seventeen. Then, freshman year, my roommate played lacrosse and I drank heavily to keep up with those guys. Sophomore year, I was on the tennis team and drifted from the lacrosse crowd, but the drinking stayed with me."

Gerry nodded in acknowledgment before waving to Karen for another round. I was uncomfortable with his questions, but sensed that he cared for me.

Karen brought over two beers and without comment, turned over my bowl of peanut shells and swept them onto the floor. The Turtle served free peanuts and encouraged everyone to throw their shells on the floor, something I couldn't make myself do. The story was that the oil from the shells helped maintain the wooden floor.

"How well do you get along with your parents?" Gerry said.

"I'm fine with Mom, but Dad thinks I'm an alcoholic. It's funny because I think he's the one who has alcoholic characteristics."

"He drinks a lot?"

I shook my head. "Just a glass of wine after dinner each night. He read that was good for his heart. The only time I've seen him have more than one drink was at dinner following my sister's college graduation. After three drinks, Dad was singing at the table."

"So how does he remind you of an alcoholic?"

"He's moody, depressed, and whenever he's home from work, the whole house is on edge. Then once something rankles him—dinner's late, I did a sloppy job cutting the grass, family plans change at the last minute, I'm watching too much TV—he explodes."

"Can you find any common ground with him?"

"It's hard being around someone who gets angry every four hours. Also, I can't tell how much I agree with him because we only talk when we disagree."

"Fair enough," Gerry said. "You said you drink because it makes you feel more comfortable?" his voice trailed, prompting me.

"It also makes me less inhibited." As soon as I said that, I started feeling paranoid. *Is this guy recruiting me for AA or a church? Maybe he really is hitting on me.* Getting defensive, I said, "How come I'm the only one who has to quit? Why don't we quit together?"

His face hardened. "Can't you see I'm trying to help you?" he snapped.

"I'm sorry, Gerry," I said quickly. "I didn't mean for that to be personal."

134

"Don't mention it," he said evenly. "I'm beyond help."

I didn't feel comfortable asking him for details, so I just grimaced at him, trying to convey empathy.

We had drunk the same number of beers, but he seemed sober. He reached for his mug and rotated it by the handle so the side with "the Greene Turtle" faced him. Staring at it, he said, "Promise me you'll try to quit drinking."

"I could drink less," I said, fidgeting on my stool. "But what's the point? There's so much pressure at the beach to drink that trying to stop here would be setting myself up to fail."

"You're setting the bar too low," he said, his voice rising. "You've got to be vigilant!"

I cringed at his tone. Not because I felt people staring, but because I was back in my parents' living room, with Dad yelling at me.

"But I don't have a drinking problem," I said. "Don't you believe me?"

"I believe *in* you, but I don't believe you."

"What's wrong with me handling this my way?"

"I thought I could handle it too," he said, sighing. "Do you want to end up like me?"

I stared at his face as I thought of something to say. "Why not? You're a good person."

He smiled, but said, "Drinking has ruined my life. It's why my wife left me."

"I'm sorry, Gerry."

"Don't be. She's better off." As he crushed out his cigar, I looked ahead, focusing at the brick-a-brac behind the bar.

He took out another cigar and struck a match, his hands trembling as he tried to hold the flame close enough to light the cigar. It was taking so long, I was sure he was going to burn his fingers, but he got it lit.

"Bruce, I'm happy to discuss your drinking whenever you want," he said, taking a pen from his jacket pocket and writing a phone number on a napkin.

"I appreciate that," I said, accepting the napkin and stuffing it in my pocket like a tip.

"Think it over. If you keep drinking like this, you're going to wind up in the hospital."

My buzz gone, I felt vulnerable and started wondering if he somehow knew that I had been hospitalized for alcohol poisoning. I left for the bathroom and when I got back, I leaned my hands on my barstool and said, "Gerry, I'm getting out of here. I have dinner plans with my roommate."

"You didn't eat enough peanuts?"

I patted my stomach. "Bottomless pit."

"Call me when you're ready to talk."

"You got it," I said, and walked outside.

But I didn't plan on calling him. Usually when people gave me advice, they didn't know me very well. Gerry knew me too well. That scared me.

That night, Tom, Erin, and I met a group from the bellstaff at the Angler before walking to the Talbot Street Café, where someone's bartender friend wrote off most of our tab. The last stop for the three of us was the Turtle.

Tom parked his old Corolla in the lot out front. As I folded my seat forward to let Erin out of the backseat, a car pulled in, two spots over. Wasted, I opened the door for the girl who was driving and said, "Welcome to the Greene Turtle."

She got out, wearing a snug black dress and a dozen black rubber Madonna bracelets on each wrist. Barely five feet tall, she looked up at me, unfazed and said, "You sure are a tall drink of water."

"I am, aren't I?" I said, too drunk to be shy. "Are you old enough to get in here?"

She smiled and reached into her purse before handing me her ID. "This says I'm twenty-one, but you can't believe everything you read. My real name is Tina."

"I'm Bruce," I said, handing her my license. "Everything on this is real."

She gave my ID the once-over and said, "Except your hair. I like it longer, like in your picture."

"Me too," I said. "Hey, if your ID's good enough, maybe I'll see you inside."

Tom and Erin got a table and I brought over two pitchers and a mug for Erin. Tom's seat was facing the bar, so he could see everything going on. I was happy with my view of the TV, which was showing the NESN replay of the Red Sox/Twins game, Clemens versus Viola. Pitching matchups didn't get any better than that.

I was a quarter of the way through my pitcher when Tom told me that *my girl* was trying to get my attention. Full of drunk confidence, I grabbed my pitcher and walked over.

After I sat at her table, her friend said, "Tina was telling me how charming you are. What's your best pickup line?"

"I don't have any," I said. "This is as far as I've ever gotten."

"I told you he was a gentleman," Tina said, laughing.

"What's *your* best line?" I asked her friend.

"I'm a girl. We don't use lines."

"This girl does," I said, pointing at Tina.

"My word," Tina said, in an exaggerated southern belle drawl. "Whatever could you be talking about?"

"I recall something about a tall drink of water," I teased.

Tina giggled. "I might've said that to a fella or two. But for me, everyone's tall."

It seemed like Tina was interested in me because she swept her thick black hair from her face as she looked at me. She was attractive and I loved how outgoing she was. But I kept thinking about the last time I saw Amy, right before she drove to the airport, and about our phone conversations where she made me feel less alone at the beach.

It felt like I was cheating on her.

I knew Tom would hassle me if I didn't ask, so I said to Tina, "Can I have your number? I'm too drunk to talk with you now."

"Now there's your best line," she said, smiling. Her friend dug a pen from her purse and handed it to Tina, who grabbed my arm and wrote her number on the palm of my hand.

Back at my table, Tom said, "What are you doing here? She looks good to me."

"Don't worry," I said, holding up my hand, fingers extended. "I got her number."

"Strong move," Tom said, nodding his approval. "Getting a number and cutting out before last call shows you're interested but not too interested."

"Showing he's interested but not too interested," Erin said drolly. "Yet another reason I'm attracted to this guy."

I smiled at Erin's futile attempt to keep Tom's ego in check. "I can't take credit for that," I said. "Clemens is down 4-3 in the sixth and I wanted to watch the game."

"Nobody ever got laid watching a baseball game," Tom said, his stern look rescinding his approval.

After last call, Tom and Erin left while I settled the tab. Outside, I was intrigued by the doorman, who was reading a book. He was wearing baggy pants and a wrinkled button-down shirt, his relaxed lean against the building serving notice that he didn't take any shit. I stopped to ask what he was reading, as if our relationship went beyond him checking my ID a couple of nights a week.

He looked up, fixing me with a stare, and said, *"Dante's Inferno."*

I nodded and said, "Who wrote it?"

That wasn't out of ignorance. I was bombed.

He stood up straighter.

Realizing my error, I said, "I didn't mean that." Then I eased away in case he was considering taking a swing. "I mean I wasn't thinking when I asked you. The second question, that is."

He kept staring and I hurried off, humiliated. But the more I thought about it, the funnier it got. Walking home by myself, I repeated the exchange out loud every thirty seconds. "What are you reading?... *Dante's Inferno...* Who wrote it?" Then I'd laugh.

When I got home, I had to call Amy. I finally felt ready to tell her how much I liked her.

"Hello?" she answered, sounding groggy.

"Amy!" I shouted. "It's great hearing your voice. I can't wait to see you at the wedding."

She didn't respond, so I said, "How's your internship going?"

"It's fine," she said, sounding different. She sounded annoyed.

"What's wrong?"

"It's late and I was asleep. Also I can barely understand you. You're slurring your words."

"Is this better?" I said, raising my voice again. "I can talk slower if that helps you."

"Bruce, you have to stop calling me when you're drunk. It's getting to be too much for me."

"Sure. No problem, Amy. I didn't mean to wake you. I just wanted to tell you something, but I can call you back another time, when—"

"Good night, Bruce," she said, and hung up.

I went upstairs. Tom had left the bedroom door unlocked, so I went in. The lights were out and they were in Tom's bed.

"Who were you talking to?" Tom said. "You didn't call that girl from the Turtle, did you?"

"That does sound like something I'd do," I said, as I walked across the dark room. When my shin banged against the sideboard of my bed, I hopped in. "But no, I called Amy."

"I always liked that Amy," Erin said.

"All you do is talk with her on the phone," Tom said. "Have you even seen her since the formal?"

"I'll be seeing her in two weeks."

"What makes her better than all the girls here at the beach?" he asked.

"Amy gets me, and I always feel comfortable when I'm with her.

Letting down my guard, I continued talking about her, but couldn't convey how special I felt having her in my life. Sitting in bed in the dark, trying to convince Tom, I felt like I was at a slumber party where I was nowhere as cool as the others, trying to defend a close friend who hadn't been invited.

We stopped talking. My head was spinning from a full day of drinking. I was so drunk, I lost count of how many beers I had that day. It must have been at least twenty.

I couldn't sleep, picturing Gerry's shaky hands as he tried to light his cigar. I wondered if that would be me in thirty years. Most things about my future scared me, but growing old and being alone like Gerry really got to me.

FOURTEEN

When I heard a knock on my front door the next morning, I knew who it was. Except for the mailman, everyone just walked into my house at the beach. I opened the door and sure enough, Paul was standing on the stoop. It was great seeing him, but I was a little disappointed that his side-parted straight brown hair wasn't tousled in some Morrissey-inspired pompadour.

After a hasty house tour, I drove us to the Carousel garage. Al, our ancient daytime guard, emerged from his booth, arm outstretched in front of him. As always, he was wrapped in his dark blue windbreaker and topped with Brylcream.

"You can't park here," he said.

"It's okay Al. I work here."

Looking puzzled, he said, "What section?"

"I'm a valet, Al," I said. He didn't have a name tag, so I kept using his name, trying to convince him that I knew him. "Call the bellstand if you want to check."

"That's okay," he said importantly. "I'll let you park."

"Thanks, Al," I said, and as I turned right and drove up the ramp, Paul said, "I can tell you're a big man around here."

"I can't believe he doesn't recognize me. He sits in that tiny booth most of the day and I probably reach over him to pick keys off the board fifteen times a week. We spend more time together than a lot of married couples."

Instead of leading Paul through the Carousel to show off its grandeur, I took the express route along the outside. After passing the drab employee entrance and then the rancid dumpsters, the concrete sidewalk gave way to sand, hundreds of loungers, and the almighty ocean.

"Ah, Coppertone," Paul said, inhaling deeply as we paused to take in a panoramic view.

Weaving between the blankets and towels, I kept my size fourteen feet low to avoid kicking sand on anyone. We found a spot and spread our blanket. Paul unbuttoned and removed his short-sleeved shirt, then slapped No Ad brand SPF-15 sunblock all over his untoned skin.

"Are most of these people tourists?" he said, looking around as he lit a cigarette. He loved the image of himself holding a cigarette. As cool as Paul looked while smoking, I was never tempted to steal one of his cigarettes and take a drag.

"Most of them," I said. "Locals travel light, so a giveaway is how little someone brings. Also, by mid-June, locals are down to SPF 2 or baby oil."

A seagull landed near us. Screeching and scurrying about with quick steps, it pecked the sand dampened by the tide. Despite plenty of food for foraging near beachgoers, the gull kept its distance. I felt a kinship with the bird. We both needed our space.

I brought up my GMATs, which were the following weekend. He asked if I was ready.

"I think so, but I haven't studied much," I said. "I'm giving up drinking for a week so I can buckle down."

"Do you think you'll be able to do that?

"You too?" I said.

"What do you mean?"

"Everyone has been on me lately about my drinking."

"Who is everyone?"

"Dad, Amy, CJ, Gerry, and now you."

"Who is Gerry?"

"Some alcoholic I met in a bar."

"Well he should know," Paul said. His sense of humor was even drier than mine.

"The way I see it, my options are choosing between drinking alcohol to get by this summer and being depressed."

He gazed toward the ocean and took a long drag on his cigarette. Then he exhaled out the side of his mouth and said, "If you aren't depressed sometimes, you'll never appreciate feeling happy."

I followed his line of sight, staring past the waves, past a distant ship, to the horizon. It was the most profound thing I had ever heard.

"I'm used to being depressed, but I feel like I'm the only one here who ever feels that way," I said. "Most nights, I go out drinking with Tom, my A-List roommate. He has high expectations for how much fun he and everyone around him should be having."

"You never enjoyed going out. But I don't think that's your problem. It's when you drink, you drink so much."

"I drink so much out of habit," I said. "I also drink to feel more comfortable, especially in a crowded bar."

"How do you know that your drinking is helping you feel comfortable?" he said. "Instead of getting wasted, why don't you drink less and focus on what's making you uncomfortable?"

"Because that sounds like a lot of work," I said, and when

he didn't respond, I said, "So you're saying I shouldn't drink so much when I'm stuck in a bar with a bunch of jerks?"

He nodded. "Being more sober, you can make better decisions about who you're with and how to handle yourself in those situations."

"I guess I can try that. What do you do when you feel uncomfortable in a bar or at a party?"

"I smoke," he said, trying not to smile as he dropped his butt into his Coke can.

"Tom tries to introduce me around, but his player friends are indifferent to me. Most people here are too cool to be quirky, so whenever I meet someone, I feel like I have to convince them I'm not a doofus," I said, lowering my voice, though it was impossible to have a private conversation among the crowd. "Those guys only tolerate people like me if we worship them."

"Being a player is like running a pyramid scheme," Paul said, lighting a cigarette. "They need chumps at the bottom to buy in."

"Chump right here," I said, raising my hand. "I feel like a loser around those guys."

He snorted. "You're not the loser in that scenario."

"If I'm not a loser, then why am I miserable and they're having a great time?"

"Because you're sensitive. You need to hang around with nicer people. You've only known Tom for a few months, right? How well do you get along with him?"

"Several days a week, we're together at work for hours a day, and more nights than not, we drink together. Considering we see each other six to eight waking hours every day and then sleep in the same room, we get along pretty well."

"How can you spend that much time with anyone?"

"One-on-one, we're good friends. But I have trouble

around his people. I can't call him on anything, or he'll bristle when I'm being too sarcastic or if I'm trying too hard to make a joke. But whenever he wants to act silly, I'm supposed to yuk it up with him."

"Why do you put up with that?"

"Because one good night out with Tom makes up for a couple of bad ones."

"If he's not looking out for you, then doesn't that make him one of the jerks?"

"I guess there are times when that's true," I said, which was something I had never allowed myself to concede.

"Getting some distance from him will help, but you still need to be more flexible around the people here," he said. "They'll relate to you better if you embrace their interests."

"You mean I have to join the valets when they play Hackeysack in front of the hotel with a piece of saltwater taffy?"

"Yes. That's a perfect example."

"Crap. Do I have to call everyone Dude?"

"No. That's really annoying."

We played cribbage and after lunch from the Carousel's outdoor grill, Paul pulled a *Car and Driver* from his backpack. I took a nap and when I awoke, he was reading *Vanity Fair*.

"I can't believe we've been here three hours," I said, looking at my watch.

"I could lay out all day," Paul said, stretching his arms.

"Not unless you put more fifteen on your nose," I said. "Actually, your whole face could use another layer."

He put down his magazine to apply sun block, deftly avoiding the cigarette in his mouth.

An hour later, his nose was glowing red. I tapped my nose and pointed at his to indicate that he needed to get out of the sun. We packed up and walked into the garage, passing Al, seated in his booth.

"Howsitgoing Al?" I said, shooting him a wave.

He looked up from his newspaper, stared at me, then looked down without comment.

As we walked up the ramps, Paul asked, "So what are the nicest cars you've driven?"

"We get a lot of Mercedes, BMWs, and Corvettes. Occasionally, we'll get a Porsche. I recently had a problem with a 944. I thought I had it in reverse—"

"Aaagh!" he yelled, as if the Porsche was his. "Do they know you can't drive a stick?"

"Hey, I've been practicing."

"I think that's the problem."

We resumed our card game on my lower deck and I brought up my "date" with Stephanie.

"The most frustrating part wasn't getting rejected, but getting rejected after I had tried so hard. On a date, I just want to be able to act like myself. Is that too much to ask?"

"That's the most reasonable thing you've asked for in a while," Paul said. "Are you going to keep dating her?"

"I don't think I was ever dating her. When I used to pick her up, I'd wait for her and her English sheep dog would nudge, push, and herd me around the room. Stephanie does the same thing to me. The only thing we have in common is a desire to make her happy."

He laughed. "Are you seeing anybody at the beach?"

"I've met some girls but I'm not seeing anyone. Lately, I've been thinking a lot about Amy, but I'm having trouble going from being friends to dating."

"You guys slept together two months ago. Doesn't that make you more than friends?"

"It should, but I was drunk, so we skipped over too many things. I need to go slow and now I can't just rewind my emotions like a VHS tape," I said, feeling terrible for not confiding in Paul about my problem initiating physical intimacy.

"From what you tell me, Amy really likes you. Any idea why she likes you so much?"

"I don't know. Maybe she had a crush on me when we were little and that never went away. I've always been afraid to ask her."

"What makes her so special?"

"This is going to sound stupid," I said, looking down sat my cards to avoid his eyes. "But when I saw her over New Year's after all those years, it felt like we were destined to be together."

"I've never heard you say anything like that about a girl."

"Amy's different. She's so great and so down-to-earth. She's also a little goofy. She says things like *cool beans*."

"Cool beans?" Paul said, puzzled.

"I know," I said, laughing. "I think it's a Midwest thing."

"Have you told her how you feel about her?

I shook my head.

"You'd better tell her. Destiny or not, if you take her for granted, she won't always be there for you."

A game ended and Paul said, "Okay. Gotta go," his abruptness surprising me. But he always ended phone conversations as if an alarm clock had just gone off in his head.

As we walked out to his car, I thanked him for playing Linus to my Charlie Brown.

"I don't follow you," he said.

"In Peanuts, Linus is always explaining life to Charlie Brown and trying to cheer him up."

"I didn't read Peanuts much," Paul said. "I liked Richie Rich though."

He drove off and I walked back to my house, shaking my head. *My spiritual advisor is Richie Rich?*

Paul was a great friend, a great listener, and he understood me as well as I allowed him. I needed someone like that at the beach. I had CJ, but I didn't share much of myself with him.

FIFTEEN

The next day at work, Tom was in a lousy mood after breaking up with Erin over the weekend. They had started dating in the fall but had been fighting on and off since Tom got to the beach. The temptation here was too much for him as girls were constantly hanging on him, looking to leave bars with him.

He came home from work mid-afternoon and swept the clutter off the eat-in counter and onto the dining room rug.

"What's wrong?" I asked him.

"Those assholes just gave me a ticket on Jamestown."

I wanted to say, "Welcome to the club," but couldn't laugh at him for getting a ticket like he did when I got one. Still, I was surprised that he wasn't able to talk his way into a warning because he seemed to go through life with a horseshoe in his pocket.

"You still up for throwing the weights around?" I asked.

"Negatory," he said. "I don't need to lift anymore."

"Come on, Big Guy. I need you pushing me," I said, disappointed because lifting was one of the few things that brought us together.

"Get CJ to spot you. Girls here don't care if I'm cut or not. All I need to do is maintain my tan."

He quickly shifted into going-out mode, asking if I was psyched for Scandals. It was Tuesday, after all.

"Nah. My test is Saturday so I'm staying in."

"You're staying in for the *rest of the week*?" he said. "I'm getting tired of dragging your ass out every night."

I didn't want him to stop dragging my ass out, I just wanted him to stop dragging my ass out *every* night.

"Don't worry, I'll be at Scandals next Tuesday. I'm not missing anything."

"What's wrong with Scandals?" he snapped.

"All we do there is stand around. It's the same thing every week."

"Why am I asking you?" he said, sounding overly dramatic. "All you ever want to do is watch TV. When we talked about living together at the beach, you said you'd be going out all the time. What happened to that?"

"Standing around in packed bars, struggling to hear conversations isn't my idea of fun," I said. "Besides, some of the people we run into are really mean."

"Like who?"

"Steev-o. He always acts like an asshole toward me."

"Steev-o *is* an asshole," Tom said. "Stop feeling sorry for yourself and deal with it."

Deal with it was Tom's answer to all my problems.

"You know half the people living at the beach," I said. "Why is it so damn important that I go out with you every night?"

He looked me in the eye. "Because I like hanging with you. So many people here are fake as hell. Dude, you're one of the most genuine people I know."

I felt guilty, although he might have just been telling me what I wanted to hear.

"Look, I've been stressed about the GMAT, but I'll be going out more after my exam."

"I hope so," he said, and as he headed up the stairs, he said, "You know where to find me."

But that was the problem. Mondays he was at Harpoon Hanna's, Tuesdays he was at Scandals, Wednesday it was B.J.'s for happy hour and then the Turtle at night for DJ Batman, and Fridays he was at Trader's. The other days, he freelanced.

After Tom left for Scandals, I studied in our room. It was my fourth day of not drinking and while I appreciated the GMAT giving me an excuse not to drink, I was getting nervous about the exam. If I didn't do well, I wasn't getting into business school. Then I'd need a backup plan for my backup plan.

Two days before my test, I was studying at the dining room table. It was mid-afternoon and Tom was deciding between happy hour and the beach.

As if blown by an ill wind, the front door flung open. In sauntered John Markey and Dave "Beast" Beason, the main agitators for our fraternity's sports rival, Hawaii 5-0. Their team jerseys were mismatched Hawaiian-print shirts for every sport, even basketball.

"Gentlemen. What's going on?" Markey greeted us. Blonde haired and barrel chested, he was brimming with mischief and good cheer.

Beast, who was thin with dark features, stopped in the kitchen, emerging with four Schaefers. Without a word, he tossed one to Tom, one to me, and as Beast handed one to Markey, Tom and I looked at each other and laughed.

"How long are you ugly mugs in town?" Tom said, as he tapped the top of his beer so it wouldn't explode when he opened it.

"We depart Sunday," Markey said, with the air of a ship's captain. Then he walked over and picked up my study guide. "What are you doing? I thought you graduated."

"Studying for the GMAT," I said.

"You're wasting your time," he said, fanning himself with the heavy book's pages. "Don't you know they design those standardized tests so you can't study for them?"

"The best way to prepare for a test is to take your mind off of it," Beast cut in. "Let's finish these beers and play some foosball at the Greene Turtle."

"You're on," Tom said.

"What are you guys, bad cop, bad cop?" I told them. "I can't make it. I have to study."

"Dude, if you don't know it by now, you aren't learning it by Saturday," Tom said, the curl in the side of his mouth showing his displeasure

"I also promised myself I'd quit drinking for a week," I said, feeling more embarrassed that I was trying to cut back than because I drank too much.

"Say it again?" Beast said. "Mr. shot of beer a minute for three hours straight is turning down a chance to drink?"

Beast knew the drill. We all knew the drill. At school, it was common for someone, generally mired with a massive hangover, to announce he was giving up drinking for a week. This would be greeted with laughter, skepticism, and often a wager.

"What's quitting for one week going to accomplish?" Tom said.

"I need to prove to myself that I can control my drinking," I told him.

He snorted. "Suit yourself, dude. Come on guys. Let's roll."

They chugged their beers and as they headed for the door, I caved. They needed a fourth for foosball and I couldn't take Tom being pissed at me two days before my exam.

"Wait for me!" I called as they headed out the door. I put my unopened beer in the fridge and caught up with them.

Tom was scowling as we walked into the Turtle. "No one's here," he said, as if every Ocean City local had just stood him up.

"You're right," I said, as we trooped past the bar and filed up the spiral staircase. "I don't see anybody here."

"You've got that backward," he said. "You don't go out to see people. You go out to be seen."

I couldn't win. But that was Tom. Once he walked into a room, he owned it.

We claimed the foosball table and soon were drinking, laughing, shouting, and talking trash. Between games, we were hanging over the railing and floating bills down to Karen at the bar, who was flinging quarters up to us. We were also tossing peanuts down at a Nerf hoop hanging behind the bar until Karen asked us to stop. Well, until she asked us a couple of times to stop.

When my cigar-chain-smoking conscience shuffled in and took his usual place at the bar, my mood went from *Animal House* to Marvin's house. By that time, Karen had refused our airmail delivery of our dollar bills, so after losing a game and then losing rock paper scissors with Tom, I had to go downstairs for change. I wasn't looking forward to facing Gerry.

"Bruce! How ya doing?" he, said, reaching up from his stool to shake my hand.

"Feeling no pain, Gerry. I'm having a few beers with some visiting friends."

"I can see that," he said, his smile gone. "I'm sorry you didn't take my advice to heart."

I thought that was unwarranted because I hadn't made any promises to him. But instead of explaining that I had just quit for six days, I asked if he wanted to join us.

"Thanks, but my knees are no match for that spiral staircase," he said.

"I forgot I was dealing with a Gerry-atric."

"Haw haw haw," he guffawed. "I'll be using that line."

"Since you can't get up there, it certainly isn't a Gerry-*attic*."

"Haw haw haw."

I told him, "I have no idea how you're going to work that second pun into a conv—"

"Dude! What's the holdup?"

I turned and glared up at Tom, who was leaning down on the railing, his palms turned up.

"I apologize for my roommate, Gerry," I said. "Let's catch up another time."

"I look forward to it," he said, staring into my eyes, his gaze intrusive.

After twisting up the stairs, I unloaded the quarters on a table. "What's your hurry, Mr. Laidback?"

"You're wasting everyone's time by talking with that beachcomber."

"I see him in here during happy hour," I said. "He gives me advice, although he's always on me about my drinking."

"Why are you telling personal stuff to some old guy you barely know?"

"Because he gives a damn about me."

"Whatever, dude," Tom said.

Markey whispered conspicuously to Beast, "Looks like there's dissension in the fraternity."

"Let's take these guys down," Tom said to me. We closed ranks and resumed our raucous game.

Between points, I'd glance down at Gerry, sitting alone. After several more beers, he settled his tab and hobbled out, probably going home to an empty house. I didn't know why I sympathized with him but not my dad. Like Dad, his views on drinking were strict, but at least Gerry was in my corner. Hell, we shared that corner.

That Saturday, I took the GMAT in Baltimore and crashed at my old row house, before driving back to the beach the next morning.

"How'd it go?" Tom said, looking up from his magazine while sunning on the back deck.

"It went okay, I guess."

"Dude, even if you're not sure, just tell people you aced it."

"I know I did well on the math sections. I might not know what *quantitative* means, but I'm great at simple math."

"*Quantitative* refers to measurement," he said, glancing back down at his magazine. "The quantitative section of a standardized exam measures basic mathematical reasoning."

I did a double take that he didn't notice. "Wait a minute," I said. "Are you smart or something?"

"I have a 3.5 GPA, so yeah, by that metric, I'm smart."

"By that *metric*?" I said. "Don't worry, dude, your secret's safe with me."

He snorted and I asked him where we were going that night.

"I thought you were done with the bar scene."

"I'm done with the GMATs, so I wanted to celebrate," I said. "With friends."

"A bunch of us are going to OC Cheers," he said, glancing up to gauge my reaction.

"Count me in," I said. I knew I couldn't keep going out just to make him happy, but I wanted to show I appreciated him trying to pull me into his crowd, though I needed his support more than his invitations.

"Have you called your father?" he said. When I looked at him, confused, he said, "Today is Father's Day."

"Not yet. I'll call him now," I said. Not wanting him to know how estranged I was from Dad, I went inside and picked up the phone.

Father's Day was never a big deal in my house because Dad wasn't good at accepting attention or gifts. A cake for his birthday was fine, but no candles and no singing.

For Mom's birthday or their anniversary, Dad always gave her a card and a lavish piece of jewelry. I viewed the generous trinket was an apology for him not being nicer the rest of the year. Over time, Mom had amassed an impressive jewelry collection that she kept stashed in a safe deposit box where it couldn't be stolen. Unfortunately, it couldn't be enjoyed either.

"What do you need?" Dad said tersely, once he realized it was me.

"Why do you ask?" I said.

"Because you only come to me when you need something."

He was right, though not quite this time. "I called to wish you a happy Father's Day."

He paused. "Well, I appreciate that."

"Are you doing anything special today?"

"Your mother is taking me to the farmer's market."

Corn was in season, so Dad could buy ten or twelve ears for a dollar. He'd buy two or three dollars' worth, depending on how much room was in the fridge. Then for the next week, he'd spend evenings sitting at the kitchen table with his shirt off, eating corn.

"That sounds good," I said.

There was a long pause, and I could tell he was organizing his thoughts.

"What are you doing now to look for a job?"

"I've been studying for the GMAT all month. I took the exam yesterday and it went well."

"That's fine, but that's not helping you presently."

"Hey, I'm sorry Dad. I have to leave for work now, but I'll see you at the wedding." I hurriedly said goodbye and hung up.

"Nice going," Tom called through the screen door.

"What are you laughing at?" I said, unaware he had been listening.

"I know you're not scheduled for work today, so you're getting better at lying."

SIXTEEN

Driving to my parents' house for the wedding Friday evening, I sped past Salisbury, Cambridge, and Easton, feeling as insignificant as the cornstalks among endless rows in endless fields between towns. I didn't know where I'd be living in September, where I'd be working, or even what I wanted to do.

I thought about trying to make amends with Dad. I could ask his advice regarding business fields that interested me and assure him that I would look for a job once I returned from the beach. But he'd ask me a bunch of questions and insist that I do research at a library. Worst of all, he'd want me to start looking right away. Realizing I couldn't satisfy him, I bagged the idea.

Then sun had set by the time I arrived their brick split level so I couldn't see if the azaleas were in bloom or how low Dad had cut the grass in his postage-stamp-sized yard.

When I pulled open the storm door, it dragged on the cement. The grinding noise reminded me of a Porsche's front-end spoiler crawling on top of a parking barrier. I unlocked the front door and pushed the door hard because it stuck in the summer.

Closing the door behind me, I felt no joy in familiar surroundings or in seeing my family. Certainly not in returning to my childhood home as a *guest*. Like every other family event, this visit would end in a blowup or by exposing a simmering issue that would carry over until my next meeting with Dad, like a cliffhanger end to a TV show. The only question was what was going to trigger Dad.

"Bruce is that you?" Mom called from the living room. "Can I get you something to eat?"

"No thanks," I said, dropping my gym bag among the potted plants by the front door. I went up the four steps to the landing and turned right, into the misnamed living room. Formal, stuffy, and *unlived* in, it had a couch, two chairs, a marble-topped coffee table, and three glass-front curio cabinets that housed Dad's fragile Wedgwood bowls and Belleek figurines. It wasn't a place for a kid to toss around a ball or set up his orange Hot Wheels track.

The living room flowed into a dining room in which we dined maybe once a year, when the cousins came over for a Passover Seder. The head of the dining room table was Dad's desk, littered with piles of papers and envelopes. The table's chairs, which were as old as me, still had their factory plastic encasing their gold velveteen cushions.

My sister Tamara, in town from Pittsburgh, was seated with my parents around the coffee table. There was no food or drink. Only guests were permitted to have a nosh or beverage in the living room.

"You must be hungry," Mom said. "Can I make you a grilled cheese sandwich?"

I shook my head.

"You're so tan," she said. "Are you wearing your sun block?"

"Of course I am, Mom," I said, lying to avoid upsetting her.

"I'm surprised at how long it's taking your hair to grow back," she said, probably concerned that I was going to mess up the wedding photos.

Tamara stood up, walked over, and put her arms around me. Surprised, I recoiled slightly. We weren't a family of huggers.

"Why are you staring?" I asked Mom.

"When you didn't come to the rehearsal lunch today, we just thought—"

"I had to work this morning," I said, cutting her off. "There's no need for me to rehearse. I'll just follow the groomsman in front of me."

Dad was sitting silently in his blue paisley armchair, which faced the stair landing, his book resting, spine up, on the floor. I walked over, put out my hand, and said, "It's good to see you."

He didn't get up. Staring poker-faced, he squeezed my hand.

I walked to the matching paisley chair across from Dad and plopped down. Mom and Tamara sat on the couch to my right, under the bay window.

Mom was chatting excitedly about relatives attending who she hadn't seen in years. Dad's disinterested expression showed he was content with letting another decade pass before seeing them.

"You seem quiet, Marvin," Mom said.

"*Maw-vin*? Who is *Maw-vin*?" Dad repeated, mocking Mom's Flatbush accent. After marrying in the late 1950s, they had moved from Brooklyn to Maryland. Dad had long-since vanquished his accent, so he picked at Mom when hers emerged.

Mom was in such a good mood, she didn't care. She talked about the guest list, the wedding details, the menu for the day-after brunch, and back to the wedding details.

As the details piled up, Dad couldn't contain himself. "I don't care if your Mahjong friend Carol had a string quartet for her daughter's wedding. If I want to hear violins, I'll turn on the radio."

"Oh Marvin, I just remembered," Mom said. "The florist called this afternoon. The calla lilies for the centerpieces aren't available. They had to have a decision, so I agreed to a more expensive lily, but it puts us over a thousand dollars for flowers."

"You authorized that?" Dad thundered. "Those bastards think they can raise the price on me the day before the wedding? I'll call in the morning and if they won't honor the agreed-on price, we'll have the wedding without flowers. Then I'll sue them for breach of contract!"

Tamara's face fell, hearing Dad's ham-handed threat. He didn't care, and continued kvetching. "Growing up, we were so poor, we had to eat lard and ketchup sandwiches. I will not be extorted by a goddamn florist!"

After Dad's tirade, Mom asked me how things were at the beach.

"I certainly hope you're enjoying your vacation," Dad cut in, his tone dripping with sarcasm.

"Please don't start now, Marvin," Mom begged.

"Start what?" Dad said, feigning surprise. "I thought spending summer at the beach was a vacation."

"I'm working full-time, Dad."

"Parking cars isn't a job." He scoffed. "Not only that, but I haven't seen any effort from you to find a real job. Tell me, what am I missing?"

"Do you really think the night before the wedding is the time to discuss this?" I said.

"It's never the right time for you," he said. "What's your plan?"

"I guess I'll be sending out resumes soon and focus on jobs in statistical research."

"You guess? You still have no idea? Why are you going into statistics? I recall you struggling in a statistics class."

"Because I love working with numbers," I said.

"Do you have any idea what a statistical researcher does all day?"

"I didn't know this was going to be a job interview."

"You should always be ready to answer interview questions," Dad said, scowling.

"I'm going upstairs," I said, and went down for my bag before running up to my room. I sat on my bed, looking around in disbelief at the four blank yellow walls. Dad had taken down my posters. The only thing left on the cork board by the light switch were multi-colored pushpins.

Mom's school supplies were piled on my desk, shopping bags with piles of new clothes all over the floor, and bags of yarn sat on my dresser. Growing up, my room had been my sanctuary. Now it was a stockroom.

I went to my closet, pulled out a notebook containing a set of baseball cards from the early 1970s, and flipped through the plastic pages.

Tamara walked in and sat down next to me. "Are you doing okay?" she said.

"I know I need to do more to find a job," I said, fighting back tears. "But it's never enough for Dad."

Three years apart in age, Tamara and I were often mistaken

for twins, although she smiled and laughed much easier than I did. She also tried harder to please others, especially Dad. She and Mom were close, like sisters, and they loved knitting and clothes shopping together. Them being so close made me feel even further from Dad.

As we talked, Dad's voice carried upstairs: "Growing up, there were six of us living in four rooms, Alice. What do I know about a country club affair?"

"Doesn't he know you're getting married at a Hilton?" I asked as we tried to ignore Dad, which wasn't easy in our snug house.

She laughed and said, "I'm keeping my mouth shut until I'm back in Pittsburgh."

"You always were the smart one. How come, on the rare occasion when Dad is happy with me, he calls me *Number One Son?* I'm his only son, so how do I lose my standing?"

"Deep down, you're always Number One Son. Dad just wants you to work for the title."

I couldn't ignore Dad's voice from downstairs as he bellowed, "... and a good-for-nothing son with no idea what he's doing with the rest of his life!"

"I'm sorry Tamara. That's my cue," I said, getting up. "I'm going to see if Amy is home."

As I hurried downstairs, Dad was threatening to skip the wedding.

"Nothing ever changes here," I yelled as I ran out, slamming the front door behind me.

I walked down the street to Amy's house. I rang the bell and waited on her stoop, unsure if she'd be home. The porch light came on and the door opened. Amy was standing there, wearing a t-shirt from her Spokeswomen cycling club and red gym shorts, her hair in a ponytail. She smiled and my heart started fluttering like I was on a date.

"You look cute as a jock," I said, picturing her jogging along the side of the street, her cheeks red, her ponytail swaying behind her, her legs chugging along.

"I thought you'd be with your family tonight," she said, stepping forward to hug me.

"That was my plan, but seeing you is much better."

She flashed an exaggerated smile and invited me in, before leading me into the kitchen and offering me a drink. I wanted a six-pack so I could feel comfortable getting closer to her but asked for a Coke.

We went to the living room and sat on the couch. I looked around at built-in floor-to-ceiling bookshelves behind an overstuffed chair with an ottoman. On one wall hung a grouping of family photographs, some showing a young Amy with chubby cheeks and pigtail braids.

My family's photos sat on a low cabinet in a corner of our living room, encased in four-by-six Lucite frames. There were two sets, taken a couple of years apart at an Olan Mills studio. In one set, I wore my tan three-piece Pierre Cardin bar mitzvah suit, with its snazzy stylized "P" gold buttons. My family wasn't nearly as happy as we tried to look in those photos. Staying true-to-form, Dad displayed his trademark scowl.

As I slumped into the cushions, Amy was leaning forward slightly, her hands in her lap. I could feel the interest in her eyes, her chin protruding when she got excited. What attracted me most was the way her mouth opened wider, showing her side teeth, just before she'd laugh.

Her dog, a medium-sized sandy-colored mutt named Sandy, ambled over. But once she realized I didn't have any food, she left the room. I appreciated not being herded, like at Stephanie's house.

Amy asked how the wedding preparations were going.

"Things are tense at my house, but that's normal," I said, extending my habit of self-deprecation to my family. "Right now, Dad is fuming over a cost overrun on centerpieces."

"Your father's such a sweetheart," she said. "Years ago, I saw him out walking and told him I was studying to be a dietician. Now, whenever he sees me, he tells me about his no-fat diet."

I didn't mention that Dad was happy to discuss his no-fat diet with the mailman, the cashier at the grocery store, or anybody else. When twenty-four-ounce cans of salmon would go on sale for a buck apiece, he'd buy dozens and stash them in the laundry room. Dad could eat the same meal every day for a year if it was low-fat, cheap, and easy to prepare.

Mom was a good cook, but after Dad's heart attack, everything had to be ultra-low fat. Dad would police the top layer of soups and sauces on the stove, scooping away congealed matter with a tablespoon, and splattering it in the sink. Mom often made a pot of potato soup that turned into a solid when it cooled. It had zero fat, zero salt, and little taste. It was perfect for Dad.

"I'm glad to hear that my dad's so adorable," I said. "We haven't been seeing eye-to-eye on much lately."

"My brother fights with my father all the time. It's heartbreaking to watch," she said, looking so somber I wanted to put my arms around her and console her. "I guess our fathers are both very protective."

"You mean controlling, don't you?" I said.

"It might seem that way when it's directed at you, but I think they're just looking out for their kids."

Amy always saw the good in me, so I couldn't object if she saw some good in Dad.

She told me about her parents flying out to Bloomington to attend her graduation. I couldn't imagine hosting my parents like that and didn't tell her that one reason I had skipped my graduation was to avoid facing Dad.

She updated me on her internship and how rewarding working in a hospital setting had been. I was happy she had found her ideal field, but was worried that she'd lose patience watching me struggle to find my career. She had a real job, educating and advising people on improving their health, while my tasks were helping hotel guests, bullshitting with the bellstaff, and staying out of Gary's way.

Since Amy was always attentive, enthusiastic, and smiling, I couldn't tell if she was giving me a signal or just being herself. After feeling so alone at the beach, I wanted to embrace her and feel some of the contentment she exuded. I was also feeling pressure to show her I was romantically interested in her, while agonizing over being too shy to hold her hand.

Her mom wasn't helping. She kept coming in to chat and check the score of the Orioles game on TV in the background. She was about Mom's age, her frizzy hair loosely tethered by an oval leather barrette fastened through two holes by a brown wooden stick. I appreciated its Wilma Flintstone practicality.

After a third interruption, Amy shot her a look that said, *Can I get some privacy?* But her mom ignored the hint so I got to watch Amy, normally poised and confident, as she squirmed and occasionally bristled at her mom's recollections. The only thing cuter than the girl next door was the girl next door when she was blushing.

"Do you see that macramé planter?" Amy's mom asked

me, pointing to a green-leafed plant hanging by a large window behind the TV.

"Oh Mom," Amy pleaded.

"Amy made that when she was a Girl Scout, but she had trouble getting her knots to line up." Her mom moved her fingers like she was tying knots. "My Amy, the perfectionist, was the only girl in her troop who wasn't satisfied with her line of knots. Oh, my word. You've never seen such tears."

"Mom!" Amy shouted. "Why do you have to tell the macramé story whenever someone visits?"

"Because you never do," her mom said, chuckling, as she left the room.

Later, her mom announced that she was going upstairs. Finally alone with Amy, I was afraid that if I didn't make a move, she'd think I wasn't interested in her *that way*.

As we continued talking, I was straining to find some opening, some rhythm or momentum that would allow me to lean in and kiss her. The more I tried to choreograph that and psyche myself up, the more immobile my body felt.

Then, as casually as if she was offering me some chips or pretzels, Amy said, "Do you want to go up to my room?"

I couldn't have been more excited. Or scared. I had my signal, practically an engraved invitation, but now I had to initiate physical intimacy. Every success with Amy posed new challenges.

"Sure," I said, trying not to seem too enthusiastic. We put our glasses in the dishwasher and I followed her upstairs. Along the stairway wall were ascending eight by ten portraits of Amy and her brother. After commenting on how young they looked, I thought, *What a stupid thing to say. Of course they look young. They're old photos.*

Walking into her room, I looked around nervously. There was a poster of Parker Stevenson and I chuckled at his perfect teeth, perfectly tousled hair, and the perfect cuff in the collar of his turtleneck sweater.

"What's so funny?" she said.

"I loved the *Hardy Boys*, but I had no idea that Parker Stevenson was poster material."

"He was so dreamy," Amy said. Then, taking a couple of steps for a closer look at his face, she added, "Still is." Grinning, she said, "What was on your walls growing up?"

"Posters of baseball players, like Dave Parker and Willie Stargell. I have a poster of Dave Parker on my wall at the beach so I guess we're both Parker fans."

"Willie Stargell?" she said, frowning. "I'm still mad at him for beating my Orioles in the World Series."

That has been eight years before. I smiled at her. She knew her baseball.

Amy's room probably hadn't changed much in years. Atop one shelf were several stuffed animals and a stack of ragged Judy Blume paperbacks. There were pale blue frilly curtains and pink ruffles on the bed skirts.

She sat down on her full-sized bed and I followed, remaining a comfortable distance away. Amy picking a stuffed Saint Bernard off the top of the headboard.

"This is Rolf. I won him at the county fair," she said, shoving the dog at me. "He protects me from monsters."

That seemed more friendly than romantic. I grabbed Rolf and assured him that I wasn't a monster.

"Here's something," she said, leaning over and picking two large thin paperbacks from a bookcase. I recognized the gold-colored yearbooks from our two overlapping years at Eastern Junior High. She handed me one and opened the other in her lap.

"Let's see ... seventh grade," she said, flipping to the pages with her class's photos. "Some of these haircuts are so dated, mine included," she laughed, as we scanned the Dorothy Hamill wedge cuts and the longer, layered Farrah Fawcetts. "There you are," she said, pointing to my eighth-grade photo. "You always were a cutie."

"But not dreamy like Parker Stevenson."

"That's a tough standard," Amy said.

I found her eighth-grade picture in my yearbook. "Here's yours," I said, handing my book to her and easing closer as I peered down at the tiny photo. "You used to be so pretty."

"What's that supposed to mean?" she said, sharply.

"That didn't come out right," I said defensively. "What I meant was that I was too self-absorbed in junior high to notice how pretty you were."

Her smile returned. "I'm relieved to hear that my looks didn't peak at twelve."

I smiled back. *Why didn't I tell her how attractive I find her now?* My head was a busy place, overthinking everything I was saying and questioning any action I was too timid to make. I kept hoping that Amy would say something direct, like, *Don't you want to kiss me?*

As I waited, I started talking about the Carousel and she asked me how the guests knew how much to tip.

"I have no idea. I also don't know why most of our tips come when we bring a car around, not when we park. We usually get a dollar but the tip amounts are all over the place. Sometimes we get stiffed, sometimes we get a soda tip, which is fifty cents, and once in a while, we'll get a fin."

"What's a fin?" she said, surprising me with her interest.

"A five-dollar bill," I said, not mentioning that it was an old term that I used to see in Archie comics. "The bellmen call a ten-dollar tip a *marlin* and a twenty-dollar tip is a *great white*. I never use those terms because I only get a tip bigger than five dollars about once a week."

Instead of moving over and finding out where I stood with her, I rattled on, detailing that we wrote the car's type, color, license, and location on our pink tickets. She listened to my favorite Garyisms, laughing when I detailed how red his face got when he bunged.

When I said that Flec was the only one who noticed me taking notes for my journal, she asked if I had written anything about her.

"Of course, but I'm not sure I can share those entries with you." It was my turn to blush.

"When am I going to get to read it?" she said.

"How about when you visit me at the beach?"

"That's one of my summer destinations," she said, which sounded nice, but still wasn't a clear sign. I had a very high standard for clear signs.

"What else do you write in your journal besides your feelings for me?" she said, grinning.

"Fairly mundane observations," I said. "For example, I'll mention seeing the seventeen-year locusts on my visit home. We don't have them at the beach."

"They aren't *locusts*, they're *cicadas*," she said in her agreeable way of correcting me. "They're so loud, but they're harmless, at least as long as they don't fly into your hair." She reached to run her fingers through my hair, but apparently it wasn't long enough, so she stopped and sighed. "Your hair was so wavy over New Year's."

That felt like a sign, so I reached for her hand. But my other hand remained at my side instead of going around her, so I was holding her hand as we sat a few feet apart on her bed.

"I'm sorry I'm so shy around you," I said.

"What do you mean?" she said politely.

"When I saw you over New Year's, I got so excited," I said,

not able to talk about why I was so shy. "Since then, I think about you all the time."

"What about all those other girls at the beach?"

"I think my haircut took care of that."

Instead of reacting to my joke, she stared at me. I thought she might have been annoyed, so I quickly said, "But seriously, you're the only girl I'm interested in."

She looked down and smiled. When she looked up again, our eyes locked. I was still holding her hand. Something was happening. I leaned closer. Then I heard footsteps in the hall. They were getting louder.

Knock knock.

"Amy? Is Bruce in there with you?" Her father sounded angry enough to break down the door and drag me away from his daughter.

Startled, I looked at Amy.

"Yes, Dad, we're talking," she called through the door. "Are we being too loud?"

"No. You're too quiet," he said, opening the door. "Why aren't you visiting downstairs?"

"I'm showing Bruce our old yearbooks," she said, smiling.

Her father's furrowed forehead looked like Gary's when I'd ask to leave work early. I hadn't seen him in a decade and all I could think to say was that his graying temples looked distinguished and that I wasn't wrestling with his daughter. Neither seemed helpful, so I waved at him stiffly and said, "Hi, sir."

"It's time for you to go, Bruce."

"Yes, sir."

"Okay Dad, we'll say goodbye," she said, her voice chipper.

"Hmmph," her father said, walking out, leaving the door wide open.

"I told you my father was very protective," Amy said, sounding apologetic.

"That's okay," I said, glad that someone was concerned that I might make a move.

As we walked down the long, straight stairway, I heard her father moving around in the kitchen. She pulled open the front door and I said, "I'm sorry about tonight."

"Why are you sorry?"

"Because I spent the whole night trying to get the courage to kiss you."

"How about now?" she said softly, as she gazed up at me.

Feeling tingly, I edged closer.

"Good night, Bruce," her father said firmly, startling me as he emerged from the kitchen. When I was a kid, he had seemed as nice as Mr. Rogers. But with his stern face and arms folded, he looked as intimidating as one of the bouncers at Trader's.

"Good night, Sir."

"It was a fun time tonight," I whispered to Amy. Then I backed away quickly, leaning into the storm door to push it open. But it was latched, so I bounced off the rigid metal, a loud rattle calling attention to my gaffe. Ignoring the pain in my side, I hurriedly reached behind me to disengage the latch, before spilling outside.

Flustered, I told her, "I'll see you tomorrow at the wedding."

"My father won't be there tomorrow," she said, grinning.

As I walked across her front yard, I was thinking, *It was a fun time tonight? What does that even mean?* On my walk home, I was kicking myself for sitting in Amy's bedroom, sitting next to her on her bed for Christ's sake, and not kissing her.

SEVENTEEN

The next afternoon, I was putting on my tux in a hotel suite with Dad and the other groomsmen. I had thought the groomsman's purpose was to counterbalance the bridesmaids during the ceremony and in the photos, but I was using them as a physical buffer between me and Dad. After sleeping late, not showing up for the rehearsal dinner, and not finding a real job, the less contact I had with him, the better.

I kept pulling my collar higher on my neck but couldn't button it. I had gotten my measurements taken near school but when I called them into the tux shop, I must have told them fifteen inches, not sixteen, for the neck.

Dad was frowning in the mirror as he watched me struggle. He started walking toward me and all I could think was, *Great, another chance to tell me I fucked up.*

"Here, take mine," he said, extending the wire hanger holding his shirt, pressed and perfect, still covered in plastic. "The sleeves will be short, but at least you'll be able to button the collar."

"Thanks," I said, in disbelief. After taking off my shirt and handing it to him, I watched him put his arms into the sleeves, then fasten the second-from-the-top button and work his way down. He got to the top button and winced as he secured it. The collar was cutting into his neck, but he refused to wear it unbuttoned.

Every day for as long as I could remember, Dad had worn a dark suit to his job at the Department of Commerce, so I was used to him dressing formally. But after putting on his wine-colored bowtie and tux jacket, he had an uncharacteristic sparkle. When Mom pinned Dad's corsage on his jacket, she made a big deal over how nice he looked, and surprisingly, he didn't seem angry at the fuss.

As soon as Ellen dropped Amy off, I got excited thinking about how the night before had ended. Her hair was down, her dress off-white with purple, red and pink flowers, and a narrow V-neck. Here, she wasn't competing with slinky cocktail dresses like at my formal. Not that she had to compete with anyone. She looked beautiful.

"You're even prettier than your eighth-grade picture," I said, as I received her hug.

"You clean up well, yourself," she said.

"Let's walk around the hotel," I said. "I wouldn't mind getting away from all the people."

We stopped in the lobby in front of a gigantic, framed print of an Italian hillside flecked with vivid reds. "This place seems nicer than the last place we stayed," I deadpanned.

"I almost killed you when you pulled up to that fleabag," she said, socking me on the arm. "How does the Carousel compare to this hotel?"

"I think the Carousel is too laid-back for a comparison," I said.

"I thought you said it was one of the nicest hotels in Ocean City."

"That's what Gary tells us, but standards at the beach are

different. We don't put a mint on your pillow—we have a glass bowl of salt-water taffy at the front desk. Towel service and umbrella availability are more important than the tone of our lobby. Actually, our most important aspect is the weather."

"I'll bet Gary bunges when it isn't sunny for the guests," she said. "The weather is one of the few things he can't control."

I smiled at her. She really paid attention to what I said.

As we strolled down the wide hallway, I was dreaming about the end of the night. Amy and I would be lounging on one of the upholstered benches along the wall, chatting, flirting, laughing, maybe smooching a little, like at my formal, with passersby thinking what a nice couple we made.

I wanted to pick things back up from Amy's coy goodbye the previous night. But as we walked, I couldn't get myself to put my arm around her or hold her hand, so I knew I'd have to rely on alcohol to help orchestrate my cozy scene with her. I'd drink enough to be comfortable around her without getting too drunk to drive.

During the ceremony, I kept glancing over at Dad. His stoic expression never changed, not even when Tamara said, "I do."

Afterward, the wedding party gathered for pictures. The photographer kept urging, "Big smiles everybody" and I laughed when he said, "Lighten up, Father of the bride. You've already paid me."

I enjoyed watching the photographer prodding Dad to pose and smile, two things Dad rarely did. He spent almost as much time directing Dad as he did with Tamara. It was subtle, but by requiring so much guidance during the photos, Dad had nearly upstaged the bride.

Once the bar stations were set up, I was in line. On a return trip, I was chatting with the bartender in the black vest, who wasn't much older than me. I was paying particular attention when he said he was making too much money as a bartender to get an office job.

Dad was proud to offer the heart-healthy dinner option of chicken or salmon. We ate a sit-down meal set with three forks, which was too grand for me. Instead of the cloth napkin in my lap, I preferred a metal box of napkins on the table, like at a diner. Having never been to a wedding, I asked Amy how this one rated.

"Your sister is stunning, the ceremony was beautiful, and the flowers are worth every penny," she said. "But weddings generally follow the same script, like the cheesy introduction of the wedding party."

When my name had been called during the introductions, I bounded onto the stage like Magic Johnson at a Lakers pregame and gave my surprised dad the first slap handshake of his life.

"I kind of liked being introduced," I said, gazing at her. "Although it would have been nicer if you were up there with me."

"That's sweet," she said. "But I don't have a title. You're the brother of the bride. I'm just the date of the brother of the bride."

"You deserve a title. You're way more polished than me. I don't even know when to button my tux jacket."

Amy reached to straighten my bowtie. "You button it when you stand and unbutton it when you sit. It's not that complicated."

When I stood to go to the bar, I buttoned my jacket and Amy smiled. As I walked over, a woman two generations older and dripping in heavy gold bracelets stopped me. In a thick New York accent, she said, "I'm your cousin, *Awdrey*, Ruth's *sis-tuh*."

"Hi Cousin Audrey," I said, blankly. "It's nice to meet you."

"We've met before. At Henry's Bar Mitzvah."

I was seven when my cousin Henry had been bar mitzvahed. All I remembered from my trip to Brooklyn was that Henry was the funniest person I had ever met and that most traffic lights in Brooklyn didn't have yellow lights.

"I can't believe you've graduated *cawledge*," she said. "Where has the time *gawn*?"

Dad would have pointed out that I had wasted those fifteen years watching TV and playing sports.

"I don't know," I said, as I waited for her next question. The one everyone asked.

"So tell me," she said, smiling. "Where are you working now?"

"I'm taking the summer off. I'll be looking for a job in the fall."

"Oh," she said, her smile gone. "What does *Mawvin* have to say about that?"

"He's not exactly thrilled."

"I'm not surprised," she said, her smirk telling me all I needed to know. I was mad at myself for thinking that my relatives would see me as an adult, and not some wayward kid.

During the reception, I had been introducing Amy as "my friend" but some relatives smiled knowingly and asked me if I was *next*. I just laughed at the question. I wasn't opposed to getting married eventually, although I sometimes joked that my parents stayed together all those years out of spite.

Mom looked delighted when she told me that her Mahjong buddies had been asking her about "the girl that Bruce brought." Amy's presence had probably caused a big move in the Mahjong betting line on whether Alice's son was gay.

The band was an African American four-piece with a woman singer whose voice sounded like Gladys Knight and looked great in her tight, shimmery dark blue sequined dress. They played mostly Motown, mixing in standards for the older folks.

I felt self-conscious as we danced. For me, dancing was harder than driving a stick. *More shoulder, less arms. Slow down. More hips, less shoulder. Now I'm too stiff.* I felt like I was using dashboard levers to operate earth-moving equipment.

After a few songs, I suggested that we take a break and asked Amy if she wanted something from the bar.

"You're getting *another* drink?" Her accusatory tone surprising me.

"I'm fine," I said. "Having a few beers helps me relax."

"Why do you need to drink so much to relax?"

I couldn't tell her the reason, so I said, "I don't want to spend all night meeting people. Everyone wants to hear about my job and my career, and I don't have much to say. All I want to do is spend time with you."

"Looks like I'm going to have to share you with your relatives," she said. "Tell them you just graduated and you're considering your options, including business school."

"That sounds fine when you say it, but they still want to know what I'm doing now. I tell them I'm parking cars at the beach and once they realize I'm not kidding, they think I'm a fuck-up."

She put a hand on her hip. "Why would you say that?"

"My dad thinks I'm a fuck-up. To him, I can't do anything right."

"I wouldn't date some fuck-up," she said. "You're nice, funny, and interesting."

Later, Amy wanted to dance again. A song ended and as we walked off the dance floor, I peeled away.

"Where are you going?" she asked.

"To say hi to my buddy at the bar. Do you want another drink?"

"No thanks," she said, her tone cool.

When I got back to our table, I put a new bottle of beer down next to the one I had just started.

Her eyes watched me closely as she said, "What do you need me for?"

"Because I enjoy being with you."

"I'm sorry, Bruce. I can't watch you drink yourself into a stupor. You have so much more to offer."

That sounded like more criticism over my stalled career. Feeling I was losing Amy's support was too much. The music and crowd noise got louder. The room seemed to be closing in on me.

"That's all I hear," I snapped. "People keep telling me I'm not reaching my potential."

She glared at me and I knew I had overreacted.

"I'm sorry Amy. I didn't mean to take out my frustrations on you."

She stared at the dance floor as we sat in silence.

"Do you like the band?" I finally said, leaning to put my hand on the back of her chair. "This music reminds me of *The Big Chill* soundtrack. I didn't see the movie, but I'll bet you liked it."

She didn't answer so I tried again, "Did you like *The Big Chill*? It's a coincidence how the movie's title applies to our current scene."

She turned to face me. "I was afraid this would happen again. I'm going home."

"What do you mean, *again*? I'm barely buzzed," I said, as she stood up. "Please give me another chance, Amy. I'll stop drinking."

"Tonight *was* another chance," she said, throwing her napkin onto the table.

"Come on, let's dance," I said, reaching for her arm. "I don't care how stupid I look."

She ripped her arm away. "My mind's made up. I'm calling Ellen."

"At least let me take you home."

Amy stared at me. "You shouldn't be driving a car right now, Bruce."

She said it without emotion, like she didn't care about me. Then she bolted out of the reception.

"What are you talking about?" I called, trailing her down the hall, more concerned with defending how sober I was than about how she was feeling. "Amy, please!"

She ignored me and went into a bathroom. I sat at a bench outside and as her amplified crying came through the bathroom wall, I leaned forward, my face in my hands.

When she came out, her eyes were red, but she looked determined as she walked past to find a pay phone.

"Amy, don't leave this way," I pleaded as she spoke to her friend.

Her conversation finished, Amy slammed the receiver into its cradle and brushed past me to sit near the front door. I sat down next to her.

"I'm sorry, Amy," I kept saying, but she wouldn't acknowledge me.

When Ellen arrived, she pushed open the door with a

clatter and marched up to Amy. Putting her arm around Amy's shoulder, Ellen quietly asked, "Are you okay?"

Amy nodded.

"I told you this would happen," Ellen said to Amy.

As they walked out, I called *goodbye* to Amy. She didn't respond, but Ellen looked back to give me an *eat shit and die* glare.

I walked to the front door, pressing my face against the glass as Ellen's car sped off. On my way back to the ballroom, I paused in front of one of the benches along the wall. My night with Amy couldn't have ended more differently from how I had hoped.

I wanted to leave but couldn't do that to Tamara. I went back to the reception and sat at my table, staring at Amy's empty seat, reliving the disappointment in her face when she saw me bring that extra beer. I looked around. My sister and her new husband Jim were talking with guests. The dance floor was crowded. It was like Scandals. Everyone was having fun but me.

My beers were no longer beading seductively. I picked one up and guzzled it, not caring that it was room temperature. I downed the other and walked over to congratulate Tamara and Jim.

"How is Dad holding up?" I asked her.

"Still behaving himself," she said. Neither of us mentioned our surprise at Dad's restraint. We didn't want to jinx things.

A couple of beers later, no longer concerned about my dancing or how upset Amy was, I took up residence on the dance floor with a few of Tamara's friends. I hit my stride, leading a conga line that snaked through the ballroom, out to the hallway, and back. As I navigated past my bartender, he handed me a bottle of beer without slowing down my train. That was *The Carousel Total Guest Experience*, Hilton style.

The highlight of the reception was Dad being lifted and carried around in a chair during the *Hora*. Hoisting one of the chair legs, I looked up as he beamed and blew kisses to the crowd with both hands. Snapping pictures, the photographer was as excited as if he had just chanced upon Bigfoot in the wild.

After the band packed up and most guests had left, I walked over to Dad. "Everything turned out great," I said. "I'll see you tomorrow at brunch."

His eyebrows narrowed. "Where do you think you're going?"

"Don't worry. I'm going straight home."

"You're not driving anywhere in your condition," he said.

"*Condition?* What are you talking about? All I've drunk in the last hour was three cups of coffee."

"I don't care how many cups of coffee you've had!"

"Dad, I'm fine!"

"You're in no condition to operate a car," he growled, extending his hand. "Give me your keys or I'll call Monday and cancel your auto insurance policy."

Tamara and Jim were nearby, watching Dad's meltdown. I shrugged at her to say, *Dad almost made it*. But for the first time all night, Tamara wasn't smiling.

Jim came over. Built like a fire hydrant, his serious manner and receding hairline made him look older than thirty-one. His groomsmen had shared stories with me about his drinking exploits his fraternity days at Penn State, but I had known Jim for being driven and successful at work; another reminder I had to get my act together.

Before he said anything, I told him, "This is bullshit, Jim. I'm not in high school. And I'm fine to drive."

He looked me in the eye. "Bruce, we both know you can drive, but do me a favor and go home with your parents."

It was his wedding and I respected him, so I walked up to Mom, who was saying goodnight to one of her Mahjong friends while trying to ignore my dust-up with Dad.

"Here you go, Mom," I said, tossing my keys to her like guests sometimes did to me at the Carousel. Though surprised, she caught them by clapping her hands together, like she was catching a moth.

Her friend was looking sternly at me. Then I told her, "It was nice seeing you, Ms. Rodder. Tell Scott I said hi."

Her face softened at my mention of her son. She said, "I will, Bruce."

Later, I tumbled into the backseat of our family car with Mom as my designated driver. I waited for Dad to resume our argument, but he remained quiet. He preferred to simmer and let his anger build up until he could no longer contain himself.

With no room to extend my legs, I laid on my back, knees in the air. As she drove, Mom was gushing about how everything had turned out as planned, while Dad was tersely answering her: *yes... yup... uh-huh.* After avoiding provocations by 150 guests, he finally had something to be mad at.

EIGHTEEN

The next morning, my parents' voices carried up from downstairs and woke me. Mom was setting up brunch for thirty. Dad was kibitzing over details.

"Can you open the pickles for me, *Mawv*? They're on the door of the fridge."

"Did you really need to buy three different types of pickles, Alice?"

My head was killing me, but I was feeling worse about Amy. After going to the bathroom, I went into to my parents' bedroom to call her and explain why I drank so much around her.

"What do you want?" she said when she answered the phone. "I can't believe you did that to me."

"I know. *I know*," I said, nervously twirling the phone cord around my index finger. "I'm so sorry that my drinking ruined last night."

"You're usually drunk when you call me from the beach and you end up drunk whenever we're together. Why do you drink so much?"

It was a perfect set-up to tell her that I needed to be drunk to be intimate with her. But I got concerned that she'd give up on me because of all my anxieties, so instead, I told her how I had quit drinking for six days the week before.

"You sure picked right back up where you left off," she said, not at all encouraged by my restraint. "Weren't you motivated to stop drinking around me after your formal? What about those times you called from the beach and were too drunk to hold a conversation?"

I cringed, sitting on the floor next to the bed. "You seemed unaffected after the formal and since you had been drinking, I didn't think that night was—"

"Yes I was drunk at the formal, but I was clearly upset each time you called me drunk from the beach," she interrupted. "You aren't that dense, are you?"

Not only was I that dense, but any concern I had over her anger when I had called her while drunk had gone away once the alcohol left my system. Now, my only chance was to tell her about my issue with intimacy.

But she was too mad to let me speak.

"Last night, you weren't just drunk, Bruce. You were wasted. You should have seen the look on your relatives' faces when you kept trying to go behind the bar to serve drinks, even after the bartender told you he could get fired for that. Then, when you asked the band to play *Bolero*, I was embarrassed to be with you."

I took the phone off its wicker tripod and put it in my lap. Leaning forward in the fetal position, I realized I had been acting like the asshole fraternity guy that everyone hated. Upset at myself, my instinct was to apologize.

"I'm really sorry I ruined your night," I said. "I promise I'll make it up to you when we see The Cure."

"I'm not going to a concert with you, Bruce. I never want to see you again."

I closed my eyes in anguish. "Amy. Please let me—"

She hung up and the dial tone reverberated in my head. My hands were shaking as I replaced the receiver on the phone cradle. *What am I doing? Amy's the best thing in my life. She was the best thing in my life.*

I thought about how quickly my cousin Audrey had sized me up after not seeing me for fifteen years. I really was a fuck-up.

The front door opened and closed quickly. It had to be Dad going for a walk, so I went downstairs. Mom was in the kitchen, arranging cheeses on serving plates.

Her was face blank, like she didn't recognize her son. "I'm disappointed by your drinking," she said.

Disappointed sounded innocuous but Mom was saying I had fucked up.

"I'm sorry, Mom. I got caught up in the celebration."

"If only it was that. But your insistence on driving home is what frightens me."

"I'm trying to control my drinking, Mom."

"I hope so," she said, but her frown showed doubt. She didn't even offer to make me breakfast.

I showered and when I returned downstairs, the dining room table, no longer a desk, was set up as a buffet. Hanging over the fireplace was a homemade paper banner reading: *Congratulations Tamara and Jim!* Dad was seated in his paisley chair below *Congratulations*. Looking up from his newspaper, he growled, "You'd better make yourself useful during brunch." Then he returned to his paper. He'd have plenty to say when the time suited him.

My parents rarely entertained and either because of the

disruption to Dad's routine or some associated stress, our family always fought before or after any event. A truce would prevail during, lest the guests suspect we were anything but a happy family.

Several older relatives made disapproving comments about my exuberant drinking and dancing. Aunt Joan, Mom's only sibling, drolly told me, "I didn't realize you were such a dancer."

Uncle Morton, Dad's youngest brother, got so close, I could smell the lox on his breath as he said, "I haven't seen drinking like that since I left the Navy. When someone asks for your keys, you refuse them at your peril." The hard squeeze he gave my shoulder wasn't out of affection.

I felt badly for disappointing my relatives, particularly my uncle, who had given me my first baseball glove when I was four. It was a hand-me-down from my cousins. I was left-handed, so I had to wear my righty glove upside down as I threw a tennis ball against the back of my house.

Once everyone had left, I cleared dishes while Mom washed piles of plates and kitschy serving paraphernalia: knives with swoopy, ornate blades, utensils with oversized wooden handles, large Lucite tongs that couldn't pick up anything smaller than a bagel, yellow and tangerine enameled hors d'oeuvre platters, and a bronze-colored fish-shaped Jell-O mold.

It wasn't a party at my house without a quivering slab of Jell-O, laced with chunks of canned pineapple. I liked Jell-O and I liked canned pineapple, but I didn't like them together.

"Bruce Talbot! Come down here!" Dad's voice roared up from the rec room.

My middle name had always embarrassed me. Dad had chosen it, thinking it sounded regal, further evidencing that as far back as my birth, we couldn't agree on anything.

I trudged downstairs. Standing at the far end of the room with his back to me, Dad was pulling aside the heavy curtains to look out the sliding glass door. Near his feet was his Scandinavian-design black leather chair. It was padded but wasn't plush and there was no ottoman. Dad didn't like getting too comfortable.

"Sit down," he barked, still looking outside. I sat on the couch next to his chair. "Your intention to drive while drunk shocked me," he said, turning. "You might not remember the end of last night, but we had to talk you out of driving home."

"Of course I remember the end of the night," I said. "I was fine by then."

"I'm not here to debate your sobriety. It's only a matter of time before you get into a catastrophic car accident. Since you're on our insurance policy, your mother and I are personally liable for damages you cause in excess of our coverage limits. One accident by you could wipe out our life savings."

"So it comes down to money," I said.

"It comes down to you being accountable for your actions," he said, talking over me. "Excessive drinking will ruin your life. You'll never be able to hold a decent job."

"But my drinking is temporary."

"How do you know that?" he said, as Mom walked in silently and sat down on the couch.

"Because my drinking habits are different when I live here."

"You don't live here anymore," Dad growled.

"Marvin!" Mom interrupted.

"Let me finish, Alice," Dad snapped, then said to me, "Your mother and I insist that you see a counselor for your drinking. We'll even pay for it."

"I'm taking care of my drinking on my own." I said, staring back, trying to appear unmoved.

"If you refuse, I will remove you from our auto insurance policy," Dad said, and walked out of the room. He returned seconds later, rubbing the back of his neck. "I'm seeing a downward spiral from you. Drinking, not looking for a job, not attending graduation, staying out until all hours at night, shaving your head, the speeding ticket..."

"You're making a big deal over a few isolated circumstances," I said, relieved that he was only aware of a few isolated circumstances.

"You have to stop this nonsense and look for a career job right now."

"I just took the GMAT. If my scores are good, that will give me an indication."

"An *indication?* Alice, he's waiting for an indication!" Dad thundered. "Maybe Moses will come through the front door and use his staff to guide your son to the Promised Land."

"I think we've discussed this enough Marvin," Mom said. "Let's not spoil the day."

"Spoil the day?! I'm looking at a ticking time bomb, Alice. Your son's actions are destroying this family."

"All this tension is making my stomach ache," she said.

With exaggerated concern he said, "Can I fix you a bicarbonate or get you a Tums?"

"Ending this conversation would help," she sighed.

"For years," he growled at me. "I've tried to motivate you, but it's like pushing on a string. I told you in March that I was washing my hands of it. That's exactly what I'm doing now. *It's nished!*" he hissed and walked out of the room.

After waiting to make sure he wasn't coming back, I looked at Mom. "Why is taking the summer off such a crime for Dad?"

189

"Your father's parents were the first in his family to come to this country. He was born two years before the Great Depression and they had to fight for everything they got."

Except for when he was railing about the cost of something, Dad never talked about his struggles growing up. I knew my grandparents as jovial retirees who had enough money to send me ten dollars every year for my birthday and again for Hanukkah.

"I didn't know Dad had grown up that poor," I said. "But he's doing fine now."

"Things didn't happen like *that*," Mom said, snapping her fingers. "We've been working hard and saving for decades. Building a life of financial security isn't quick and it isn't easy."

"But you guys did it and now you can relax."

"Where you come from stays with you. Back then, the father was the provider, and the mother looked after the house and kids. That mindset was unfortunate because your father missed a lot of time with you and Tamara."

"Missed a lot of time?" I said, my voice rising. "If he had spent *any* time with me, he might have imparted in me some of the deference and drive that he cherishes."

"You're not being fair to him," Mom said.

I looked into her eyes. They were the same hazel-brown as mine, but we didn't see Dad the same way. "Do you know I was six the last time Dad took me to a baseball game?"

"You remember that?"

"The Senators lost to the Red Sox 4-3 and Frank Howard hit a home run," I said. "Uncle Morton drove us and the cousins to RFK on ball day. I still have the giveaway baseball."

"If you could have retained knowledge like that while studying, you would have made the dean's list."

"Can we talk about what a terrible student I was another time? How come Dad never took me to another game?"

"Your father doesn't drive. And didn't the team leave town soon after that anyway? They weren't very good."

"Mom, the Senators stunk but that's not the point. Dad never bothered to watch an inning or a few minutes of any game on TV with me," I said, standing to look out the sliding glass door at the magnolia tree in the neighbor's yard. I hadn't climbed it since I was ten, when my best friend Peter Boyer and I would sit high in the branches and look down on the roofs of two-story houses. The tree used to seem gigantic, but it was no longer so imposing.

"I know he doesn't like sports, but I always felt that he didn't like me either."

"That's nonsense," she said, and gave her usual excuses for Dad.

I sat back down next to her. She was caught in the middle, so instead of arguing, I said, "You know, it's not easy being a twenty-two year old."

"It's not easy being the parent of a twenty-two-year-old, either."

"That's pretty good. Did you get that from a book?"

"You'll find out someday. In the meantime, I wish you'd listen to your father more. It doesn't take that much to please him."

"The problem is, it doesn't take much to set him off, either."

We shared a smile and I knew she still cared for me. Dad may have been the king of the house, but I was the prince.

NINETEEN

That night, I met Paul after his restaurant shift in downtown Silver Spring. We walked to Tastee Diner, a run-down, authentic railcar diner. The food was marginal, but it was *our* diner.

He was telling me about how Tastee was losing its fight to stay open due to the renovation downtown.

"I've been away for too long. I didn't realize things were so dire," I said. "I'll come back and chain myself to a booth if that will stop the bulldozers."

"There have been other changes," Paul said. "The Royal has gone up twenty cents."

"They have to keep up with inflation," I said.

"The patty is also a little smaller."

"Sticking it to us on both price and portion size?" I said in mock anger. "Is there no end?"

It was midnight, a little before the after-hours crowd would be rolling, stumbling, or limping in. We walked past the cash register inside the two sets of doors and seated ourselves in Marge's section.

My first visit to Tastee had been with Paul in high school

on Halloween night. That night, Marge took our order wearing a Muumuu on her 250-pound body with the menu written on her arms and legs in ballpoint pen. The next time I went to the Diner, I was relieved that Marge's Muumuu menu had been her Halloween costume.

"I think I blew it with Amy," I said. "She broke up with me this morning."

"Oh no," he said, and stopped flipping through the tabletop jukebox, which featured artists ranging from Patsy Cline to Prince. "What happened?"

"I drank too much during the reception. There was an open bar, so you know—"

"Free booze is never an excuse for irresponsible behavior," he said. "What's okay at the beach or at school isn't acceptable at your sister's wedding."

"I get that, but last night was different. I had to drink."

"What was so different? Your father?"

"I wanted to be close to Amy. I can't do that without drinking."

"What do you mean? I thought you were attracted to her."

"I am. It's not that, exactly," I said, taking a deep breath. "It's because ... I'm too shy to kiss a girl or to lead her from kissing to being more physical."

"But you've told me about several girls that you've had sex with."

"That's because I was either drunk or the girl led me. My problem with Amy, with girls, is that I have to be drunk to initiate intimacy with them."

"What if she wants to go further?" he said, lighting a cigarette. "Can't you tell?"

"Two nights ago, we were sitting alone on her bed and I couldn't even kiss her."

"Who initiated sex at your formal?"

"We both did," I said. "But I was drunk, so I didn't have any problem."

"Maybe if you told Amy about your difficulties, she could make the first move."

"I've tried, but I always stop because I get scared that she'll reject me."

"She wouldn't reject you."

"She just did."

"That was because of your drinking. This is different."

"I don't even know what makes me feel this way. I think it's my brain telling me I'm not ready for a relationship. If I don't know the reason, how can I expect her to understand?"

"If you want Amy to give you another chance, you'll have to tell her. You also need to share more of yourself with her."

"I know, but except for right now, I've never told anybody about this. I usually just break up with a girl instead," I said, stopping when I heard shoes shuffling behind me. I knew it was Marge because she had trouble lifting her feet.

"Where have you been, Sweetie?" she said, her ponytail half-gray, her face free of make-up and evidencing fifty hard years of living.

"I'm living in Ocean City this summer," I said, smiling after seeing her. "Nobody there serves a Cheeseburger Royal like you."

"Ocean City," she said, a gleam in her eye. "I used to raise hell there years ago."

"Tell us a story, Marge," we begged.

"I better not. These walls have ears. You boys need menus?"

I looked at Paul, then said, "We're ready."

She took our orders and when she left to check on another table, I brought up my fight with Dad.

"Toward the end of the night I stopped drinking and had

three cups of coffee," I said. "Dad didn't care. He took my car keys and now he wants me to see a counselor for my drinking."

"That's not a bad idea," Paul said.

"Whose side are you on?"

"I'm on the side that wants you to be happier. What's wrong with seeing a counselor?"

"I don't know. I guess I hate doing what he tells me to do," I said. "Do you think I'm an alcoholic?"

"I don't know, but you can have a drinking problem and not be an alcoholic."

"You aren't making this easy."

"I'm just trying to help."

"Besides, my drinking isn't hurting anyone, not even me. I always get up and function the next day."

"Your drinking does hurt you. It makes you act very differently. When you're drunk, you're much more outgoing and louder."

"So what's the problem with that?"

"You always complain that people misunderstand you. Well, when you're drunk, they don't have a chance to get to know the real you. But I don't even think drinking is your main problem."

"Great. There's more?"

"I think you're too afraid to fail. You only do things that you're very good at and avoid everything else. Have more confidence in yourself and try some new things. If you fail, then learn from it. Trusting yourself might also help you overcome your difficulty with intimacy."

"Now that you've solved all my problems, what will we have to talk about?" I said, smiling. "No wait. I've got one more. This afternoon, Dad cut off all support."

"He kicked you out?"

I nodded. "After this *visit*, I'm not allowed back to Flower Avenue."

Paul reached into his pocket and took out his keys. He removed a bronze-colored key from the ring, put it on the table, and slid it to me.

"Your house key?" I said. "What are your parents going to say?"

"They probably won't notice."

"I appreciate that," I said, adding it to my keyring. "I can't see reconciling with Dad any time soon."

"Before you can reconcile with him, first you'll have to be his son." Then, smiling, he said, "If you guys became closer, what would you do together?"

I exhaled audibly while considering that.

"Dad and I would have to talk, which means I'd have to listen to him. That would be weird. I'd have to cut back on sports, drinking, TV, and playing spades and poker."

Marge returned with our coffee and sat down, filling my side of the booth.

"How have you been Marge?" I said, concerned. "You look tired."

"Well, my doctor's on me about my weight again, but asking me to lose it around here is like asking an accountant not to embezzle."

We smiled politely and shortly afterward, Marge unwedged herself from the booth to "spread herself around," as she called it.

I resumed talking about Dad. "Last night, Dad had a few drinks and was enjoying himself so much, I couldn't believe it."

"Why is that so unusual?"

"Dad has tons of grudges with Mom's family. I'm sure being around them was awkward for him."

"Why doesn't Marvin get along with your mom's family?"

"To be fair, Dad also fights with his family. He never forgets a slight, perceived or real. His first date with Mom was a double date with Mom's sister Joan and her husband Stanley, who insisted on paying for the fancy dinner. This humiliated Dad, so Dad calls him a *macher*, a big shot. I think he's jealous because Uncle Stanley is so successful and sociable, which sucks because I really like him and rarely get to see him."

"Uncle Stanley's a player?"

"You could say that," I said. "Why are you smiling?"

"Because neither you nor Marvin like players."

"So?"

"Don't you see? You have so much trouble dealing with him because you two are so alike."

"Are you serious?" I said, looking for him to tip off his joke with a tell-tale grin. "Dad and I don't get along because we're so different."

"You guys have different interests, but deep down, you're the same. You're both introverted, sensitive, stubborn, moody, depressed, avoid social settings, hate trying new things…"

A chill went down my spine. "We're also both worriers."

"Oh, god yes," he said. "That was so obvious, I didn't mention it."

"So you think I'm stubborn?"

I was kidding, but he didn't take much time to think before saying, "You're about as flexible as a crowbar."

"Well you're as matter-of-fact as—" I said, laughing because I couldn't think of anything. "A straight piece of iron used to pry open things."

"Good one. Those garage fumes must be getting to you," he said. "But seriously, this summer has to have been difficult for Marvin, with your sister's wedding and your graduation. You guys are growing up and he's losing his influence."

I hadn't thought about that. But I never thought about Dad's feelings.

Marge came back and brusquely dropped our plates onto the table. After she left, I told Paul, "The food here isn't great but it's always served with love."

"Have you ever told Marge you loved her?" he said, as he dunked a French fry into our side bowl of gravy.

"A couple of times, but only when I was drunk."

He stared. "And you've never told your parents you loved them?"

"Well, except for last night, I'm never drunk around them."

Marge kept bringing us coffee so we remained there for hours. I was asking Paul a question, but instead of listening, he was shaking his pack of Marlboros, hoping to coax out one more.

"I'm out of cigarettes," he said. "Can we stop at the Texaco on the way home?"

"Sure, but I should get going. It's almost 3:30 and I can't afford to wake up Dad."

When we said goodbye to Marge, I promised her that I wouldn't let them close the diner. After dropping off Paul, I drove home and saw through the bay window that my parents had left the living room lamp on for me. I walked inside and quietly closed and locked the door behind me. I trotted up the stairs to the landing and cautiously looked to my right in case Dad was sitting in his paisley chair, waiting up for me.

His chair was empty. Relaxing, I turned off the lamp and went upstairs, holding the wrought-iron railing so the stairs wouldn't creak so much. I passed my parents' door before tumbling into bed. Through the wall separating our rooms, I heard rustling in their bed. Dad might have been checking his clock, but he didn't come out to yell at me.

TWENTY

On my drive back to the beach the following morning, I thought about how stupid I had been for getting wasted at the wedding. It was raining and my left wiper blade was shot, so every swipe left behind two concentric arcs of water. When U2's *With or Without You* came on the radio, I got lost in the song until I noticed tears dripping off my chin. I felt all alone without Amy.

I rehearsed conversations where I'd tell her why I drank so much. I'd promise to stop drinking around her and beg for another chance. I had been apprehensive about dating Amy, but now that she didn't want to see me, I wanted to date her more than anything in the world.

The next night, CJ came over and we made tacos for dinner, which we tried to do every week. We were finishing cooking when Jon strolled in the front door, wearing beige linen shorts and a white polo shirt. Like most locals, CJ included, Jon usually wore light colors to accentuate his tan.

He had a lot of Eddie Haskell in him and relished acting as a wedge between Tom and me. When Tom was around, Jon gave me more crap than usual, marking his territory like a dog. That meant pissing on me.

"When did you move in?" Jon asked CJ in his condescending tone that made everything sound like an insult.

"We're making dinner," CJ said. "You got something against eating?"

"I'm just looking out for you," Jon said, as he headed up the stairs to get Tom. "If you're still paying rent at your other place, you should get that money back."

When they came back downstairs, Jon was obviously talking about CJ and me when he told Tom, "Those two have been handcuffed together so long, they must have lost the key."

"You fellas going to Scandals?" Tom asked, sounding sincere, but he was taunting us because everyone knew that CJ had no chance of getting in.

"You guys go ahead," I said, opening the oven and removing a baking sheet of taco shells right before they burned. Wearing puffy blue and white checked oven mitts, I felt like a spinster.

"What happened to you going out all the time after your test?" Tom said.

"I did say that," I admitted. "But after the wedding, I decided I needed to cut back on my drinking."

"You and CJ got married?" Jon said. "I didn't get an invite, so I hope you guys eloped."

Tom laughed at Jon, then told me, "Dude, I told you that you're not an alcoholic. You don't have to prove it by staying home all the time."

"You have to go out, Bruce," Jon said, with mock urgency. "Who's going to point out typos in take-out menus or explain to us why two large pizzas are such a better deal than three mediums. And how will I ever remember whether it's *ice* tea or *iced* tea?"

Laughing, Tom and Jon ducked into the kitchen to grab beers from the fridge. They poured them into plastic cups and left.

"Pi r squared. It's pretty simple," I said to CJ. "Actually, it's just r squared since pi is a constant."

"You don't have to remind me," he said. "I know not to order a medium pizza around you."

After we brought our plates into the living room, CJ picked up the TV remote and said, "What the fuck does Jon care where I hang out? He can be such a dick sometimes."

"I'm surprised to hear you say that. I thought you liked Jon."

"I do like Jon. When he's not acting like a dick."

"How can you like him when he acts like a dick to you?"

"You're one to talk," he said. "Tom rags on you and you still follow him like a puppy."

"He's just mad because I don't go out all the time," I said. "Percentage-wise, Tom hassles me much less than Jon does. Plus, Jon is much more annoying. I've stopped calling him on his bullshit because no one else cares whether he's lying, as long as his stories are good."

"You sound jealous," CJ said.

"Maybe a little, but I'm not going to lie or exaggerate about what happened the night before just to make it sound more interesting. What really bothers me is that it bothers Tom that I don't go out often enough."

CJ closed his eyes and shook his head rapidly several times. "Then stay in and do what you feel like doing," he said, then took a bite from his taco.

After dinner, we hung out in my room, drinking beers and

listening to my stereo. My housemate Lisa joined us and when CJ fell asleep on Tom's bed, Lisa and I were stacking beer cans on CJ's head. They'd topple over and he'd stir at the clattering, then go right back to sleep.

We gave up after not being able to stack more than three. Lisa was sitting on the floor, her back propped with a pillow against the sideboard of Tom's bed. I sat on my bed, getting up to change the record. I was playing individual songs, sharing with her what I liked about each one.

"Why do you have a plastic lawn chicken in here?" she said, pointing to a shelf at the foot of my bed.

"That's Señor Pollo, our fraternity's mascot," I said, and told her about his Eastern Shore roots.

"You weren't perchance the individual who purloined him, were you?" she said, eyeing me suspiciously.

"*Perchance? Purloined?* You should have been coaching me on vocabulary for the GMAT," I told her. "I swear, I didn't purloin him."

"Then why is he in your room?"

"He just took to me. I think he knows I'm a kind soul."

"Señor Pollo sounds like a good judge of character," she said, smiling.

I smiled back. "We're well-matched," I said, picking up Señor Pollo and cradling him like a football. "I like kitschy stuff and he has kitsch in spades."

I was drinking beer, while Lisa was working on a Diet Coke. She rarely drank. Her vices were cigarettes and pot, but Tom wouldn't let anyone smoke in our room.

She had lived in Ocean City the past two summers but wasn't a party girl, so I asked what she liked so much about the beach.

"I love lying in the sun and feeling the waves come in," she said, breathing in deeply, as if she could sense the ocean from a mile away. "The only downside here is all the crazy stuff people do."

"I apologize for being part of the crazy stuff," I said. "Staring about two weeks ago, I've cut back on my drinking."

"That's great," she said. "It must be hard dealing with your inner struggles."

Reflexively, I smiled back. After processing what she said, I asked, "What do you mean?"

"You're uncomfortable here at the beach, and you deal with it by drinking. Based on how much you drink, you must really be struggling."

I looked at her and she stared back, her lips puckered around a straw, casually sipping from her can of soda. She offered a tight smile and said, "When I get stressed, I find a quiet place and read. The library is great for that."

"I don't want to insult Ocean City, but it never occurred to me there was a library here," I said.

"That's more of a reflection on you than on Ocean City," she said, and feeling foolish, I nodded.

She crawled over and reached under my bed. "What's this?" she asked, pulling out my composition book.

"It's my journal," I said, feeling apprehensive as she held the book that documented some of my deepest feelings.

"Can I read it?" she asked, one eyebrow raised, as she opened it.

I wanted to scream *no!* but since she had already started glancing at my green ink entries, I said, "I guess so. Maybe I can read yours sometime."

"I couldn't let you do that," she said. "Mine's too personal."

As she read a few pages. I was trying to remember the most embarrassing things I had written.

"Is Amy your girlfriend?" she asked.

"I was hoping she was. But not after last Saturday."

She shrugged. "Here's what you do. Apologize for the stupid thing you did. Tell her how much you care for her; I mean deep down, like when you're falling asleep at night and you're thinking about her. Then don't do that stupid thing again. Ever."

"I've already tried to apologize and it didn't work."

"You either didn't communicate all your feelings or you guys weren't meant to be," she said. "If she can't see how great you are, then move on."

But I couldn't move on. It was destiny.

I let Lisa record an entry in my journal. She wrote: *12:20 on a mellow Tuesday night – ah morning in all actuality. Bruce was so kind as to allow me to peruse his journal, I'd like to say I found his writing truly entertaining – a definite bestseller, no doubt.*

"That's very polite of you," I said, after reading.

"I like your writing style," she said. "But there isn't enough juicy stuff in there."

"I don't kiss and tell," I said.

"Well then I respect your propriety."

"Thanks," I said. "It's also because I don't kiss that often."

She laughed. "I also appreciate your candor."

I enjoyed spending time with Lisa. She was easy to talk with and after living together, she knew me pretty well, so I didn't feel pressed to impress her. Also, I wasn't particularly attracted to her, although I really liked the way her light brown hair was streaked with blond from all her time in the sun.

As I put on a song from the new Violent Femmes album, I was telling her that when I saw them at the 9:30 Club in D.C., I was standing in the front, so close to Brian Ritchie, I could see a tiny Servomation sticker on his bass. When I looked up from my turntable, she was yawning.

"Sorry. It's not you. I had a long shift today," she said. "I'm going to bed."

"I'll see you around," I said, as she stood up.

Stopping at the door, she looked back and said, "Yeah you will."

Saturday morning, as Dave walked up to the front of the Carousel, Flec tapped the face of his Swatch and said, "One hour late, Mister."

"I overslept," Dave said, with a sheepish grin. "I didn't even have time for my Captain Crunch."

"That's *Cap'n* Crunch to you," I said. I was right on it.

"What are you, the fucking publicist for Kellogg's?" Jon said. He was right on me.

"Nah. I just do this as a public service."

"Since when was being a pain in the ass considered a public service?" Jon asked.

He was the Geek Police (policing *of* the geeks), while I was the Police Geek (policing *by* geeks). Everyone laughed with Jon. Since his force was much bigger than mine, I didn't point out that Kellogg's didn't make Cap'n Crunch.

After we dispersed, I was writing down Jon's line on a valet ticket. Distracted, I didn't notice Gary until he was on top of me.

"Didn't I tell you the other day not to lean?" he bunged. "The next time I see you leaning against the facing, I'll make you paint it."

"My definition of *leaning*," I said. "Is if the wall is suddenly removed and that causes me to fall over, then I was leaning."

"My definition of *unemployed* is going to be you in five

minutes if you don't stand up straight," Gary said, and returned to the lobby.

As I wrote down Gary's line, Flec came up to me and said, "What's up with all the writing you do?"

"If you must know, I'm keeping a journal."

He snorted. "Let me see what you just wrote down."

"No way," I said. "I'm not offering my written insights for public ridicule. If I'm going to be mocked, it'll be in the traditional manner—because of something I say or do."

Later, while Flec and I were eating lunch in the cafeteria, he asked a lady at the next table if he could borrow her pepper.

"Here you go," she said, handing him the pepper shaker. "Got any salt?"

"No, go fish," he told her. Then he said to me, "Put that in your book."

"Alright, I will."

As we worked on our plates of chicken à la king, I was complaining about Gary's bunging, telling Flec, "I can't believe Gary insists we say, 'Welcome to the Carousel' to every guest."

"You muttonhead," he said, laughing. "You still say that?"

Embarrassed, I said, "Sometimes."

Muttonhead was Flec's signature insult, which I loved, even when it was my head that was full of mutton.

He asked me if I was going to the fireworks that night.

"I'm not big on fireworks or crowds," I said. "I get annoyed by the way people react when they see fireworks—oohing and aahing like they're overacting in some porno movie."

"What are you, a communist?" he said.

"Because I don't like fireworks shows?"

"To hell with the fireworks. You were trashing porno movies."

I didn't tell Flec that one of the few normal things my

family used to do together was go see fireworks every Fourth of July. But beforehand, we'd fight over where to go, when to leave, what to bring, what to eat, who had forgotten to return the flashlight to the shelf over the washing machine in the laundry room....

We'd actually fight over picnic food. Seeing fireworks should have been a nice family activity, but we weren't built for outdoor fun. We needed walls. And doors to slam.

TWENTY-ONE

That Thursday, our house was hosting a party for all Carousel workers. Word had gotten around so well that all week, people that I didn't know kept telling me about it.

I know, dude. Shipwreck Road, fourth house on the right. I crash there all the time.

I got home from work that night around 10:30 and had to push my way to the stairs and then through the crowded hallway to reach the keg in the upstairs hall bathroom. At work, Flec and I had dared each other to go to the party in uniform, complete with a name tag, but after showering, I put on my favorite bowling shirt: royal blue with red and white trim, and chain-stitched with the name *Jay Ferguson*. After finishing my shower beer, I tapped another and went downstairs.

Playing quarters at my dining room table was Gary, wearing a burgundy Carousel baseball hat turned sideways and feeling no pain. Perched in front of him was an empty fish-shaped bottle of wine he had brought. It was like seeing my principal at a high school party, but then the party was for *all* Carousel employees and Gary was a strong company man.

I shoehorned myself into the chair next to him. "Can I get you a beer bong?" I shouted to him over the stereo.

"What I want, you can't get me," he said, sloppily patting me on the back.

"Gary's looking for love," Tom said from across the table. Then, puckering his lips like Dana Carvey's Church Lady, he added, "Well isn't that special?"

"Is that all?" I told Gary. "I thought you were going to ask me to clean the windows."

Gary looked at me and did something he rarely did. He laughed at something I said. That made my night.

Later, my housemates and I had to meet with two police officers on our front stoop who were giving our house a noise warning. Lisa was next to me, her arm loosely around my waist. I didn't think much of it because we were packed into the narrow hall.

When Tom first saw the cops, he asked them, "What kept you?" and then flashed his big grin. He wasn't letting them spoil his good time.

One officer suppressed a smile, while the other was all business as he explained that a second violation would result in the arrest of any resident present.

After they left, Tom crumbled our copy of the citation and threw it into the crowd in the living room. I started pushing through the masses to reclaim my spot at the dining room table, but Lisa grabbed my arm.

"Let's go out on the deck," she said, and I noticed she was wearing a pastel-green sundress, not the baggy t-shirt or sweatshirt that she usually schlepped around in. She also had on makeup.

To be polite, I agreed. She was giggling as we walked outside. Then she put her arm around my waist. Lisa wasn't a giggler.

"How much have you had to drink?" I asked.

"Plenty," she said, laughing.

We walked along the wooden deck behind our house, next to the shallow inlet. I was flattered that Lisa wanted to be with me, but I wanted to hang out with the bellstaff.

"Look, there's the big dipper," Lisa slurred, pointing to the sky.

As we walked, she occasionally veered toward the water that was sloshing against the bank at our feet.

"Let's watch where we're going," I said, getting between her and the edge and putting my arm around her to guide her.

"You really need to spice up your journal," she said, throwing her arms around me. "I can help you with content."

"I appreciate that," I said. "But right now, I'm going back inside for a beer."

"Don't you want to stay out here with me?" she asked. Then she reached up to kiss me, but her lips landed on my chin. "You're taller than I thought," she giggled.

With Lisa being so assertive, I wouldn't have had any problem being intimate with her. But I was sober enough to know I didn't want a physical relationship with her. She was my housemate; someone I divvied long-distance phone bills with, someone who reminded me when it was my week to clean the kitchen, someone I drove to Food Lion because she didn't have a car.

"Come on," I coaxed, pulling her arm. "You should be at the party."

Back inside, I steered Lisa to a group in the living room that included Sue, her loft mate. Then I snuck off upstairs to the keg.

Paul's strategy of drinking less was working. I had started late and was drinking in moderation. Being more sober than most people, I didn't feel so rushed during conversations. But I was having trouble turning down persistent beer offers and by the time we had drained the fourth keg, I was filling my cup out of habit.

As our house thinned out, I was hanging out on the deck with a group from the bellstaff, including Lab, our valet supervisor. A pear-shaped six-seven, 240 pounds with spindly legs and a flat top haircut, Lab played basketball for Salisbury State. He claimed his nickname came from a basketball tournament at Spingarn in D.C. when he was a high school sophomore. The emcee dubbed him "Baby Skylab" because he was big and he dunked.

Tom went inside and when he emerged with a 1.75 bottle of Bacardi 151, a stack of Dixie cups, and a big smile, I knew I was in trouble.

"I can't start doing shots," I told Tom as he cracked the seal. "I've got court at 9:00 tomorrow morning for a speeding ticket."

I sat out the first round, but people were toasting me for having the crappiest morning ahead, so I gave in and grabbed a paper cup and had my first of many shots.

Gary had left the party hours before, so I asked Lab if there was a lot of money out there after I had left work that night.

On slow days, Gary tried to motivate us with a narrative along the lines of: "I knew a valet working on a day like today. Two hours before quitting time, he had fifteen dollars in his pocket, but kept hustling, swept when I asked, was polite, didn't steal runs, and left with fifty dollars."

We'd smile at him. *Riiiight Gary.*

Gary always closed with: "There's a lot of money out there." Then he'd walk over to the bellmen and make a similar pitch.

There's a lot of money out there had become our answer to just about anything:

"I can't believe that guy in the Vette just stiffed me." *Don't worry. You'll make it up. There's a lot of money out there.*

"Lab, can I leave early?" *Think you should? There's a lot of money out there.* "But Flec just ran over my foot with that station wagon and I think it's broken." *Go to the hospital after your shift's over. You don't want to miss out because there's a lot of money out there.*

With a thirty-two ounce plastic cup of beer in hand, Lab smiled as he answered my question. "Around midnight, I had twenty-five dollars in tips. But instead of leaving early, I changed the oil in the old van and vacuumed Al's booth in the garage. Then I did two bellruns..."

Bam! Lab slapped his hand on the wooden table in front of him. "Twenty bucks each. Next, I parked two Ferraris and a Lamborghini, did a bellrun for Richard Pryor, and punched out with three hundred bucks." He started pulling out his wallet to show us, but we told him not to bother because we believed him.

Lisa came out and sat on the wide arm of my wooden chair. She was the only girl with us and didn't say anything for a couple of minutes. Then she leaned toward me, spilling into my lap.

"Let's go inside and watch TV," she whispered.

She knew my weakness, and as I stood up to go with her, Tom said, "Where are you going, dude?"

"To watch TV with Lisa. I've got to sober up before court anyway."

"Stay out here with us, dude," he said. "You're better off with us."

"I'll be back," I said, too drunk to understand what he was telling me.

"Bruce, there's no money in there," Lab called.

Once inside, I was surprised that everyone had left. Lisa

and I sat on the couch and I turned on ESPN, but she was looking at me, not the TV. She started kissing me, but I wriggled away and said, "I'm going back out on the deck."

"I thought you liked me," she said, her voice high-pitched.

"I do like you," I said, feeling terrible for rejecting her. "I want to watch TV with you."

We resumed watching TV, but a minute later, she hopped into my lap. "Let's go upstairs," she whispered, and then started kissing my ear. I knew I shouldn't go with her, but I couldn't tell her no.

As we were kissing in my room, I could hear the guys talking on the deck below and wanted to go back outside but didn't want to hurt Lisa by rejecting her. I wasn't thinking about whether I still had a chance with Amy. In the moment, I wasn't thinking about Amy at all.

We sat down on my bed and Lisa got on top of me. As she unbuttoned my shirt, I didn't do anything to stop her.

I was shocked when my alarm went off the next morning. Not because I had only slept a couple of hours or because I was so hungover after getting wasted for the first time since the wedding. It was because Lisa was asleep in my bed. Usually I slept in a shirt and shorts, but that morning, I only had on boxers and socks. Lisa was wearing one of my t-shirts. I didn't know what she ordinarily slept in, but assumed it wasn't one of my t-shirts.

As I sat on the edge of the bed, trying to piece together the end of the night, Lisa was lying on her side, snoring softly. Her snoring would have been funny if she had been lying on our living room couch, but not in my bed after we had slept together. I was mad at myself for not being able to say no to her.

I went into the bathroom to brush my teeth and tamp down my hair with water. Then I tiptoed to my dresser to change, before sneaking off to court without turning back to see if I had awakened Lisa.

I couldn't get comfortable in the courtroom's narrow, high-backed row seating. I expected the place to be jammed, given the level of enforcement on Jamestown Road, but the forty of us present had room to stretch out, if not relax.

Tom had assured me that they'd throw out the ticket if I went to court, although I couldn't remember why he had been so confident. I didn't think I had been going that fast but was having trouble wording my story for the judge.

It might have been my hangover, but the acoustics were making everyone in the courtroom seem like they were shouting.

One guy gave the judge a sob story about an overgrown bush blocking a speed limit sign. He looked my age and wore khaki pants, a white button-down shirt, and a black knit tie with tiny waffle dimples. I hadn't brought dress clothes to the beach, so I wore shorts and a collared shirt. The judge let that guy slide, so I figured I'd be sliding as well.

As I waited, I was thinking about Lisa. *Did she really like me or was she just drunk? What if she wouldn't let me read her journal because of something she had written about me?* I was also thinking about Amy. She had dumped me, but I was still holding on, so I was feeling like I had cheated on her.

I was lost in thought when the clerk read a citation number and butchered my last name.

"Here, sir," I said, snapping to attention.

He gestured upward with his hands. After I stood, the judge said, "How do you plead, Mr. Margulies?"

I'm guilty. Guilty of sleeping with Lisa.

"Not guilty, your Honor."

Tom's buddy Joe, the ticketing officer, stood to address the court. He looked very official in his uniform, especially since I was used to seeing him casually dressed at Harpoon Hanna's on two-for-one drink nights.

"Your Honor, using hand-held radar, I clocked the defendant's vehicle traveling thirty-six miles per hour," Joe said. "The posted speed limit on Jamestown Road is twenty-five."

"Are you trained to operate that radar detector?"

"Yes, your Honor."

"Was it operating properly on the day in question?"

"Yes, your Honor."

"What say you?" the judge sayeth to me.

"Your Honor, I was watching my speedometer the whole time. I never went as fast as thirty miles per hour," I said, relying on the five-mile-per-hour cushion the cops always allowed.

"Were you aware of the twenty-five mile per hour speed limit?"

"Yes, your Honor," I said, steadying myself by holding onto the seatback in front of me.

"And yet you admit to driving as fast as thirty miles per hour on Jamestown Road?"

"Yes, your Honor. Actually, not more than twenty-nine miles per hour," I said, in order to avoid a tie at thirty.

The judge appeared to wink at Joe. My body tensed as it hit me that the five miles per hour wasn't a hard-and-fast rule. I started sweating.

"Do you have any extenuating circumstances to bring to the Court's attention?" the judge said.

He's giving me a chance. All I need is an excuse.

But I couldn't lie. I certainly couldn't perjure myself.

"No, your Honor," I said, grabbing the seatback in front of me more tightly, as murmurs rippled around me.

"So to confirm, you're pleading *not* guilty to exceeding the posted twenty-five mile per hour speed limit. Yet you admit to driving twenty-nine miles per hour?"

"Yes, your Honor," I said, barely audibly. The murmurs got louder, reminding me of a lecture hall class after someone had just given the professor an obviously incorrect answer.

The words had barely left my mouth before the judge rattled off his decision. "The defendant admits to traveling twenty-nine miles per hour in a posted twenty-five mile per hour zone yet presents no mitigating circumstances. The court accepts the de facto guilty plea. License points are reduced from two to one. The fine is reduced to forty dollars plus court costs."

In a conversational tone, the judge asked if I would be driving home.

"Yes sir. I mean yes, your Honor."

Then he returned to his loud voice. "In that case, be sure to obey all posted speed limits and all applicable vehicle laws en route."

He slammed down his gavel as laughter filled the courtroom.

When I got home from court, Tom was eating a bowl of cereal at the dining room counter. The downstairs was as clean as the day we moved in.

"Nice job cleaning up," I said, inhaling deeply. "How'd you get rid of that party stench?"

He looked up and smiled. "You slept with Lisa. You slept with Lisa," he taunted.

"Thanks Dr. Ruth," I said, trying to seem unaffected. "I figured that out this morning."

"I tried to warn you, but you wouldn't listen," he said, laughing. "Hey, how'd court go? You got them to throw away the ticket, right?"

"They dropped one point," I said, without any details.

"You still got a point?" he said, in disbelief. "You didn't argue against the radar detector, did you? Everyone knows you just have to give them an excuse, *any* excuse, like you were late for work. You gave the judge a simple excuse, right?"

Everyone knew that but me. But then if I had been cool and hadn't tried to shake Joe's hand, I wouldn't have gotten the ticket in the first place.

"The judge didn't buy my excuse," I said, too embarrassed to share my legally flawed defense. "The legal system around here sucks. Meaningless speed traps, stupid noise warnings—"

"Dude, don't mess with those noise ordinances," he said, his face looking earnest. "If they bust our house for noise again, they'll put anyone here who's on the lease in jail."

"You serious?" I said.

He nodded. "I know plenty of guys who went to jail for a second violation."

When I came home from work the following afternoon, Lisa was sitting on the living room couch, reading a book in her lap. We hadn't seen each other since the party and once she realized I was the one who walked in, she nearly pulled herself into a ball.

"Hey Lisa," I called.

"Hey," she said, not looking up.

I took a deep breath and walked over to sit down next to her. We were on the same couch where we had been making out two nights before.

"What are you reading?"

She held up a thick paperback with a tree on the cover.

"Do you want to talk?" I said.

She shrugged, still looking down.

"I'm sorry about the party," I said.

"I feel really stupid," she said, looking at me briefly.

"We were both drunk," I said, which was my justification for most of the stupid things I did.

"I thought you were into me," she said, nervously twirling her hair around her finger. "I guess I was wrong."

"I think you're great but I'm still interested in Amy," I said. "I'm going to take your advice with her and do a better job apologizing."

I was hoping she would say something like: *I hope that works out for you.*

When she didn't, I started sensing how lousy she felt and was struck by how hard it must have been for her to face me when she obviously felt so vulnerable.

"I don't want to talk about it now," she said.

I couldn't think of anything more to say, so I stood up and said, "I'll be around if you want to talk."

She didn't respond and I trudged up the stairs instead of bounding up two at a time like usual. As I shot baskets at the Nerf hoop in my room to blow off steam, I was thinking: *First Amy. Now Lisa. My drinking really is hurting people.*

TWENTY-TWO

Friday night, instead of going to Trader's, I stayed home and watched baseball. I had the house to myself, pleased to be managing my drinking, though avoiding Trader's was a bonus.

CJ came by after work around 11:00, which was too late for him to go to Trader's. After the game, I turned off the TV and went upstairs to put a Cars album on my stereo. I didn't mind going up every twenty minutes to flip the record because CJ and I both loved the Cars. Hell, maybe Jon was right about us being married.

An hour later, the front door opened and my neighbor rushed in, shouting, "Two policemen are measuring the noise level behind your house!"

I ran upstairs and when I turned off my stereo, I noticed the screen door on my balcony was open. I went downstairs and my neighbor was gone. Two cops were standing at my front door.

"Are you a signor on the lease?" one asked. He was heavy-set and middle-aged.

"I am," I said, walking through the entranceway toward them.

"It's after 10:00 p.m.," the other cop said, squeezing in front. He was younger and looked comically skinny next to his partner. "We took a reading fifty feet from the street that exceeded fifty-five decibels. You're under arrest for violating Ocean City noise ordinance number…"

I didn't catch the number, but it was a safe bet it was one of the ones highlighted in yellow when I signed my lease.

"Don't I get a warning?" I asked.

"You received one last Thursday," Skinny said, looking smug. "Are any other lessees present?"

"No, it's just me," I said, looking over at CJ, whose normally sleepy eyes were wide open. And for the first time since Tom had told me in March, I was glad that CJ wasn't living with us.

Heavy read me my rights, sounding as serious as Joe Friday. I thought the whole thing was bullshit, given the innocuous circumstances.

Trying to lighten the mood, like Tom had done at the party when we had gotten the warning, I said, "Does that mean that if I say anything, regardless of what I say, it's held against me? Or is it the content that matters, like if I said something incriminating about the noise, such as the volume level or specifications of my stereo?"

They frowned at each other, like I had made a joke about cops eating doughnuts.

"You'll find out soon enough," Heavy said tersely. Under his breath, he told Skinny, "Let's show this guy the routine downtown."

Skinny handcuffed me. My hands were behind my back, the cuffs digging into my wrists. I looked back at CJ, who said, "Call me and I'll pick you up."

Skinny pulled me outside. After opening the door to their squad car, he shoved my head down, forcing me into the backseat.

As Heavy drove, I braced myself in a corner of the backseat, trying to avoid being thrown about. Waiting at a light, I heard people shouting much louder than my stereo. I turned and identified the culprits: two college-aged guys holding open beers outside a bayside bar.

"Look at that meathead throwing a football in the bus lane," Heavy told his partner. "That idiot's going to get himself run over."

"Then there's no need to arrest him," Skinny said, laughing. "Why don't we weigh anchor and see how many we can pull in?"

"In the immortal words of Roy Schieder," Heavy said. "You're gonna need a bigger boat."

While they were cracking up, I was thinking, *Why am I getting arrested? This is bullshit.*

Heavy drove a few more miles downtown and parked in a fire lane alongside City Hall. Skinny opened my door and pulled me out of the car.

"Every weekend, I babysit dozens of drunk college kids. I've got enough trouble with my own two," Heavy told his partner as we walked. "What are you doing this weekend, single guy?"

"I'll be out on the bay in Stacy's boat tomorrow," Skinny said.

"I thought you were breaking up with her."

"I'm having second thoughts."

"Yeah?" Heavy said. "You'd miss her?"

"I'd miss her parents' boat," Skinny said. "I'll re-evaluate in the fall."

"You're too young to be tied down. After the season, put them both in dry dock."

We stopped at a poorly lit side door. Heavy pulled a keychain loaded with dozens of keys from his pocket and unlocked the door. We walked inside and downstairs to a basement that smelled like wet laundry left in the washer for days. We entered an open room with two uniformed cops sitting at desks.

"What's the charge?" one asked, standing up.

"Noise violation," Heavy said. "But this one's a real cutie pie. Take special care of him."

The booking cop nodded and I had my answer. After being read my rights, I should have kept my mouth shut.

The guy removed my cuffs and as I rubbed my wrists to get my circulation going, I watched as he squeezed ink onto a square glass pane and spread the ink with a roller.

"Fan your hand," he said, grabbing my right hand and firmly rolling my finger side-to-side into the ink. Then he pressed my inked finger onto a white card. After five iterations, plus prints with multiple fingers, he repeated the process with my left hand, before handing me a moist towelette. I tore open the foil packet and sniffed the clean-smelling antiseptic. Then I removed and unfolded the damp wipe and scrubbed my fingers, with little success removing the ink.

"Stand over there," he said, pointing toward the wall. I complied and after he snapped a frontal and a side view photo, I figured I was done but he told me to empty my pockets. I looked at him, confused.

"You'll get a claim ticket," he said, which didn't address my concern. But afraid to say anything, I took off my Swatch and handed it to him with my wallet and keys.

"I also need your shoelaces."

"What for?" I had to ask.

"So you can't hang yourself," he said. "Lawyers make us do that."

That made no sense to me, but I didn't understand why they were making such a big deal about my stereo. It wasn't even that loud. In no position to object, I sat in a chair and removed my shoelaces. He put everything in a manila envelope, twisting the red string around the red button to secure the flap.

"Okay, let's go," he said, our footsteps echoing as we walked down an interior hallway.

As we approached a jail cell with a bunk bed and a sink next to an exposed toilet, I looked at him and he nodded. I was in shock as he opened the lock with a key as wide as a tongue depressor.

The hallway light illuminated part of the cell. There was a guy, about thirty, leaning against the iron bars near the door. As the officer prodded me inside, the guy moved into my path. His arms were folded, showing a barbed wire tattoo around his muscular right biceps. I didn't have any tattoos. I didn't know anybody with a tattoo.

The officer ignored the guy's aggression and slammed the cell door behind me. As the officer walked off, the guy was staring at me like a butcher sizing up a side of beef. It seemed foolish to say, "Pardon me," so I dropped my shoulder and brushed past him, knocking his arm.

"What's your fucking problem, you skinny shit?" he said, sidling around and bumping up against my chest.

"What are you talking about?" I said, the intensity of my voice nowhere near his.

"Don't fuck with me, college boy. What're you in for, huh?"

I looked down before responding. "Noise violation."

He snorted. "Figures. You college boys got it so tough at the beach."

"How about you?" I said, but as soon as I asked, I realized I didn't want to know. The clacking of the officer's footsteps faded. I was on my own.

"Not some candy-ass noise violation. Don't ask me any questions, huh?"

I nodded and when he smiled, I was relieved that he was leaving me alone.

"How's your stomach?" he asked.

"What?" I said, and as I spoke, he lunged and sucker-punched me in the stomach. A pathetic *ooof* escaped from inside me and I went down on one knee.

Standing over me as I gasped for air, he said, "That's a down payment. If you tell anybody about it, I'll find your ass and give you the balance."

I looked up at him, unable to tell if he was drunk, high, or crazy.

"I'd beat the shit out of you right now," he said. "But I'm having enough trouble making bail without that *compleecation*."

When I straightened up, he sprang at me again. I jumped backward, almost falling over.

But he had faked this attack and remained standing in his tracks. "You're such a pussy," he said, laughing. "I'm embarrassed to be in here with you."

I waited until he climbed onto the top bunk before I walked over and fell into the lower bunk. Shivering, I reached for the blanket folded at the foot of the bed, but the wool was scratchy, so I only pulled it over my legs. I curled my body around the thin pillow and felt the bedsprings through the mushy mattress.

Unable to sleep, I was further distracted by a clock loudly

ticking each second. Hundreds of ticks later, I had to go to the bathroom. Then I realized: *I can't go to the bathroom. There is no bathroom.*

Despite my squirming and adjusting, I couldn't stop my urge to pee. I got out of bed and modestly angled my body with my back to the guy before loosening the drawstring in my shorts.

As I hunched over a tiny toilet I could barely see, he said, "You'd better not miss, boy, or I'll make you lick up anything you get on the floor."

I was startled, partly because he sounded close enough to reach out and grab my neck.

Steadying my nerves, I spit into the bowl for perspective. But my mouth was so dry, the spit dribbled out onto my shirt. With all that pressure, I couldn't pee, so I stood there, waiting.

"Just sit down, you pussy," the guy mocked.

Finally, pee came out and my accuracy was fine. Afterward, I rinsed my hands in the metal sink, but after touching the handle to turn off the water, I felt like I had to wash my hands again.

I tumbled back into my bed, thinking about what Dad would say if he knew I was in jail: *Nobody will hire you with a police record.*

The bed springs above my head started squeaking.

"What's your name, boy?" The guy said, his tone raspy.

My eyes opened wide but I ignored him and tried to calm myself by counting the clock's ticks. Four, five, six...

"What's your problem, boy? Huh?"

I didn't answer.

"Since you're being a little bitch, I'm gonna call you Rich. Then as soon as that cop stops walking people past, I'll make you my bitch. Rich the bitch. Rich *my* bitch."

My body started shaking and I counted twenty more ticks.

"You've seen *Deliverance*, huh?" he said.

Whenever someone I knew brought up *Deliverance*, it was referring to one thing: a guy getting sodomized.

"Have you?!" he shouted.

I remained silent, trying to stop shaking.

In a sing-song voice, he said, "Are you ignoring me, Rich because you're scared about getting raped?"

My heart was pounding in my throat and I felt like I had to throw up.

"Answer me, Boy," he said, his voice gravelly, "Or I'll come down there and show you my favorite part."

Oh shit. Oh shit. Oh shit! He's going to rape me.

"I've heard about the movie," I said, straining to sound calm, arms folded across my chest, squeezing the sides of my shoulders, trying to stop shivering.

"There's this scene where some local boys tell an out-of-towner to squeal like a pig. Sounds *juuust* like us, don't it? Huh?" He cackled loudly, reminding me of the PCP guy from Trader's. Then he stopped abruptly.

Why did he stop?

I didn't understand why. Then I heard footsteps. They got louder as the booking officer walked by with a guy my age.

I rushed to the cell door. "Officer!" I yelled, grabbing the bars, but he didn't slow down or acknowledge me.

After they passed, the guy said in a low voice, "If you tell him anything about me, I'll slit your throat."

A minute later, the officer walked back alone from the other direction.

I extended my hand through the bars to get his attention. "Officer! I've got to get out of here."

"They told me about you," he said, slowing his pace. "Some time in there will teach you some respect for the police."

He walked off and I stood there, my head pressed against the bars. I couldn't believe they were treating me like a criminal because I had made a joke. When I realized my back was to the guy in my cell, I hurried back to my bed.

I tried to distract myself by focusing on the ticking. I was picturing the clock's gears meshing and then disengaging with a burst. I imagined some ticks sounding slightly longer, some a bit deeper.

In a high-pitched girl's voice, the guy said, "Please don't play hard to get Richie."

My eyes popped open.

His voice got raspy. "Why'd you go and do that Rich? Huh? Now I can't trust you anymore. That was dumb Rich. Real dumb." He stopped for a few seconds and then whispered, "You wouldn't tell anybody, would you Rich? It could be our little secret how I made a man out of you."

I couldn't speak. I couldn't even move my head. Frantic, I was thinking, *What do I do if this dirtball tries to rape me?*

He stopped talking.

Hundreds of ticks later, I heard footsteps, and the booking officer came by with another detainee. I ran to the cell door and yelled, "You've got to put me in another cell!"

He passed without looking at me. When he returned, I pleaded for him to stop.

"I told you to settle down and wait!" he barked, as he stared me down.

"But this guy's threatening me!"

The officer stopped and called into the cell, "Is there a problem?"

"No problems here, officer. We're just *fine*," the guy answered, his voice syrupy sweet. "Fine as wine and twice as nice."

"Keep it that way," the officer replied. Then, matter-offactly, the officer told me, "You're going to hear some tough talk in jail. That's another reason people avoid breaking the law."

"Please, officer. You've got to let me out of here."

"I can't do anything until the magistrate is ready to see you."

"When will that be?"

"I'll get you when it's time," he said, and walked away.

I went back and fell into my bed. My heart was pounding, my body taut as I waited for the guy to resume harassing me. Minutes passed. I strained to listen for his breathing, hoping he was asleep.

There was rustling above me.

"*Riiii-iiiich*," he taunted.

Laying on my side, looking at the cell door, I folded my arms tightly across my chest.

"I hope you're ready," he said, his tone now raspy. "Once that donkey stops walking people past here, I'm coming down to pop your cherry ass."

Getting desperate, I weighed my options. I couldn't win a fight with the guy. I couldn't reason with him so I'd have to confront him without fighting him.

"Look motherfucker," I said, as low as I could get my voice. "You want to fight? I'll fight you."

"Are you standing up to me Rich?" he said, sounding amused. "I didn't know you were so scrappy."

"Come down here and find out. But if you do, you'll never make bail. The cops will never believe I started the fight."

"Shut your goddam mouth!" he yelled. "Or I'll put my first down your throat!"

"You talk a lot, don't you?" I said, pushing my bluff.

"You'll see, once that cop stops coming by!"

"Keep talking," I said. "That tells me you aren't going to do shit."

Terrified, I braced to defend myself in case he came down. As I waited, I wondered what would happen once they stopped walking people past the cell. The guy remained quiet as the procession of detainees continued.

As I listened, his breathing became consistent, so I figured he had fallen asleep, though each time he started mumbling and thrashing, I was on alert. After my initial shock, I'd assure myself that he was just a restless sleeper.

Tick... tick... tick.... I had a long time to think about what a fuck-up I was, about how smart Amy had been to dump me, and how Dad had been right all along. I was a failure.

The scraping of a key in the lock jolted me awake. A different officer opened the cell door with a loud creak I hadn't noticed on my way in.

"The magistrate will see you now."

"Me?"

"You."

Without looking back, I scrambled out of bed. I didn't need a reminder of what my tormentor looked like. His voice would be with me forever.

TWENTY-THREE

The officer led me into a room with two men seated behind a desk, facing the door.

"Sit down, Mr. Margulies," said a solid-looking guy, about fifty, with a sun-creased face. He identified himself as the magistrate and introduced his court reporter.

The magistrate looked down at an open folder on his desk. "Are you familiar with the *Scared Straight* documentaries?" he said, his eyes not leaving the folder to gauge my reaction.

"Bits and pieces, sir."

"I see you shared a cell with an individual charged with armed robbery, so you likely just received a comprehensive lesson," he said, chuckling. Then his voice rose. "Let that be a warning. You will not fare well with that crowd."

"Yes sir," I said, shuddering.

"What are you doing Mr. Margulies?"

"Sorry, sir," I said, sitting up straighter. "I'm nervous. I'm also tired."

"With your life, Mr. Margulies! Or should I say, 'What are you doing *to* your life?' You're twenty-two and," he looked down at the folder. "In the past two months, you've been taken by ambulance to Penn Regional, you've received three speeding tickets, and last night, you were arrested."

"I don't know, sir."

As the court reporter typed, he was shaking his head slightly.

"You need to be accountable for your actions, Mr. Margulies," the magistrate said. "I need you to answer some character questions now. I trust you attend college Mr. Margulies?"

"No sir, I just graduated."

"Congratulations," he said without enthusiasm. "Where are you employed?"

"At the Carousel, sir. I'm a valet. In September, I'll be looking for a job in the DC area."

"Hummmph," the magistrate scoffed. "Do you take any illegal drugs?"

I paused. "What happens if I decline to answer your questions, sir?"

"Then I won't be able to determine your fitness for release and you would remain in custody," he said, his eyes looking over his reading glasses at me. "Are we clear?"

I nodded but was thinking: *Anything you say can be held against you.* I was afraid that by acknowledging drug use, I'd be giving them a real reason to arrest me.

"I've smoked marijuana, but not often, sir, I swear. I've never done any other drugs. Mostly, I drink alcohol."

"How often do you drink alcohol?"

"Not as much as a month ago, sir."

"That's not responsive, Mr. Margulies."

"Sir, I recently concluded that I drink too much and over the past few weeks, I've made a lot of progress moderating my drinking."

He looked into my eyes. "Were you drinking last night when you were arrested?"

"No sir. Just stupid."

The court reporter couldn't help but grin.

"Very well," the magistrate said. "I believe you are being forthright. When we next meet, you can give me details of your new job and progress at reducing your alcohol intake."

"Yes sir. Will we be meeting again sir?"

"We will indeed, Mr. Margulies. I will be presiding over your arraignment on January 7."

His voice boomed, "There will be no more incidents between now and then. Are we clear?!"

"Yes sir," I said. He maintained his stare, so I added, "Thank you, sir."

"Very well," he said and turned to the court reporter. "The subject is cleared for release."

The court reporter nodded as he concluded typing. Then he walked me to the room where I had started, and a different booking officer handed me the envelope containing my belongings. The officer asked if I needed a dime to make a phone call.

I wasn't sure if I had been released, so I stopped myself from telling him that I thought that they only did that on TV. I nodded to him and put out my hand for the dime.

The wall clock read 5:56, so I was worried because CJ wasn't an early riser. Six rings. Seven rings. I was thinking I'd have to take a bus home, but CJ finally picked up.

After speaking with CJ, I walked outside. It was starting to get light. Sitting on the curb, putting the laces back in my hi-top Chucks, I looked left, toward the sunrise. Mom used to wake me by telling me to make that day my day. I wished I was a kid again so I could develop a closer relationship with her.

A guy walked around the corner, holding his young daughter's hand. Judging by his bouffant hair and flip flops, he had just rolled out of bed. The girl, who looked kindergarten age, was wearing a pink dress, pink boots, and a floppy white sun hat with a plastic daisy.

As they approached, I smiled at her and in my five-year-old voice, told her I liked her hat. It was *my* day, but I was willing to share it with her.

The guy's eyes widened, apparently realizing why I was relacing my sneakers. Tugging at his daughter's arm, he dragged her away from me and across the street.

"It was only a noise violation!" I shouted. Then I put my head down, repeating the magistrate's question. *What am I doing with my life?*

I looked up when I heard the Doge. After getting to my feet, I hopped in and greeted CJ but didn't say anything else.

After several blocks, he said, "I've never seen you so quiet. I expected you to be joking about getting sprung, or having paid your debt to society, or finally being able to taste freedom."

"That was the worst night of my life. The guy in my cell threatened to rape me."

"No shit? What did you do?"

"At first, I didn't do anything. Then when I felt like I couldn't take it anymore, I told him to come down and fight me."

"What do you mean, *come down*?"

"He was in the top bunk," I said.

CJ started chuckling.

"I know," I said. "It sounds like we were at summer camp."

"Then what happened?"

"The guy backed down. He would have killed me, but I assumed that he couldn't afford to add assault to his charges. Luckily, I was right."

"Man, that sounds intense," CJ said. "I'm proud of you for standing up to him."

"Thanks. After they let me out, I faced a magistrate who went over all the stupid things I've done this summer. Man, I'm such a fuck-up."

"Don't be so hard on yourself," he said. "Even though you are kind of a mess right now." At least he said it in a nice way.

We pulled up in front of my house and I thanked him for being there for me. Then I went inside, hurried up the stairs, and jumped into my bed. It felt warm and plush.

Hours later, Tom woke me by rattling around our bathroom as he got ready for his 10:00 a.m. shift. He opened the door and came out, brushing his teeth.

"Where'd you sleep last night?" he said, seeing that I was awake. "Don't tell me you got lucky while watching your baseball game."

"I was in jail," I said, casually stretching my arms as if it was any other morning. "Noise violation."

"You're fucking lying to me," he said, ducking back into the bathroom. *Thwumph!* He spat in the sink and came back out.

"I wish I were," I said. "Ask CJ. He was there. I mean he was here."

"Was anybody else arrested?"

"Nope. I was the only one home."

"What happened?" he said, sitting down on his bed.

"CJ and I were downstairs. My stereo was on up here," I said, pointing to it like I was identifying a suspect in a police lineup. "It was just loud enough for us to hear downstairs, but I didn't know that our screen door was open."

"So you stayed home to avoid drinking and got arrested?" he said, starting to smile, but caught himself. "Dude. Sorry. That's rough."

I continued to answer Tom's questions about my arrest, though I didn't mention my cellmate. I was annoyed because he seemed entertained and not at all concerned about how I felt. Listening to me recap the night before made him late for work, but he had a great story to tell the guys. I knew I'd be answering their questions for days, just like after I had been hospitalized.

My shift wasn't until 5:00 but I couldn't get back to sleep, worrying about how to tell Dad I got arrested and how disappointed Mom would be.

I thought about Amy. How instead of getting to know her better, I kept disregarding her and getting wasted. I was ashamed for being so offensive and wanted to call her and apologize, but she wouldn't pick up my calls or answer my messages.

Trying to feel some connection to her, I pulled out my photo album to look at pictures of her. One showed us slow dancing at the formal, our foreheads touching. She looked completely content. I stared at the photo, trying to imprint Amy's face into my memory, thinking, *I have to make her feel that way about me again.*

There was a picture of Tom and me chugging beer from our pitchers and one of me, Tom, and some other brothers with our white shirt tails hanging out through the fly in our pants. I had thought the photo was cheeky, but now it angered me. Not because I was acting like a fool but because I was acting like a fool while ignoring Amy, my date.

Flipping through the album, I realized that I wasn't addicted to alcohol. I was addicted to being Drunk Bruce. He always had a good time while I was the one waking up the next day full of regrets. I no longer cared how much fun my drunk guise was having because my real life sucked.

Not only was Drunk Bruce having fun at my expense, he had gotten close to Amy, something I couldn't do. He laughed and flirted with her, whispered in her ear, and was confident enough to touch her arm, her shoulder, and her waist. Drunk Bruce was comfortable with Amy. He was intimate with her. I dearly wanted all those things.

TWENTY-FOUR

A couple of nights later, I got home from work around midnight. By the phone was an official-looking envelope addressed to me. I got about one piece of mail a week: postcards from Paul, letters from Mom, the cable bill, speeding tickets from Worchester County, and my membership card to the Chester Cheetah Cheetos Big Cheese Club, which I had joined with Dave.

The return address read: *Educational Testing Service, Princeton, NJ*. I took the green ink as an omen.

My hands were trembling as I ripped open the envelope and pulled out my GMAT score report. There were numbers everywhere: raw scores, corrected raw scores, questions right, questions wrong, questions omitted.

My verbal score was in the 63rd percentile, my quantitative in the 94th percentile, and my total score was in the 86th percentile. Plan B was still viable.

I wanted to call Amy and tell her, but doing well on a standardized test wasn't enough to get her to talk with me. Instead, I called Paul.

"Those are very good scores," he said. "Why don't you sound more excited?"

"The Cure concert is less than two weeks away and Amy won't even talk to me."

"You can't just call her. You need to drive to Richmond and surprise her at work. Then apologize and ask her again."

"That's ten hours roundtrip. What if she says no?"

"Then it'll be a long drive home. If you want Amy to forgive you, you'll have to put yourself out there for her. The only way to find out if you can trust someone is to trust them first."

"Where'd you get that?" I said.

"Hemingway."

"That's a great quote but Amy's too mad at me."

"She won't say no."

"How can you be so confident?"

"Because she's never going to forget the time you drove to Richmond and asked her."

"What's going to be so memorable about it?"

"I don't know yet, but it'll have to be some big romantic gesture. You'll have to be completely vulnerable, so she can laugh in your face or squash you like a bug if she wants."

The conversation drifted. Paul told me about a remote segment he had just seen on *Letterman* featuring Larry "Bud" Melman. I brought up how much I liked The Cure's new album but was disappointed there were only two upbeat songs.

"They only do a couple like that for radio play," he said. "If you want pop, listen to Duran Duran."

"Duran Duran doesn't need my—"

"I've got it!" Paul interrupted.

"You've got what?"

"How you're going to ask Amy to the concert. You'll be wearing makeup like Robert Smith."

I groaned. "Are you kidding?"

"You'll need black eyeshadow and eyeliner, white foundation, dark red lipstick. A wig would be perfect, but you'd have to get it styled."

"You're enjoying this aren't you?" I said. "You must want me to look ridiculous."

"You looking ridiculous is part of it," he said. "Her pity may be the only thing that keeps her from squashing you like a bug."

"Stop saying that!"

"Sometimes you have to risk getting squashed."

On my next day off, I grabbed some Q-tips and cotton balls from my housemates' bathroom and tossed them into a plastic shopping bag with the makeup I had bought the day before with the help of an elderly dime store clerk, who had never heard of Robert Smith. Short and stooped, with bifocals hanging from a beaded chain, she oddly smelled like Scotch tape.

Late in the morning, I filled my tank at Seven-Eleven, grabbed a Super Big Gulp, and took off. Instead of the quicker route south along unfamiliar roads on the Eastern Shore, I drove west, within a mile of my parents' house, trying to avoid getting lost.

An accident on I-95 had me running late and I hit rush hour traffic outside Richmond. Minutes before 5:00, I arrived at the hospital parking lot, worried that Amy had already finished her shift and I had missed her. Since I hadn't brought her apartment address, my only chance to see her was at her work.

Cramped in my front seat, I hurried to put on my makeup, but had no idea what I was doing. I had been too embarrassed to ask my housemates for tips on applying makeup. If Tom had heard about my plans, he'd have asked me why I was putting myself through all that for anybody.

Even with the air conditioner cranked, my face was glistening with sweat. After putting on too much eyeliner, I was stabbing at the globs under my eyes, but that was smudging everything. I hadn't brought any cleanser, so I was sucking on Q-tips and dabbing at the splotches, futilely trying to erase them. My foundation was just as bad. I didn't know where it should stop, so I put it everywhere, even on my ears and neck.

After I finished, I sat back and peered into the rearview mirror, hoping that everything would somehow come together, like a mismatched quilt.

But my face looked scary, not avant-garde. My eyes were raccoon black, my foundation was ghostly white and as uneven as a bad spray-on tan. I couldn't even wash my face and start over. Amy would have to appreciate my effort, if not my execution.

As I walked to the hospital, I could feel everyone staring but I had come too far to turn back. When Paul had talked me into the makeup, I only envisioned Amy seeing me, not a dozen people in the parking lot. Even a squirrel in the grass by the walking path got on its hind legs and eyed me up.

Inside the hospital, I stopped in front of the information desk, where a woman with short hair and gold-tone glasses was seated.

"What are you supposed to be?" she said, leaning forward.

I grinned sheepishly, too embarrassed to say anything.

"I don't know what you're expecting from me," she said, easing back in her chair. "I looked at the calendar this morning and today is not Halloween. I don't have any candy for you and there had better not be any tricks."

"Yes ma'am. I'm here to see Amy Lawson. She's a dietetic intern."

"Is this a joke, son?"

"No ma'am," I said, shuffling uneasily from foot to foot. "Can I see her please? I just drove six hours to see her."

"I guess I'll let you through. But only because I don't want you to get upset and start to cry. You might ruin your eyeliner."

Shrieking with laughter, she slapped the table in front of her. Then she pointed to the elevators behind her. "Third floor. Turn left off the elevator and follow the signs to Room 307."

She put on the table a visitor's pass, encased in a plastic holder with a metal clip on the back. I grabbed it and hurried off.

On the elevator, a woman in scrubs gave me a *Stay back or I'll use my mace* stare. I got off and followed the signs to Room 307. Printed in black letters above the room number on the frosted glass door was *Dietetics*. Taped to the wall near the door was a magazine ad for *The Incredible Edible Egg*. Written in red marker on the ad was: "Good cholesterol ... Fact or fiction?"

I took a deep breath and opened the door. Inside was a large room. It was empty and as I wandered through a maze of rooms, looking for someone to help me, I was thinking, *Is this a joke, son?*

Finally, I saw a girl my age, wearing a white lab coat, her hair in a bun. She had just pulled a notebook from a bookcase and sensing my presence, she turned and almost dropped the notebook when she saw me.

I was afraid that she was going to scream for help, so I slowly extended the visitor's pass in my hand and said, "I'm here to see Amy."

Seeing the pass, she relaxed somewhat. "Is she expecting you?"

"I don't think so."

"Are you Bruce?"

"Huh? Yes. How did you know my name?"

"Amy's talked about you. She said you were tall and had very short hair. She didn't mention anything about makeup."

"Until a half an hour ago, I had never worn makeup," I said, smiling nervously. "I obviously don't know how to put it on."

"Try not to smile. You don't want to crease your foundation. Oh, and when it comes to makeup, less is generally more."

"Thanks for the tips, but I'm never doing this again. Is she here? Can I please see her?"

"Amy's attending a department lecture, but I'll see if she can come out," she said, walking away and closing an interior door behind her.

I was relieved that Amy was still at work, but as I watched the second hand on a wall clock go around a second time, I was thinking that Amy was probably somewhere in there, begging her friend to come out and tell me to go away. I couldn't believe I had let Paul talk me into such a stunt.

The door opened and I turned. Amy was standing in the doorway wearing a lab coat and brown glasses. She looked like a doctor, another reminder that she was a success and I was a loser.

Our eyes met. She didn't smile or even offer a shrug to invite an explanation for my makeup.

On my drive, I had practiced what I'd say when I first saw

her: *Amy, I'm so sorry. Please give me a chance. I'll do anything to be with you.*

I had imagined that after hearing that, she would rush over to and squeeze me tight against her.

But she just glared. Clearly, she hadn't returned my calls because she wanted me to disappear from her life. Now her last memory of me was going to be me showing up at her work looking like an axe murderer.

I opened my mouth to deliver my heartfelt lines, but her frosty stare rattled me. Instead, I said, "You look so official in your lab coat."

"What are you doing here?" she said, folding her arms. "Why are you wearing that ridiculous makeup?"

"I came to ask you to go to The Cure concert with me."

"So you're supposed to be Robert Smith?"

"It's a loose interpretation," I said, smiling, hoping to remind her of the guy she used to adore. "Can we talk?"

"I'm attending a lecture," she said, cooly. "I'm working, you know."

"I didn't mean to interrupt you at work. I came here to speak with you in person."

"I need to go," she said, turning to leave.

"Wait!" I called. "You don't owe me anything, but I drove all afternoon just to see you. Please at least give me a chance to apologize."

She turned back, still looking angry. "I really have to go now but my shift ends at 8:00."

"You'll meet me? Where?"

"At the information desk in the lobby," she said, and hurried off.

The door closed and I exhaled deeply. I had figured that she might be pissed when she first saw me, but seeing her that livid was horrible.

I found a bathroom in the hallway. After pulling a handful of beige paper towels, with their accordion folds, from the metal wall dispenser, I hunched down, my hands resting on the sink's rounded corners. Looking into the mirror, buried under all the junk on my face, I saw a smile.

I stopped at the front desk and placed my pass on the table in front of the woman from earlier.

"What happened to your makeup?" she said.

"I don't need it anymore."

"Well any fool could've told you that," she said, and stared at me until I left.

To kill time, I drove around downtown, stopping for a burger. Then I started worrying that I'd get lost and be late to meet Amy, so I drove back to the hospital and walked around the grounds, looking at my watch every five minutes. At 7:45, I went inside and sat near the information desk, happy that the lady from earlier wasn't there.

My stomach was in knots as I thought of what to say to Amy. I'd be sincere, I'd be myself, and that would have to be good enough. But after that moment of clarity, I thought about her scowl when she saw me and wondered whether she'd even show up and if she did, whether she'd squash me like a bug.

At 8:00, Amy walked up from the hallway behind the desk. I stood up, my legs wobbly.

"What did you want to say to me?" she said, stopping several feet away. She looked less annoyed than earlier. Still, she wasn't happy.

"Well, Paul told me if I cared for you as much as I tell him, that I'd better drive here and tell you how much you mean to me."

Amy's expression didn't change. "Whose idea was the makeup?"

"That was Paul's, but don't blame him. He probably thought I'd put it on better."

"Did Paul write your apology as well?"

"No. I'm winging that," I said, smiling. "I'm truly sorry I didn't control my drinking around you, Amy. I promise I'll never do that to you again."

"I can't begin to tell you what a nightmare that wedding was for me."

I nodded and said, "I'd do anything to take away your pain from that night."

She stared back. It felt like ten seconds.

"I don't think I can—"

"You have to give me another chance," I blurted. "It's destiny."

"What does that mean?"

"When I saw you over New Year's after all that time apart, I knew we were destined to be together."

"That seemed more like a chance encounter," she said, unmoved.

"You got something against destiny?"

"I don't have anything against destiny," she said. "My issue is with you."

I swallowed hard. I had hoped I was making progress with her.

"Are you hungry?" I asked.

"I was going to eat something in the cafeteria," she said. "I guess you can join me."

"Destiny thanks you," I said, smiling. "So do I."

We sat down with our trays and Amy unwrapped a

chicken salad sandwich on wheat, to go with her cup of water. My second dinner was another cheeseburger with fries and a large Coke; a shameless meal to eat with a dietician.

She was guarded, her warmth missing, so our meal felt more like a job interview. But unlike job interviews, I was motivated to sell myself. I wanted to join Amy's *organization* more than I had ever wanted any job. My responsibilities would be supporting and intriguing her; being someone she was proud to be with, not some guy she used to think was cute but was drunk all the time.

"You looked so mad upstairs," I said. "I was afraid you weren't going to meet with me."

"It was an important presentation, so your timing was particularly bad," she said. "Also, I was beyond mad at you."

Was. Is she no longer beyond mad or is she referring to the past? Afraid to ask, I said, "I didn't have your schedule, so I just showed up. I feel fortunate I was able to catch you."

She fixed me with a stare. "So what's changed with you in the last few weeks?"

It was like those interview questions I was never prepared for. Luckily, Paul had suggested that she would ask me something like that.

"I miss having you in my life," I said, but she didn't look impressed. "But what's really changed is that I now understand what you were telling me at the wedding."

"I didn't think you were listening to me that night. What was so striking?"

"You said I could rely on you; that when I was with you, there was no reason for me to drink."

"So why does that mean so much for you now?"

"Because now I realize those weren't just words. They were a commitment. I didn't understand it then because I thought I

246

had been committed to you, but I realized I hadn't been," I paused. "I want to be fully committed to you now."

Her face softened slightly.

"Amy, I want to show you that you can rely on me," I said, stopping to wipe tears from my eyes. "I know I messed up, but I can control my drinking, especially if it means being with you."

"I appreciate you coming here and telling me that."

What does that mean? It sounds like something an interviewer says before turning me down.

Usually, I'd be too embarrassed to be crying in front of someone but I didn't care. I was crying about Amy. I was crying for Amy.

"Does that mean that I'm still in your *Boy Book*?" I said.

"Boy book? What does that mean?"

"*Are You There God? It's Me, Margaret.*"

"That's one of my favorite books," she said. "Why are you bringing it up?"

"When we were in your bedroom last month, I noticed your Judy Blume books. Last week, I missed you so much, I went to the library and asked a librarian what her favorite Judy Blume book was. Then I sat down and read it."

"That was sweet of you," Amy said, smiling with her side teeth showing, the way she used to smile at me. Her smile made me feel so good.

"That was my idea, not Paul's," I said, eager to take credit for something thoughtful. "I would really appreciate the chance to show you I've changed. Will you go to The Cure with me?"

"I don't know. That's a long way to go in the middle of the week."

"You used to hop on a plane just for a date with me." I said, allowing myself to smile. "Come on, it'll be a great show…"

She stared at me for a long moment. Then she said, "Okay. I'll go. But you'd better not wear that ridiculous makeup. And you'd better not get drunk."

"No makeup. No drinking. I promise." I'd have promised her anything. "Having you forgive me is all the motivation I need."

"Oh, it will take more than that for me to forgive you," she said. It was a blunt reminder not to take her for granted. Again.

I was a slow eater and she politely waited for me to finish. Then she said, "I should get going. I have an early shift tomorrow."

"Of course," I said, hiding my disappointment since things seemed to be going well.

I went back through the line for coffee for my drive to the beach. Then I walked Amy to her car, relieved that there was no expectation of me kissing her goodbye.

She got in her car and closed the door. I motioned with my hand and after she rolled down her window, I wanted to make sure I hadn't imagined her agreeing to go to the concert.

"I'll call you and we can finalize our plans for The Cure, okay?" I said.

"Cool beans," she said.

I felt tingly. I had been afraid I'd never hear her say that again.

TWENTY-FIVE

Days later, a familiar voice greeted me from two checkout lanes over at Food Lion.

"Bruce, how ya doing?!" It was Gerry, with an unlit cigar in his mouth.

He waited just inside the automatic front doors for me to finish checking out. "It's a small world," he said, as I approached. "You have time to talk?"

"Sure," I said. We walked out and sat on a wooden slat bench, dropping our bags at our feet.

It *was* a small world. The Carousel was across Coastal Highway, two blocks to our right was the Greene Turtle, and my house was a half-mile behind us.

Gerry struck a match, cupping his hands to shield his cigar from the breeze.

"Have you made any progress with your drinking?" he said, shaking the match and then spiking it into the gutter.

I nodded. "In the three weeks since my sister's wedding, I've only been drunk once."

"That's real progress," he said. "Keep that up."

I felt relieved, because I had been thinking that Gerry was going to hassle me for being drunk that one time.

"You were right about me choosing between drinking and the girl that I really cared about," I said. "I think she's giving me a second chance."

"Looks like I couldn't inspire you to quit drinking, but she did," he said, smiling. "That must be quite a girl."

"She is," I said, smiling back.

"It means a lot to me to know that you're really working on your drinking."

"Thanks," I said, not used to being affirmed.

We discussed whether the Celtics could have beaten the Lakers if Kevin McHale had been healthy. Then, despite my usual deference toward Gerry, I had to ask him something that had been bothering me since we met.

"Why are you so interested in me, Gerry?"

He paused as he flicked unseen ashes onto the pavement. "I guess because I miss my son."

"You have a son? How come you've never mentioned him?"

"I also have a daughter," he said, looking straight ahead, following the traffic. "My wife made me leave our house because of my drinking. We're divorced eleven years now."

"I'm sorry, Gerry."

"Don't be. Just don't make the same mistakes I did."

"How old is your son?"

"He'll be twenty-nine in April, but we haven't spoken in years," Gerry's voice trailed. "He doesn't want me in his life."

"What would you say to him if you could?"

"That I'm sorry that things turned out the way they did."

"You mean your drinking?"

"That's a big part of it, sure. But until kids experience real responsibility, it's hard for them to understand the life decisions a parent has to make. I always did what I thought was best for my family. Except for my drinking, of course."

"I can relate because I never understand why my dad does what he does," I said. "I've stopped trying."

"Pushing him away is the worst thing you can do."

"I'm not pushing him away," I snapped. "He's the one who pushed me away."

"It doesn't matter whose fault it is," Gerry said, his voice rising. "Put aside your pride and let him into your life. A father feels his son's pain in addition to his own. I know that firsthand."

"I'll try, Gerry," I said, though I knew there was no way I could relate to Dad's way of thinking.

"Don't try. Do it," he said, staring at me.

Gerry usually gave me good advice but his insistence that I reconcile with Dad seemed futile.

A few minutes later, I pointed to my bags and said, "It's been great talking with you Gerry, but I need to do something with these frozen pizzas."

He smiled. "I guess now we'll be running into each other at the grocery store instead of happy hour."

I smiled back and said, "In the immortal words of Joachim Andujar, *Youneverknow*."

He laughed. "That's his favorite English word, right?"

I nodded. When it came to sports references, Gerry and I spoke the same language. I got up, gave him a caring pat on the shoulder, and walked to my car.

The following week, I drove home for the concert. Mom made me promise I'd stay with them, so I arrived at my parents' house late in the afternoon and visited with her, then cleared out before Dad got home from work. I hadn't spoken to him since the wedding brunch and didn't need another lecture on my career.

Driving around my neighborhood, I was thinking what a big effort it was for Amy to drive all that way just to go to a concert with me. I remembered how she had smiled after I had told her I had read the Judy Blume book and allowed myself to hope that she hadn't given up on us.

After a fast-food dinner, I drove a mile past my house down Flower Avenue, passing my elementary school on my left. After pulling into the Giant grocery parking lot, I grabbed two quarters from my ashtray and went inside. I walked to the far-right aisle, passing by packaged meats and the dairy section. At the end of the aisle, I looked to my left. The machine was still there, with its faux woodgrain front and "Cold Drinks" spelled out in groovy semi-cursive blue font.

Starting when I was small enough to sit in the grocery cart seat, whenever Mom dragged me there, I'd beg her to buy me a drink from that soda machine. It used to cost ten cents, but she only gave in two, maybe three times.

The price was now thirty-five cents, but I'd have paid a dollar.

I inserted my two quarters and pushed the button for orange soda. As I bent down to collect the three nickels the machine surrendered, I watched the cup slide down the metal guide into position, followed by the rattle of ice pellets as they dropped into the wax-lined cup. Finally, the syrup and soda squirted down from rubbery white nozzles.

Is the foam going to rise over the lip of the cup? I watched, transfixed. *Nope. Not this time.*

Once the foam settled, I slid open the Plexiglas window and removed my beverage. I took a sip but it didn't taste so special since Mom hadn't bought it for me.

I went to the floral section at the front of the store and waited for a woman, who was arranging roses in a vase, to acknowledge me.

"Do you need assistance?" she said, finally looking up. She seemed stuffy, like she would always use *perhaps* and never use *maybe*.

"I'll take all the help I can get. I have a big date in less than an hour."

She frowned, as if thinking: *I hope Casanova here will be changing his clothes beforehand.* Then she said, "These beautiful red roses arrived earlier today. Would those be appropriate?"

"Appropriate?" I said. "I'm sorry, I'm not following you."

"I beg your pardon," she said, raising her nose slightly. "Red roses symbolize love."

"Unfortunately, they wouldn't be appropriate. Is there a color of rose that says *I'm really sorry and you're great and I'll do anything if you'd forgive me*?"

She cleared her throat importantly and strode from behind the counter. Picking a bouquet of yellow tulips from a bucket, she held them in front of me, as water dripped off the stems. "Perhaps these," she said.

"Those are nice, thank you," I said. "Hopefully, she'll give me a chance to come back later and buy her red roses."

"Hope springs eternal," she said, sliding the tulips into a cellophane sleeve and handing them to me.

I drove around until it was time to pick up Amy. Walking up to her stoop, I was thinking: *Trust her. Be open with my feelings. Make sure she's happy. Do whatever she wants.* I laughed because the last couple sounded like Gary's advice for treating Carousel guests.

I rang the doorbell and glared at the storm door. The one I had banged into the night before the wedding.

When Amy opened the door, I was melting inside.

"Are those for me?" she asked, pointing to flowers I had forgotten I was holding.

"Here you go," I said, extending the bouquet as the cellophane wrapping crackled.

"Tulips are my favorite," she said, as she accepted them.

I followed her inside and into the kitchen, where she put the flowers in a vase. We walked back toward the front door and as she picked her purse off a table in the foyer, she called, "I'm going to the concert!"

"Have fun," her mother called from another room.

"We will. Bye!"

I couldn't believe the exchange. My parents never let me out the door without a public service announcement about drinking and driving. And a warning about coming home late.

Amy was wearing a white cotton sweater over a pale blue dress and a wide brown headband in her hair. Not yielding to my florist, I hadn't changed my pinstriped lime green 7-Up driver's shirt, black gym shorts, and red hi-top Chucks.

"What are you laughing at?" she asked, as we crossed her front yard.

"You look nice," I said, smiling. "But you're dressed for a garden party and I'm dressed for the skate park. Meanwhile, the rest of the brooding, goth crowd at the show will be shrouded in black for the apocalypse, the afterlife, or whatever it is they're into."

As I opened the passenger door for her, she said, "If the world ends tonight, I'm glad I'm wearing sensible shoes."

We had a good conversation on the forty-five-minute drive to the arena. The subject of alcohol didn't come up, but right after we walked inside, we passed a concession stand serving beer and wine. Unsure whether I should acknowledge it, I asked Amy if she wanted a drink.

"No thanks," she said, looking wary, as if I had just offered her heroin.

"Don't worry, I'm not having anything," I said, well aware that me not drinking was as much a condition to my admission as the ticket stub in my pocket.

She smiled, relieved that I had cleared that hurdle, low as it was.

On the way to our seats, I stopped counting all the guys with Robert Smith inspired hair and makeup. After passing one with impeccably poufy, yet wispy hair, I asked Amy, "How did my makeup compare to that guy's?"

"His looks great. Yours looked like a three-year-old had gotten into his mother's cosmetics."

"Not a chance," I said. "Growing up, two things were definitely off limits in our house. Mom's makeup and her fabric scissors. She'd have spanked me if I touched her Lancome."

The venue seated about 10,000 and was filling up, except for the nose-bleeds. We had great seats, twelve rows back on the floor. There was no warmup band and as we waited, I was looking around at all the couples comfortable with each other, holding hands or swaying together to the recorded music. Then there was Amy and me. *Will we be a couple again by the end of the night?*

Mid-song, the recorded music cut off and all the lights went out, like there had been a power outage. As we waited, the pitch-black arena was dotted by lighters and peppered with cheers and whistles. Then the speakers produced a grating mix of guitars, drums, and the groan of twisted metal. It sounded like a theatrical bus crash.

As the noise continued, I felt disoriented, like I had just

climbed out of a shattered window on that wrecked bus and was wandering down a dark country road looking for help.

Dimly lit images flickered on a screen behind the stage as muddled talking was mixed with eerie wailing. The screen flashed with ghastly close-ups of lipstick-red lips and teeth, likely Robert Smith's, licking, biting, snarling, and talking. I reflexively slipped my arm around Amy's waist and she leaned toward me. I was holding her but it didn't count. I wasn't being romantic, I was unnerved.

The video went on for a minute or two, then people up front started cheering. Apparently, The Cure had come on stage in the darkness. They began playing and after dim stage lights went on, Amy pulled away from me to dance.

I kept looking over at her. As she watched the stage, she'd smile or grimace, and I'd wonder what she was thinking. When she danced, her head would rock side to side, or she'd swivel her hands in front of her. Then she'd get hot and push up the sleeves on her sweater and run her fingers through her hair. I fantasized about embracing her for a long kiss while everyone in the arena ignored us to watch the concert.

When Amy would catch me gazing at her, I'd smile, and she'd smile back. Or I'd yell, "Can I get you anything?" And she'd shake her head.

After making it through the prequel, I was enjoying the show, but got bored. I didn't have the attention span to sit through an entire concert or movie, so toward the end, I was one of the few hoping there wouldn't be another encore.

As we walked to the parking lot, I asked Amy if she wanted to stop for something to eat.

"Thanks, but I'm driving back to Richmond early tomorrow so I can't make it a late night."

This can't be the whole date. Things seemed to be going well, but I couldn't help feeling that she was rejecting me. I didn't know when I'd see her again and was running out of time to show her how much I cared about her.

As we exited the Beltway, I asked if she had time for a walk around the block.

She agreed, which gave me some confidence.

It was after 11:00 mid-week so it felt like we were the only ones outside. The darkness was pierced by streetlights, porch lights, and an occasional car's headlights. The cicadas were quiet but there was a persistent hum from cars on the nearby Beltway.

As we walked, I had to keep slowing my pace to match Amy's. I had a long stride and was so excited, I was walking faster than normal.

"You know, this is really our first date," I said, as I reached for her hand. My heart fluttered faster when she didn't pull hers away.

"What about your formal and the wedding?" she said.

"Those weren't dates, they were *events*," I said, nervously swinging her arm. "This is the first time we've gone out when we weren't formally dressed."

"I was thinking that you dressed up whenever you went out," she said.

"My cummerbund is at the cleaners so I couldn't wear the tux. Besides, even James Bond wouldn't wear a tux to a Cure concert."

We talked about the concert and I asked if she would have changed anything about the show.

"When Robert Smith introduced the songs, he'd say, 'This is called *The Walk*. This is *A Forest*.' I wanted to hear what the songs meant to him. I mean, we're at your concert. We know the names of your songs."

"You're right," I said. "His introductions didn't speak to me at all."

"Did you expect him to talk to you?" she said playfully. "He didn't have time to get to everyone, so you'll probably have to see him at a smaller place."

I smiled at her. I loved her sarcasm.

We had circled back to her house, but I hadn't told her how much I cared for her.

"We sort of had another date the night before the wedding," I said, looking into her porch-lit eyes. "I had the best time talking with you."

"Would you have enjoyed the concert more if you had been drinking?" she asked. Her question seemed off-topic to me, but it may have been on her mind all night.

"I felt lost when the show started," I said, trying to give her more than a defensive *no*. "But with you there, it was easy to stay calm. If I had been drinking, I might have cheered more and I might have danced a little, but I wouldn't have enjoyed it more. You were right. When I'm with you I don't have any reason to drink."

"None at all?" she said, looking at me intently.

What is she getting at?

"That's not exactly true," I said, clearing my throat, as I tried to find inspiration from Paul's advice or from Hemingway himself. "I guess the reason I drank so much around you ... is because ... I have trouble with physical intimacy. When I'm sober, even though I really want to, I can't get myself to kiss you unless you kiss me first."

She smiled and put her arms around my shoulders. "You mean like this?"

As she kissed me, I imagined her smiling contentedly like the picture in my photo album.

After our kiss, she said, "I've been waiting for you to say something about your difficulty."

"You knew?"

"It was pretty obvious when we were in my bedroom," she said. "When you aren't drinking, we have this amazing chemistry, but you're too shy to touch me."

"Then why didn't you say anything about it sooner?"

"Because I needed you to tell me."

"Is that why you broke up with me?"

"Of course not. I stopped seeing you because of your excessive drinking. I don't even mind if you have a couple of drinks around me. Just don't get drunk."

"Don't worry. In Richmond, I promised I wouldn't drink when I was with you and I'm keeping that promise. I was so happy when you said you'd go to the concert. I had been afraid that I was never going to see you again."

"I was afraid of that as well," she said. Then she smiled.

Sensing that she trusted me, I felt different. I was no longer just a guy on a date, I was part of something bigger than myself. I felt like a boyfriend.

I wanted to kiss her again but couldn't, so I propped my forearms on her shoulders. "Are you sure you can't stay out a little longer?" I said, holding her shoulders and dancing her side to side.

"Sorry. I promised my parents and I really should get some sleep."

"Would it be okay if we kissed again?" I said.

"I think I've got time for that."

I leaned down and kissed her. Afterward, I kept holding onto her. "I don't want to lose you," I whispered.

She hugged me tighter. "I know you don't."

Amazing chemistry, I said out loud, savoring the expression on my three-block drive home. Amy knew my secret and it didn't affect our relationship. It was my best date ever.

As I approached my parents' house, the traffic light at the far end of the block was flashing red, which it started doing every night at midnight. I slowed to make a U-turn to park in front of my house, but was too excited to sleep, so I drove to Paul's.

The lights at his house were off, so I went to the Diner to see Marge.

"Are you meeting friends, Sweetie?" Marge asked, as she approached my booth.

"No, it's just me," I said, not concerned that she would banish me to a counter seat because I was alone.

"How come you're in here by yourself?"

"I was in such a good mood I had to come see you," I said, smiling.

"Why are you so happy?"

"Besides seeing you?" I said, and Marge's haggard face lit up. "I just had a nice date with a girl I've been interested in for a long time."

"How come you never bring a girl in here, Sweetie?"

"Aw Marge," I said, probably blushing. "I don't want to make you jealous."

"That's a good thing," she said, leaning down and playfully putting her hand on my shoulder. "Because I'd probably scratch her eyes out."

Then she gave me a look that made me think she might have been serious.

After finishing my Cheeseburger Royal, Marge kept warming up my coffee, so I stuck around.

There was a crash in the kitchen. Apparently, someone back

there had dropped a plate, startling some customers. Others applauded, which I always thought was mean.

"That's okay," Marge yelled toward the kitchen. "Just rinse it and put it back in the rack."

Mae, the frail, elderly, blue-haired waitress who handled the left side of the diner, laughed and said, "Margie, please."

But trying to subdue Marge was futile. She was spreading herself around, holding court like Don Rickles presiding over a lounge audience in Vegas, and no one was off-limits.

At a nearby booth, one guy was ordering a burger and asked Marge, "Can I get that rare?"

Her eyebrows lowered. "We'll see how it comes out. But by the time our cook comes back inside from smoking his cigarette, the burgers are usually well-done."

I loved the Diner's atmosphere but couldn't drink coffee all night, so I said goodnight to Marge. I didn't want to go home, but I had no other place to go. As I eased my car to the curb in front of my house, I saw the living room lamp had been left on for me.

Opening the storm door, I pulled up on the handle to avoid waking anybody with the dragging sound. Once inside, I locked the front door and exhaled in relief at the stillness. Then I quietly made my way up the stairs.

"Do you know what time it is?"

I jumped after hearing Dad's low voice from the living room. Standing on the landing, I turned to my right. Sitting in the blue paisley chair, Dad was glaring as he carefully placed his book on the floor.

TWENTY-SIX

"Do you know what time it is?" he repeated, an octave lower.

"It's probably after 2:30."

"You realize I have to be up for work in a few hours," he growled. "But after waiting up half the night for you, I won't be able to get back to sleep."

"I didn't ask you to wait up."

"This is my house. It's my responsibility to make sure you make it home safely."

"*Make it home safely?* Don't worry, Dad. I can take care of myself."

"What was so damn important that caused you to stay out until all hours of the night?"

"After the concert, I went to the Diner by myself. I didn't call you because it didn't make sense to wake you to tell you not to wait up."

"There is no upstanding reason to be in a diner at 2:30 a.m. I have allowed you to visit, but you have no appreciation for me or my rules. Starting tomorrow, you're out on your own."

"Is my presence here that offensive?" I asked, although the answer was obvious.

"Watching your inaction—" he paused to rub his chest. "Watching as you waste your life has been nothing but a slap in my face. When I was your age—" he stopped and took a breath. "When I was your age, no one paid for my education. No one had to tell me to look for a job. I went out and knocked on doors. You, on the other hand, have everything handed to you!"

"I know things were tougher for you," I said, my shoulders heaving because Dad had never yelled at me like that. "I can't change that, but I have my own struggles. Not that you care."

"When have you ever told me about your struggles?" he snapped.

"Dad, whenever we talk, all we do is fight," I said, unable to keep from crying. "You don't know me, and you've given up trying. I'm just a liability for you now."

"When you stopped listening to me, I stopped trying to understand you," he said, ignoring my tears.

My anger, which had always covered up my feelings of rejection from him, wouldn't let me admit to him that he had been right about my failure to plan my career, so I just stared at him.

Grimacing, he stared back. I was surprised that he didn't have more to say.

I went upstairs, grabbed my toothbrush from the hall bathroom, then re-packed my overnight bag. I passed Mom, standing in their bedroom doorway at the top of the stairs. Thin as a fencepost, her threadbare, light blue nightgown draped loosely from her shoulders.

"I knew it was a mistake to stay here tonight," I told her, as I hurried past. "I'm sorry, Mom. I'll call you sometime."

"You woke up your mother?" Dad yelled up, as if

surprised that she wasn't able to sleep through our yelling. As I hurried down the stairs, he said, "You cannot imagine the stress you have caused your mother and me!"

I stopped on the landing to face him. "Your stress? Have you ever cared about what I'm feeling?!"

"I have, but what you need is a wallop on your backside, not sympathy."

"All you do is bark orders!" I yelled back. "You know, if a farmer beats his mule once, it's the mule's fault. If the farmer beats his mule every day, it's the farmer's fault."

"Get out of my house you ungrateful son of a bitch!" he shouted, getting up. My body tensed as I watched him take a step toward me. But he stopped walking and seemed to wince. After taking a deep breath, he stiffly sat back in his chair.

His confused expression distracted me from my anger. "Are you okay, Dad?"

"I don't need your help," he barked, and took another deep breath, his eyes fixed on me.

"Fine," I said, and went down the last four stairs. I unlocked the front door and slammed it behind me, vowing to never speak to him again.

Too upset to drive, I sat in my car, cursing Dad. All my life, I had known the rules at home and for the most part, I had complied. But yelling at him like that put me over the line and I knew I wouldn't be permitted to just hop back.

Coming home in the middle of the night represented everything that was wrong between me and Dad. He demanded order and accountability, like being rested so you could give your employer a fair day's work the next day. I had planned to change my habits once I got a job, but not before. I knew that once I started working, my carefree life would be over.

I drove to Paul's house. There were no lights on, so as I

stood on the welcome mat, I pulled his house key from my pocket and had to feel for the keyhole before unlocking the door. In the darkness inside, I extended my arms, bumping into furniture in the front room. His parents were upstairs, but they slept through anything. I turned left and squeezed behind the dining room chairs. After a few strides through the kitchen, I opened the basement door. There was light.

Walking down the bare wooden stairs, I was surprised at how cool the basement was in summer. Paul was lying on a mattress on the floor along the far wall, buried under a comforter covered with Kliban cats, the cartoon ones with red sneakers.

He had his run of the unfinished basement. It had gray painted cinder block walls, exposed rusty pipes, and two small head-high windows with tiny cobwebs and dead bugs in the recessed sills. On the other side of a patchwork partition was a laundry area, two windows looking out at the backyard, and a bathroom that hadn't been serviceable in years. It was dreary, especially for someone as creative as Paul, but all he needed was his stereo, magazines, books, and the keys to his mom's car.

I walked across an area rug and peered down on him.

"Stop hovering," he said, without looking up from his *Rolling Stone* magazine.

"How do you see in here?" I said, pulling a string dangling from one of the exposed overhead bulbs, my light consuming the clip lamp on his makeshift bookshelf. "My dad's always telling me to turn off a light, but what's the point when electricity is so cheap?"

"Everything's cheap when you aren't paying for it," Paul said, squinting at me for effect. "What are you doing here?"

"I went to see The Cure with Amy tonight."

"That's right," he said, sounding more engaged. "How was it?"

My euphoria from the date was long gone, which had always been my pattern around Dad. Any positive feeling was offset by my house's gloom and doom. Like a casino, the house always won.

"*That* went well," I said, sitting down on Paul's guest bed, which was another single mattress on the floor, perpendicular to his mattress, my legs splaying onto the floor. "After I said goodnight to Amy a couple of hours ago, I stopped by here. But your house was dark, so I went to the Diner. I got home after 2:30 and Dad was waiting up."

"Oh no," Paul said, putting down his magazine and sitting up. He knew what a big deal that was for Dad.

"We were yelling at each other. I called him a bad parent. He called me a son of a bitch."

"Marvin called you a son of a bitch?" he said, grinning.

"I know. His go-to is *bastard*. I've never heard him use *son of a bitch*," I said, almost smiling myself. "What do I do now? There's no way he'll let me move back home."

"Why do you want to live there anyway?"

"Maybe because I always wanted us to feel like a normal family before I moved out for good. The problem is that I could do everything right: stop drinking, stop staying out late, get a career job, and that still wouldn't be enough for Dad."

"You don't have to plan your whole life right now, just your next step," Paul said, yawning. "Tomorrow morning you should go to College Park and get an application for business school."

"Why tomorrow?" I said, stretching my legs in front of me, inches above the floor.

"Because if you wait until September, you'll annoy Marvin even more."

"Why should I care?"

"Because this time, he's right."

I stared at Paul for his betrayal. "I can't give in to him."

"Then do it for your mother," he said, rewrapping himself in his comforter and lying back down.

"You win," I sighed. "I can't believe I'm taking career advice from a waiter. Am I in trouble or what?"

"Or what," he said. "After that, you'll need to update your resume and start looking for a job where you have to wear a tie every day. But don't think of it as giving in to him. Think of it as figuring out what you want to do."

"Right now, I want to go to the Diner," I said, clapping my hands and standing up. "Come on. We can discuss my career plan and you can make a bunch of lists."

From under the covers came a muffled, "I'm sleeeeepy."

"Are we going?"

He didn't answer and remained rolled up, looking like a gigantic, padded caterpillar.

"Paul?" I asked again, standing for a closer look.

He was asleep.

I turned on his old twelve-inch TV. It didn't have cable, so I kept turning the dials, passing the same eight or so snowy channels, looking for something to watch.

The next morning, on my drive to the beach, I stopped by the University of Maryland's business school, five miles from my parents' house. The woman helping me said that my GMAT scores should get me accepted, but she was so enthusiastic about everything, I couldn't gauge her sincerity. I left with an application and a glossy folder containing more school information than I would ever read.

When I got to my place, I saw a note that Mom had called. I picked it off the counter in disbelief. She could barely wait twelve hours before nagging me to apologize to Dad.

The note said: *Bruce, Call your mother at Holy Cross.* As in Holy Cross Hospital.

That got my attention and I immediately dialed the number. Mom picked up and said, "Bruce? Where are you?" Her tone urgent, as if her son was a fugitive.

"I'm at the beach. Why are you at Holy Cross?"

"It's your father. He was having chest pains this morning, so he stayed home from work."

"Dad didn't go to work?" He never missed work, his ethic forged by a Depression-era fear that the day he called in sick was the day they'd find someone else to do his job.

"His pains got so severe, I called 911 and they sent an ambulance. They think he had another heart attack."

I took a deep breath. "Is he going to be okay?"

"They don't know. He's in surgery now."

"I'll leave right away. I can be there in three hours."

"Oh, don't feel like you have to come back," she said, her passive-aggressiveness on full display. "But it would be nice if you were here for him this time."

This time was because when Dad had his first heart attack a few years before, I had been away at school and they didn't tell me about it until after he got home from the hospital. Since they had waited so long to tell me, I didn't make a special trip home to see him.

"Are you kidding?" I said. "I just have to let my boss know."

"If it's not too much trouble," she said. "That would mean a lot to your father."

My bag was at my feet, so I went upstairs for clean clothes.

Then I called the bellstand and asked them to take me off the schedule for a few days, and left a note for my housemates.

I drove extra fast on Route 50, figuring I had a valid excuse if I got pulled over. But it wasn't just an excuse. I was afraid that Dad would die before I could see him. At one point, I was crying, thinking that I'd never hear him say that he was proud of me.

———

Walking into Holy Cross and seeing the concerned faces on other visitors, I felt the gravity of being in a hospital.

"I'm here to see my dad, Marvin Margulies," I told a retiree wearing a blue blazer at the reception desk. "He had a heart attack this morning and was brought here by ambulance."

He directed me to intensive care in the coronary care wing. I walked off, pausing outside the gift shop. *Flowers, balloons? Nah, too impractical for Dad.*

I got off the elevator and walked down the hall, looking at room numbers, while trying not to gawk into open rooms. Dad's door was open and I walked in, expecting an intensive care room to require masks and gowns, but it looked like an ordinary hospital room.

It was dark, though it was mid-afternoon. The window shade had been lowered to expose only the window's bottom two inches. I frowned, thinking this represented how Dad viewed the world and how little of it he let into his life. Scribbled in black marker on a grease board on the wall to my left, was *Cora*, with a smiley face in the middle of the "o." Apparently, she was Dad's nurse.

Dad was asleep, propped up in bed with pillows and wearing a hospital gown. It was jarring to see the plastic tube in his nose and his chest hooked up to several monitors, one beeping importantly every second.

Without his glasses, Dad looked about one hundred years old. His eyes were sunken, his face heavily wrinkled. I felt uncomfortable as I stared down at the shell of the man who had called me a son of a bitch the night before.

Mom was sitting bedside, her back to the door. I silently walked around the foot of Dad's bed. Once in her view, I nodded.

"I'm glad you made it," she said, smiling grimly, her cream-colored face paler than usual. She stopped knitting and put the sweater she had just started for Dad into the bag at her feet.

"How's he doing?" I whispered.

"You won't disturb him. He's heavily sedated," she said, standing up. "Wait here. I'll get you a chair."

"That's okay Mom," I said, glancing down at Dad to make sure he was breathing. "I've been sitting in a car for hours. I don't mind standing."

"How was your drive?" she asked. "You got here so quickly. I hope you weren't speeding."

"My drive was fine, Mom," I said, ignoring her speeding remark.

Minutes later, I walked out to a waiting area to grab a heavy wooden chair, then planted it on the window side of Dad's bed, facing Mom. I told her I had gone to Maryland's business school that morning and picked up an application for the following fall.

"You went to the University of Maryland to apply to business school?" she said, sounding as shocked as if I had told her I had just applied with NASA to be an astronaut.

"Yes Mom. I just said that."

She sniffed. "Will they accept you with your grades?"

It was no wonder I had issues with self-esteem.

I asked her if anything had changed with Dad lately. "He seems angry all the time, although that might be due to my proximity."

"Your father was under a lot of pressure with the wedding and of course, he's still been grieving since Grandma Helen's death in December."

Grandma Helen had been my last living grandparent, but I hadn't been thinking about her lately. Looking at Dad lying there helplessly, I felt badly for him.

"Dad never shows weakness, so I didn't think her death was still affecting him."

"Your father loved his mother dearly," Mom said.

"I know, Mom. He took good care of her."

I reflected on that as we sat in silence. Then I said, "How come Dad never talks about his dad?"

Dad's dad had died when I was a toddler and I knew little about him.

"They had a complicated relationship," she said, choosing her words carefully, as if Dad was eavesdropping.

"Can't you tell me anything about it?"

"Your father wouldn't want me to repeat this, but after graduating high school, he asked his father for a loan to attend college."

"What did his dad say?"

"He told your father to join the Army."

I laughed, but Mom's stern look made me realize that she wasn't joking.

"So what did Dad do?" I said, fascinated, as I rarely heard stories about Dad, especially from when he was growing up. That was probably why I could never picture him younger than his mid-forties.

"When your father turned eighteen, he enlisted in the Army to become eligible for the GI Bill."

"Dad was in the Army?"

"He was an Army cook," she said, and we smiled at the absurdity of it.

"How could Dad be a cook? He can barely boil an egg."

"He was only in the Army a few months," Mom said. "They discharged him because of his poor eyesight."

"I guess he couldn't see well enough to read the recipes," I said, and we shared a laugh. "How come Dad never told me he was in the Army or that he didn't get along with his dad?"

"He doesn't like talking about himself and he avoids discussing his father."

"Is Dad's lousy relationship with his father the reason he never spent time with me?"

Mom stared at me, punctuating my callousness. "You just remember things differently. Your father used to play cards with you. And checkers too."

"That was a long time ago, Mom. Where has he been the last ten years?"

"Since before you were born, your father has done all he could, sacrificing and saving, just to make your life easier," Mom snapped. "Have you ever considered that?"

"No," I said quietly.

"Then you should appreciate the advantages you have and that you never had to consider the Army as your way up and out. We have a nice house in a safe neighborhood, and we've given you and Tamara everything you needed."

Instead of appreciating Dad, I had always bristled at his strictness and frugality. Each day on his commute to work, he'd take a longer bus ride just to save a dime each way on the Metro fare. He'd reuse a teabag, leaving it sitting in a Pyrex glass dish by the sink and he never gave up on a tube of toothpaste. He'd eat around green mold in a block of cheese and gleefully claim he was *recycling*.

Dad was prosperous enough to own a house free and clear, that had central air conditioning, but was too thrifty to turn it on.

Throughout the afternoon, Mom kept getting up and fussing with Dad's blanket or taking his temperature with her hand. His breathing was choppy and periodically, when he'd snort loudly, Mom would stand for a closer look and we'd exchange worried glances. But as long as the machines didn't start beeping more, she'd sit down.

Nurses and orderlies came and went. They'd greet us, check the monitors, write down numbers and brief notes, make up the bed around Dad, and occasionally replace his IV bag. They were friendly, but had no answers for us.

As the afternoon wore on, I kept expecting Dad to wake up and ask why dinner wasn't on the table.

Around 8:00 that night, a doctor came in. He shook Dad's shoulder and then more gently, he moved Dad's chin, but Dad didn't wake up.

"How is he doing?" Mom asked, her tone fearful.

"He had a significant event," the doctor said. "If he makes it through the night, I would be optimistic."

If he makes it through the night?

"Do you know what caused it?" I blurted.

The doctor looked at me, apparently not appreciating being interrupted.

"The heart is like an engine," he said, gesturing like he was holding a softball in both hands. "A cardiac event can appear to be caused by a shock or sudden action, but generally, the culprit is a long-term blockage. Mr. Margulies had a previous cardiac event, so his elevated risk factors were likely exacerbated by his diet, exercise, or stress."

Stress? Like his son not getting a job? Like his son coming home late at night and yelling at him? I thought about how red Dad's face had been the night before and now feared that calling him a terrible father would be the last thing I'd ever say to him.

The doctor left and as Mom and I sat there, I looked at Dad and promised to stop pushing him away. In return, he just had to recover.

"Do you think I caused it?" I said, breaking our silence.

"You've added to your father's stress, but at your father's last physical, Dr. Weintraub had referred him to his cardiologist for screening, but your father kept putting that off."

"Why didn't Dad see the cardiologist?"

"Your father doesn't like doctors. He insisted on handling it himself."

"I can't believe he'd risk his health like that." But I couldn't say anything critical because I hated going to doctors. That reminded me of Paul saying that Dad and I were so similar.

It had been dark for hours when Mom yawned and said, "He isn't going to wake up tonight. There's no sense in both of us staying here, so go home and get some rest."

"I'm going to Paul's tonight." I said and wrote his phone number on the grease board. "Promise me you'll call if anything happens."

I left the room feeling helpless. I finally wanted to help Dad but there wasn't anything I could do.

I got three dollars' worth of quarters from a change machine outside the cafeteria. It was after midnight when I dialed Amy's number. The operator made me deposit a dollar before she would connect my call to Richmond.

"Hey Amy. I'm sorry to disturb you, but I have to talk to you."

"What's going on?" she said, sounding groggy, probably trying to determine if I was drunk.

"I'm at Holy Cross. My dad had a heart attack this morning."

"On my God! Is he okay?"

"We're not sure yet. Overnight will be the big test."

"I'm so sorry. How are you doing? How is your mom?"

"We're okay. I always thought Dad was indestructible, so this is a shock…"

I stopped talking, reflecting on how dire Dad's health was.

"Can I do anything?" she said, bringing me out of my thoughts.

"Thanks. Just thinking about you helped get me through the day, but it's all up to Dad now."

I told her about my fight with Dad the night before and how I felt that his heart attack had been my fault.

"Don't dwell on that," she said. "Focus on helping your mom and then after that, you'll be able to make amends with your father."

Throughout the call, the operator kept prompting me to deposit more quarters. After five minutes, my supply had been exhausted.

"Call me tomorrow when you get news," she said.

"I will. Thanks for being there for me."

The operator let us say goodbye before cutting off the call.

I stopped at Seven-Eleven and downed two chili cheese dogs in my car before driving to Paul's house. The lights were on in his front room, so I tapped on the front door as I walked in.

"What are you doing back in town?" Paul said from his stepfather's chair next to the couch.

"Dad had a heart attack this morning. He's at Holy Cross."

His jaw dropped. "Wow. I'm sorry. How's he doing?"

"He was in surgery this morning and he's not awake yet. They say he's stable, but I don't know. He looks so frail."

"How is your Mom?"

"She's holding up as well as can be expected. She's staying overnight with him."

"How about you?"

"You know, I never thought I'd miss him. But now I'm thinking I'd have a lot of regrets if he died."

"What would you regret the most?"

"That I didn't try harder to reach him. Also, that I don't remember him saying he was proud of me."

"Marvin isn't much of a talker, so he's probably been proud of you but just didn't tell you. Are you proud of him?"

"I'm proud of all that he's overcome in his life. So yeah, I guess I'm proud of him."

"You should tell him that."

"I will. If I get the chance."

TWENTY-SEVEN

Things felt familiar as I walked into Dad's room the next morning, though I was more fearful than when I had arrived the day before. Each time I had started falling asleep at Paul's, I woke up, anticipating the phone was about to ring. Then I'd lie there worrying that something bad had happened, but that Mom wasn't calling because she didn't want to tell me over the phone.

Dad was asleep under several blankets and Mom was seated in her chair. She had finished the body of her sweater and was making good progress on one sleeve.

"How is he doing?" I whispered.

"He woke up around 6:00," she said, smiling.

"Thank God," I said. "That's when he usually gets up. Did he say anything?"

"Not much. I told him it was Saturday, and he went back to sleep."

Mom and I talked for a while, then I opened my book and she focused on her knitting. We had settled in for another long day. Then Dad started moaning.

"*Mawv*? Are you okay?" Mom asked, as we stood to look closer.

"It's hot," he mumbled, and Mom peeled away two blankets, folding them below Dad's knees.

I wanted to thank him for all he had done for me but was afraid I would cause his blood pressure to spike and make his monitors go crazy, so I said softly, "Hey Dad, I'm here."

He didn't say anything.

Mom must have noticed my disappointment because she said, "I think he went back to sleep."

Late in the morning, Tamara arrived from Pittsburgh, carrying her knitting bag, her Mary Poppins optimism lifting our spirits. The three of us were catching up when Dad said, "Is that you, Tamara?"

Our heads spun to face him. His eyes were closed, but he seemed to be smiling.

"Hello Pa-Pa," Tamara said, as casually as if we were gathering around our faux butcher block kitchen table for dinner.

"How are your wedding plans going?" Dad said, opening his eyes slightly.

Tamara and I exchanged worried looks.

"It's probably the medication," Mom whispered.

Dad looked down at his chest. "Alice, why am I wearing a gown?" he said, befuddled.

"You had a heart attack yesterday morning," Mom said.

"The doctor said you're recovering well," I said.

"Bruce? You're here too?" Dad said. "How is your semester going?"

"It's wrapping up," I said, concerned by how out of it he was. But at least he wasn't yelling at me.

Dad fell asleep and a few hours later, a different doctor came in and woke him.

"Are you feeling any pain?" the doctor said, reaching down to grasp and "shake" Dad's hand, which remained at his side.

"I don't think so," Dad said. "When can I leave?"

"We'll get you home as soon as possible, Mr. Margulies," the doctor said, shining a pen light into Dad's eyes and then examining his chest. "Your vital signs are stabilizing. Keep that up and you'll be leaving us."

Dad looked at him blankly and the doctor turned to Mom. "This was a close call, but I believe the worst is behind him. After another day or two with no setbacks, he should be able to go home."

Dad had drifted back to sleep by the time the doctor left the room. Finally, we had a sense that he was going to recover. When I asked if anyone wanted something from the cafeteria, Tamara said she'd go with me and put away her knitting.

It was between lunch and dinner and the cafeteria was empty. As we sat in the dining area, we could hear the banter from the servers from across the dining hall.

"I think Dad's heart attack is my fault," I said as we ate. "Two nights ago, Dad and I had a big fight. His face was red, and he was probably having chest pains then."

"I heard all about it. Mom told me on the phone."

"She's such a gossip," I said, and we both chuckled.

"Dad's been having chest pains for years," Tamara said. "He takes an aspirin daily but he pops an extra one whenever his heart flares up."

"I always wondered why he kept a bottle of Bayer under his paisley chair," I said, feeling a little less guilty.

"That still doesn't explain the toenail clippers he keeps there," she said, smiling. "You can't blame Dad's heart attack on one fight. Besides, Dad thrives on stress. He needs to be aggrieved so he can revel in it."

"He does relish his conflicts," I said. "Remember when

those raccoons kept getting into our backyard trash cans and Dad tried to scare them away?"

Tamara smiled. "He put on those plastic safety goggles and went after them with the hose and a rake."

Imitating Dad's deep voice, I called, "Alice, where did those kids put the goggles?"

The cashier stared at me from across the dining area. I smiled and waved at her.

Joking around seemed inappropriate in a hospital, but at least we were sharing happy memories of Dad.

After our carefree meal, the walk down Dad's hallway brought me back to reality. "Now that Dad's going to recover," I said, "I want to apologize to him but I'm not sure what to say."

"What are you apologizing for?"

"Everything."

"Just tell him what's in your heart. Dad isn't very nurturing, but deep down, he loves you."

"You think so?"

"I know so," she said, smiling. "Whenever we talk about you, he asks if I'm concerned about you."

"What do you tell him?"

"I tell him that you'll be fine. You'd better not make a liar out of me."

With Dad seemingly out of the woods, everyone was waiting for more signs of his recovery. He was more awake, but wasn't saying much. We had all resumed our individual activities when Tamara stopped knitting and told me, "Now's a good time."

"You think so?" I said.

"A good time for what?" Mom said. She hated being left out.

I leaned forward in my chair. "Dad? Hey Dad," I repeated louder to get his attention. "I want to apologize to you."

"What for?" he said, his face blank.

"For two nights ago. I shouldn't have yelled at you."

He remained quiet; his eyes directed toward the wall behind me.

"And for only coming to you when I needed something. I'm sorry I haven't listened to you more."

"You're here for me now," he said, looking at me, his voice without its usual edge. "As long as you're listening now, it's not too late."

"Are you feeling okay?" I asked, unsure if he was coherent.

"I'm touched that you drove all this way to see me. I know it can be hard dealing with your old man."

"I can do better, Dad."

"We can all do better," he said, and closed his eyes.

———

Right before 6:00, an orderly wheeled a dinner tray into the room. Dad hadn't eaten anything for a day and a half, and the smell of hot food woke him.

Mom adjusted Dad's bed so he could sit up as the orderly guided the tray in front of Dad. Then with a flourish, Mom picked the beige plastic dome off the plate, revealing Dad's main course: baked chicken and mashed potatoes. It looked pretty good for hospital food.

Dad glanced down at the food.

Tamara and I leaned forward, anticipating Dad eating, a milestone in his recovery.

"They put gravy on the mashed potatoes!" he bellowed, as

if the potatoes had been laced with cyanide. "You told them no gravy, didn't you, Alice?"

The orderly looked stunned. I got his attention and nodded my head toward the door. He took the hint and left.

"I specified no gravy," Mom said firmly, disassociating herself from the debacle.

"Are they trying to kill me?" Dad said, highly agitated.

Tamara and I exchanged glances. Dad was back.

Mom worked hard, scraping away nearly all traces of gravy with the flimsy plastic knife and though Dad must have been hungry, he only picked at the chicken.

After dinner, with Dad more alert, Mom was smothering him with attention: *Do you want a sip of your tea? Do you need another blanket? Are you in pain?*

Dad didn't complain, and surprisingly, he seemed to appreciate her pampering.

Who are these people? I thought. For once, it looked like they really did love each other.

"Do you want me to put on a show, *Mawv*?" Mom asked. She had failed to curb her Flatbush accent, but Dad didn't even criticize her.

"TV show? Dad?" I whispered to Tamara, "He doesn't even know how to turn on the TV at home."

Dad didn't answer Mom, which was his answer. She grabbed the TV remote, which was dangling by its cord from the side of Dad's bed and put on *Jeopardy!* I had never watched TV with Dad and wondered how my family would react while watching a game show. Luckily no one tried to be first to call out the answers.

During a commercial, Dad turned to me and said, "Do you know I'll be turning sixty in two months?"

"I sure do. October second. The pressure's on for me to find you a thoughtful gift for under ten dollars."

Mom and Tamara were knitting, trying not to look like they were listening, though Tamara laughed out loud at my comment.

Dad continued, "My old man worked like a bastard his whole life and dropped dead of a heart attack at sixty-two."

"I didn't know that," I said, feeling uncomfortable at the turn in the conversation.

"He lived a hard life. After he died, Sylvan took care of my mother for fifteen years and she drove him into his grave at sixty."

"I really liked Uncle Sylvan. He was always nice to me."

"Sylvan was a mensch," Dad said.

It was nice hearing him praise his older brother. Dad didn't seem to revere many people.

"How come you never talk about your father?" I asked, as I fidgeted in my chair.

"We weren't that close," he acknowledged. "There were four kids and at home, he spent most of his time reading and studying religion."

"Is that why you never spent time with me?" I asked, and out of the corner of my eye, I saw Mom almost drop her knitting.

"On Father's Day when you were seven or eight," he said, his voice getting even quieter. "You gave me a pencil holder you made with Popsicle sticks. It's been sitting on my desk at work ever since. I look at it every day."

My eyes were riveted to Dad, but I knew Tamara was smiling because fifteen years before she had helped me glue that pencil holder.

"It reminds me that I have to be a provider," he continued. "My family struggled through the Depression. My father could barely scratch out a living and keep us fed. I wasn't letting that happen to my family."

His face softened and he looked down. I turned away, embarrassed for him because I knew how much he hated to show any cracks in his facade.

"Every night, I go to bed worrying about you," he said, his voice hoarse and fatigued. "I just want to pass along what I've learned and make sure you kids have opportunities in life. I see you making mistakes." He paused. "It's hard to watch."

My eyes started watering. I had to look at the TV to try to keep from crying.

"I think that's enough for now, *Mawv*," Mom said. "You should be resting."

I had never noticed Dad's interest in me because he wasn't engaging like Andy Griffith, Tom Bosley, or Fred MacMurray, who made parenting look so easy every day on TV. Dad couldn't equal those fictitious fathers. No one could.

It no longer mattered to me who had pushed the other away. What mattered was that we both wanted to get along better.

Dad awoke later with more energy because he wanted to talk about my job search.

"It's getting late," Mom interrupted, her decade-long habit of keeping the family peace kicking in.

"Don't worry Mom," I said. After hearing about Dad's upbringing, I felt I understood him better and wasn't angry at him like usual.

I leaned forward in my chair to look him in the eye. "Dad, I went to the University of Maryland yesterday. They were impressed by my GMAT scores, so next fall, I'm going to business school like you did."

"What would you do with an MBA?"

"I've always been interested in marketing and finance," I said, stretching the truth.

"How are you going to pay for graduate school?"

"Tuition is only about two thousand dollars a semester. I have money saved and I'll be working for a year before school starts."

"That sounds like you could swing it," he said. "But you'll need a more specific plan."

"I agree," I said. The words felt strange. "They said that after I'm accepted, I can meet with one of their guidance counselors."

Dad didn't have his usual vigor and didn't press me like usual, so I tried to get a rise out of him. "You know, Dad, I'm also considering becoming a stockbroker."

"Ah, those guys are crooks," he said, swatting his hand at the air in contempt. "They just keep moving your money around and make hay on commissions. If those bums had any idea where the market was going, they'd be retired and—"

"Living in Tahiti," I finished. "Dad, you've been investing for forty years. Why aren't *you* living in Tahiti?"

"Your mother doesn't like the sun," he said.

As Dad and I enjoyed a rare laugh together, Mom and Tamara were smiling as they knitted. For the moment, I was Number One Son.

Things were calm and we seemed like a normal family. It was nice. And strange. After a couple of hours of relative bliss, I said goodbye to Mom and Tamara. As I got up, I leaned over and told Dad that I was leaving.

"Your visit means a lot to me," he said quietly, his eyes closed.

"Dad, since I'll be getting a job in the fall and then starting business school, can I move back home in September?"

He didn't answer.

"*Mawv?*" Mom prodded.

"You'll have to ask your mother," Dad finally said.

That's it? Mom's a pushover for me, so that's as good as a yes.

I was so relieved, I leaned down and kissed him on the top of the head. His hair was thinner than I expected and with his hospital gown hanging loosely around his neck, he looked feeble.

I took a couple of steps, then turned back, intending to tell him I was proud of him. Instead, I said, "I love you, Dad."

"I've always loved you, son," he said casually, as if this was understood.

Mom gave me an *I-told-you-so* look while a beaming Tamara gave me a *thumbs up*.

Getting choked up, I nodded at them and left. Feeling unburdened, I bounced down the hallway to the elevator, hoping to pass someone I could share a smile with.

I got quarters and called Amy.

"How's your father?"

"Much better. He might be discharged tomorrow."

"I'm so relieved," she said. "You sound so much better than last night."

"It's been a great day. Dad's going to recover and I've realized that he hasn't been such a bad father."

"I'm so happy to hear you say that. What changed your mind?"

"In the last two days, I've spoken a lot with Mom and Tamara about the sacrifices Dad has made for me. It also brought back some good memories."

"You know I have to hear some of those memories. Don't keep me in suspense."

"I remembered one Saturday when I was eight or nine, he walked me to the park behind the church on Franklin Street to play basketball with me. But he had no idea what he was doing so I had to show *him* how to shoot baskets."

"What's wrong?" she said when I paused.

"Nothing," I said. Then, trying to be more open with her, I said, "My eyes are getting teary thinking about Dad growing up and never playing basketball."

"I'm starting to get teary as well," she said.

The operator wasn't moved. She cut in to ask me to deposit fifty cents.

"Dad was always there for me in his detached way. Whenever he was hammering me about my grades or my job search, he was just trying to make me a better person."

"That's how he shows he cares," she said. "Your father would do anything for you if he could."

There was a silence as I considered that. Then she asked, "What are you thinking?"

Usually, when she asked that, I avoided her question. But I said, "I was thinking that before I met you, I never shared my feelings with anyone. I'm glad I have you to share them with."

"*Awwww.*" Amy's sugary reaction made me glad I didn't say something evasive, like *I'm not thinking of anything.*

After making sure no one was walking by, I told her, "I also wish I wasn't so shy around you."

"You've known me since second grade. You can talk with me about anything."

"Well, I don't mean just talking. I mean–"

"In an intimate way?"

"Yes," I said, glad she couldn't see me blush. "You know, since I saw you over New Year's, I've been worrying that I wouldn't be a good enough boyfriend for you. There were so many things I wanted to change about me before we started dating."

"Just be yourself and show me you care. And don't be too shy to hold my hand. I like it when you hold my hand."

My quarters exhausted, we said goodbye. I walked through the quiet lobby around 12:30 a.m. Outside the entrance, no one was pacing or smoking a cigarette. There were no sirens, no emergencies, and no one walking to their car after a difficult visit. Today was my day. But it wasn't just mine. All felt right in the world.

———

I drove to Paul's and like the night before, he was in his front room, watching *Letterman*.

"How is Marvin doing?" he said, as I walked in and sat on the couch.

"He's been awake much of the day and should be leaving the hospital tomorrow or the next day."

"That's great. I'm glad you were there for him."

I nodded. "I also got my lease at home renewed."

"Now all you need is a job."

"Thanks for reminding me," I said. "But that's not even my biggest news."

"Your dad's recovering from a heart attack and he's letting you move back home," Paul said. "What's bigger than that?"

"I told him that I loved him. He said he loved me, too."

Paul cocked his head to the side. "That's a lot of breakthroughs for someone as non-communicative as you. What brought that on?"

"Hospitals are great places to talk. Also, I allowed myself to listen to some of the good things people were saying about

Dad. Like yesterday, Mom told me that after high school, he joined the Army to pay for his college."

"How come you never told me Marvin was in the Army?"

"I didn't know until yesterday. He was honorably discharged after a few months because his eyesight was too bad."

"Is that why he doesn't drive? Because of his eyes?"

"I don't know. He has a driver's license, but I've never seen him drive a car.

"You never asked him why he doesn't drive?" Paul couldn't believe it. "How could you grow up in the same house with him and not know that?"

I turned up my palms. "It's hard to explain," I said, looking at the TV.

I could feel Paul's stare as he said, "Give it a try."

"It never came up," I said, trying to understand it myself. "I probably walked past his open bedroom door hundreds of nights without sticking my head in to say *hi* or *goodnight* to him. We were like housemates who barely acknowledged each other."

Paul started laughing, so I said, "What's so funny?"

"You and Marvin are going to be housemates again."

TWENTY-EIGHT

The Saturday before Labor Day, Ocean City was ready for hibernation. For the past week or two, seasonal locals had been clearing out to get ready for their fall semester, though most were back in town for the final weekend. All week, guest traffic at the Carousel had been so slow that even Gary couldn't claim that there was a lot of money out there.

Valets had been going through the motions since early August. Instead of attacking and *getting those doors*, we were waiting for cars to stop and a "Welcome to the Carousel" was rarer than a five-dollar tip. Gary couldn't discipline us like in early summer because so many of the staff had given notice, he couldn't risk having anyone else walk.

The main reason for valets to keep working until Labor Day was to remain in Gary's good graces for a bellman job the following May. I had stuck around because I was making much more in tips with fewer valets working each shift.

Gary came out mid-afternoon and stopped right in front of my face, which still made me uncomfortable. Instead of bunging because I had been leaning on the facing, he sounded somewhat deferential when he said, "Did you pick up the trash like I asked?"

"See for yourself Gary," I said, sweeping my arm behind me toward the garage.

"That looks fine," he said, after a cursory look. "I'm leaving now, but Lab will be in at five, so he'll have other tasks for you."

He wasn't scheduled Sunday, and I was off Monday, so this was goodbye. As we faced each other, I waited for him to say something. My relationship with Gary, like with Dad, was based on his expectations, which meant that unprompted, I didn't have anything to say.

Finally, he said, "Thanks for staying until the end of the season."

"You were a fair boss and I respect your drive at work," I told him. "I'm sorry if I was a pain in the ass for you at times."

He looked at me, probably expecting a punchline. But when I didn't make a joke, he cleared his throat and said, "Thank you. Well, good luck in the future."

It was awkward, but then things between Gary and me usually were.

Watching him walk to the garage, I felt badly that he didn't want me back the following summer, although if I had told Dad I was working as a bellman the following season, it would have sent him right back to Holy Cross. Besides, I had survived Gary's bunge camp. I didn't need to re-up.

Gary hadn't gone to college and that drove him to work harder than anyone else who had *that piece of paper*. Since I had a diploma, I had career opportunities that he would never see. I had Dad to thank for that.

Shortly after 5:00, Lab emerged from the lobby. Smiling, he greeted me: "I knew a valet working on a day like today. There was no money out there, so they canceled valet service."

"You serious? We're done for the season?" I said. He nodded, so I said, "Now that you don't have to work Monday, the holiday should be called *Lab* Day."

There were only ten keys in the box and as soon as a parking space opened up in the front lot, one of us stood in the space while the other brought around a car from the garage and parked it in the saved spot. After relocating the last car, we walked inside and Lab gave the front desk a manila envelope containing the keys and their corresponding front lot locations.

We went downstairs for dinner and as we waited in line with our trays, I told Lab, "It's been such a whirlwind afternoon, I'm expecting Gary to pop out from behind the serving line and present you with a plaque, an engraved squeegee, or an autographed copy of *The Carousel Total Guest Experience*."

"I hope not," Lab said. "I haven't prepared any remarks."

"Just modify your Oscar speech," I said. "Replace *The Academy* with *The Carousel* and *My director* with *My bellcaptain*."

He laughed and I said, "You know you're going to miss me around here."

Lab would be staying on at the Carousel in the fall and working part-time as a bellman.

I felt I had made some friends at the beach and was glad that they had made the effort to get to know me. My expectations had been high in March and I wound up having a great summer, if not a great time at the beach.

The next morning, I woke up feeling an urgency to get out of town. My job was done and I had said my goodbyes. There was no need to stay for Labor Day.

Packing dredged up some forgotten beach acquisitions, like a pair of beachy black and gray striped JimmyZ pants with their black Velcro belt waistband and price tag still attached. I had bought them at South Moon Under during a two-week stretch in June when CJ had a crush on the store manager. After spending more than $300 at her store, he finally worked up the nerve to ask her out, but she turned him down.

When will I ever wear these? I thought, as I tossed them into my *keep* pile. I was able to throw away some items, including Gary's empty fish-shaped wine bottle.

After finishing packing, I asked Tom to help me load my car. He couldn't believe I was leaving before Labor Day and I couldn't believe he didn't try to get out of helping me. As we trooped up and down the stairs and out to my car, he kept going on about our house's end-of-season blow-out the following Saturday.

Fuck that, I thought. *I'm not coming back for another party.* All I had in common with those people was proximity to Tom and a propensity for consuming too much alcohol; two things I was trying to eliminate from my life.

Since the wedding, Tom and I had been hanging out together much less as I gravitated to people from the bellstaff who accepted me more than Tom's bar crowd. It wasn't Tom's fault that I didn't flourish at the beach, but as I struggled, he could have supported me more.

Though he was helping me move, he was getting on my nerves by going on about returning to school in a few days. When he asked if I had a job yet, his tone casual, as if my lining up a job was some minor errand, I couldn't hold it in anymore.

"Not yet," I said. "Things don't magically fall into place for me like they do for you."

"Things work out for me because I make them happen,

dude," he said, then started laughing. "Don't forget to apply at the Hallmark Store. I'll bet they have a sweet employee discount."

That pissed me off because he never cared about how anxious I had been about looking for a job. I didn't say anything. It was a waste of time and I wanted to leave without another blowup. We were too different to have spent so much time together. At least after today, we'd have our space.

We finished loading my stuff and as we drank water in the kitchen, he brought up that damn party again.

"I haven't heard of any other comeback parties," he said. "So ours could be as big as our party in July."

Frustrated, I unfastened my house key from my ring and dropped it onto the eat-in counter. I had anticipated a satisfying metallic *clink*, but the key hit the Formica with a hollow *clack*.

That was it. I was no longer an OC local. I had never really been one, but now it was official.

Tom glanced at the key, then stared at me. "What are you doing?"

"Turning in my key."

"What about our party?" he said.

"I'm going to pass."

"If you're worried about the house getting another noise violation, the cops won't bust anybody for noise after Labor Day."

I believed him because he was well versed in what he could get away with. "It's not that," I said. "I'll be in Silver Spring, so it's three hours each way."

"Come on," he said, flashing his grin. "One last blowout."

But I wasn't budging. "Like I said, I'm not going."

"You had me fooled," he said, his jaw set. "If I had known you were such a loser, I never would have roomed with you."

"I wasn't trying to fool you," I said, bristling because Tom had never called me a loser, at least not to my face. "Don't feel hurt."

"Hurt? Why would *I* be hurt?" he said, scoffing. "You're the one who can't hang."

"If you're not hurt, then why did you call me a loser?"

"Because you *are* a loser," he snapped. "All summer, I tried to get you to go out and when you did, you'd beg me to leave early. When you started bitching about struggling at bars, I knew you were a lost cause. You were out of your league here. That makes you a loser."

"Leaving a bar early doesn't make me a loser. I told you that sometimes when I went out, I was getting physically anxious. Why is that so damn hard for you to understand?"

"Dude, all I know is once we got here, you turned into a shut-in."

"That wasn't my *choice*," I said. "I used to like hanging out with you, Tom. But at the beach, you're all about you. Not that any of that matters anymore."

"Your loss," he said. "Man, arguing with you is like arguing with a girl."

Comments like that from him used to devastate me, but now I saw him for the shallow person he was. He needed to bully people into acting the way he wanted them to, so he surrounded himself with people who would prop him up. He was insecure, just like me, but he overcame it by projecting confidence.

"Everyone tries to be your friend," I said, as we faced each other across the dining room counter. "But you only see others for what they can do for you. You hang with people you don't care about; they're only your supporting cast."

"Bottom line," he said, folding his arms, "I have a good

time whenever I go out and I get more girls in a week than you get in a year."

"I only need one," I said. "And I'm very happy with her."

He laughed. "I also have tons of friends and no one cares about you."

"You accumulate followers, not friends," I said. "Friendship is what matters to me. Being there for each other. I've got real friends. I don't need dozens of *friends* like you have."

"Who are you to judge my friends?!" he said, edging closer, leaning against the sink. "All you did this summer was stay home and pout."

"You know, back in March, you were the blood brother I never had," I said, shaking my head. "You were the one fooling me. You were only using me for playing time in basketball and softball, and for acceptance with the fraternity."

"You're crazy."

"Then we got to the beach," I said. "At first you did try to help me adjust until you realized I wasn't helping you socially. I was never your friend at the beach. I was just another one of your entourage where the only thing that mattered was making you look good."

"Dude, I never needed your help to look good."

"You never needed me for anything. And if you gave a shit about me, you'd have been more supportive."

"I wasn't going to hold your hand all the time. If it hadn't been for me, you'd have sat home with CJ every night."

"At least CJ has my back."

"You guys make a great couple," he said.

"I hope your life stays perfect, Tom, because once you have to face something that you and your buddies can't justify away in a bar, you won't know what to do."

"I can justify away anything in a bar," he said, laughing.

"Not everyone's life sucks like yours," he said, turning toward the stairs. "It's time to move on, dude."

"I have moved on. I'm getting control over my drinking and working on my relationship with my dad. Those mean more to me than going out to bars."

"That's great. You no longer get shitfaced all the time and you can hold a conversation with your father. Do they give out medals for that?"

I stared at him, and for the first time I could remember, he looked away first.

When he walked off, I said, "God, you're so fragile."

He turned back, his face looked distant, like I was another nobody in a bar.

"Whatever, dude," he said.

"You always have to get in the last word, don't you?" I said, as he turned and walked to the stairs.

"Always!" he yelled back.

The bedroom door slammed and his stereo cranked up. Walking toward the front door, I ran my hand along the top of the dining room table. It had been perfect for quarters. But the party was over for me.

Driving up Jamestown, I stopped at the light on Coastal Highway, craning my neck for a last look at the Turtle on my left. I made my right turn and barely acknowledged the Carousel, now on my left, and then in my rearview. There'd be no valets out front until May, when the Carousel would again defend Gary's title as Ocean City's top resort.

Three miles down Coastal Highway, I turned onto Route 90, a fifty-five mile an hour highway connector with no median, so there were signs directing drivers to turn on their headlights in the daytime to alert oncoming traffic. Two bridges later, nothing but trees surrounded the road and I settled in for my drive.

Every few miles, I passed a blue and white "Evacuation Route" sign. They were for hurricane evacuation, but I imagined they were guiding me home. Thirty miles inland, I stopped seeing the signs, but I knew my way. I wasn't sure where I was going in life, but I had a great girlfriend and for the first time in a while, I wasn't running from anything, not even Dad.

ACKNOWLEDGMENTS

With gratitude to Lauren Faulkenberry, who taught me in painstaking detail how to write a novel. Painstaking for me, likely excruciating for her. Thanks also to my friend Ben MacNeill, who graciously read many terrible versions of this book. Finally, thanks to my wife Marlee, the most fervent reader I know, for challenging me to write a good book.

ABOUT THE AUTHOR

I grew up in Silver Spring, Maryland and live in Chapel Hill, North Carolina. Go Terps. I'm fortunate to have four kids and an understanding wife. My favorite activities are playing pickup basketball and eating in diners.

Well into my career as an attorney, I went to a college graduation party for a friend's daughter. The guests were asked to write on their nametags what they had wanted to do for a living when they grew up. I had no idea as a kid and still have no idea. After a lot of thought, I wrote down "writer". It seemed like a joke at the time. It still sounds like a joke. But maybe not.